Flame

Marie Herman

ISBN:1480105988

ISBN-13:978- 1480105980

DEDICATION

I'd like to dedicate this book to my family and friends, no matter what life throws at you, remain strong guys!

ACKNOWLEDGMENTS

I'd like to thank my family for all the love and support they have shown to me throughout the whole time of writing this book, they supported this book even when I wasn't feeling too good about it myself. Thanks a lot guys!

PROLOGUE

A drop of perspiration dripped down the edge of my forehead as I continued jogging the average route that I usually jogged on. The sun was burning down on me, its light shinning in my eyes and its heat making the jog ever more unbearable. But I continued on, firstly, to let off some steam I had after the counseling meeting I went to just a half an hour before now, as usual, it never strikes my fancy. Secondly, so that I can stay physically active, which was more than needed for the events that happen every night in the alleys of New York City.

My lungs indeed didn't feel as if they were burning like the rest of my body was (as much!), for they were kept strong from my weekly routines (including the jogging). Though I had to admit, this was one of the problems with the coming hot months of the summer, heat, and lots of it. I huffed out as I finally neared the more rural (as much of a rural place New York City can be!) part of New York City, I turned the corner and out gaped a big piece of land, possibly five acres of land, all fenced in with a "no trespassing" sign. It was Government property.

Before I made it my routine to come down this route, it made me uneasy doing so, every time I stepped foot onto this area, I felt a bit spooked, like I was doing some crime or something and was going to be tackled by a bunch of men in swat uniforms, but of course that never happened. Obviously it was a stupid thing to be worried about, for I never ACTUALLY went onto the land that said "No Trespassing" and was fenced in with a chain-link fence, but rather went around the area, where a small side-walk type path laid, but still, not the safest thing to do unless you'd want to be questioned, though I never have.

As I began getting lost in thought, I realized that my pace decreased dramatically, rolling my eyes I began to speed up a little bit once more, trying ever so hard not to give into the heat of the sun. I keep promising myself a special stop to a coffee shop to pick up a nice cold-beverage after I am done jogging the route, as I begin to near the middle of the course of the path, when suddenly I spotted movement out of the corner of my left eye, I stopped abruptly and turned myself to see what it was that caught my eye.

My jaw gaped open as I saw three little kids (possibly only 3 years younger than myself, but still stupid enough to be doing what I see them doing), INSIDE the chained-link fence that clearly stated "no trespassing"! My eyes widened, as my heart, even though not working as much as it had to while on the jog, began to pound deeply fast inside of my chest, its beats were heard pounding inside of my ears.

Thinking as fast as I could, I quickly decided to try and call out to them, maybe persuade them to get off the land. "Hey, you guys SHOULDN'T be on that land, you can get severely hurt and in trouble!" I yelled at the top of my lungs, hoping honestly that they'd listen and come running back, saying how they didn't read the sign or something. But obviously, with my lovely luck, that did not happen.

Looking towards them, one of them turned around, gave a big grin, then began walking after the others, like it was some type of big adventure game, really?! I give a big huff, this really IS not good, for a number of reasons, that without those reasons, I would've probably have just left them there and allow them to gain their punishment, for that was quite frankly, and most certainly what they deserved, but nope, it wasn't the punishment that was the problem, it was the huge pond of who-knows-what that they were heading for. Dangerous, first of off, they can most certainly drown, which would be catastrophic to their parents, but then, to top it all off, that pond, is most definitely not filled with water, but with what ever the government choose to throw in there(which seeing that this is the site of a nuclear energy testing facility, it won't be good, at all).

I kept on looking around, just waiting for SOMEONE to show up and take them off the land, for how can't something like this place not be closely monitored by surveillance cameras? To my utter dismay and shock, no one came. Why was it when they are needed, they never actually show up?! Children's lives are possibly at stake, and so they believe that it's better off coming to a drug-notified area to try and stop people, who choose to use drugs, from using them, rather than

trying to stop a very clear catastrophic event from taking place on their very grounds! The nerve of some people...

So it was then decided, by myself of course, to go and stop those kids myself. I dropped my water bottle on the side of the fence, wishing desperately that I had enough time to take a sip out of it so that I can relish the cooling-relieving sensation of it running down my so very dry throat. Of course every moment counted, and I'd rather not be the reason why three kids were injured(at the LEAST and BEST) in front of my eyes and I could have done something to stop it. I jumped up and slid my fingers through the openings of the fence, balancing myself and I tried to find a hold for

my feet to go, as I finally got into the position I needed, I began to climb to the best of my ability. It wasn't necessarily that I COULDN'T climb, but more or less it wasn't one of my more-practiced "skills" especially seeing that a chained-link fence was rarely seen outside of this place in the inner depths of New York City, where most of the non-road covered land was covered by buildings and sidewalks, closely crammed together to use up as much land as possible.

My hands were burning from the friction and the heat of the metal fence by the time I got to the very top of it (which was about 15 feet, too high for my liking), looking down with a huge sigh as I saw the journey of climbing now DOWN 15 feet until a plausible jumping height was fit. Climbing down, not as hard as climbing up, as long as you have good foot-eye coordination so that you can place your feet in the right places without having to look down every second, so that you can spend your time on bringing your hands into the right places (which of course I do, thankfully). But all I have to say is that these kids BETTER be thankful for what I am doing for them right now after all the effort I'm putting into it, of course they won't be, they'd probably won't even think that they were in danger in the first place and that I was just ruining their fun, but still, I GUESS at least they will be safe.

I jumped down, and quickly collected my bearings, not sure exactly how much time I had to do so. I looked into the slight-distance to see where they were now, of course they had to be at the far side of the pond, yet thankfully, it looked as if they were just skipping stones into the pond, so I allowed my heart rate to slow down just a little bit as I jogged towards them, taking in the area for it was hopefully the only time I was ever going to have to see this place from an inside perspective again. It was quite an odd place, no trees, no grass, no pavement, no nothing really. It was just a bunch of dirt and stone, a long with a small little shack-looking building to the far corner, judging by it's size, it was only used for maintenance and led to a bigger area underground. Which indeed, is now making me uneasy, for who knows what kind of trouble I'd be in if I got caught trespassing on their land, even if it was for more than a good cause.

It's interesting how no-one has caught me yet, which has me thinking that this place must be dormant for a week or something, maybe it's just dormant every summer because of the hot weather that might be a huge problem when it comes down to nuclear energy and junk like that... maybe... But it still wouldn't make sense why on Earth they'd leave it here with NO ONE watching it. I took a deep, content breath in as I finally got within ear-shot of the three boys, I opened my mouth to speak, when suddenly the unthinkable chain of events began to unfold.

One of the boys, from what I can see the tallest of the three thought that it would be funny to push the other boy, most definitely the shortest of the three, over, then that boy, after getting up, to my amazement, began laughing, after getting shoved what looks like pretty hard to the ground. I tried to blurt out to stop, I just KNOW what's going to happen, confirming my thoughts, the short one pushed over the tallest one, and they began tackling each other.

I began to run, I know for a fact that my yelling at them from this point on won't stop them what so ever, my best options is to run and hope that I can make it before----

My plans and thoughts being brutally cut off as the taller kid ended up kicking the shorter kid off of him, landing that short kid into the water. No. This CANNOT be happening right now, it is as if I just walked into a horror movie. Of course one kid can't swim. Of course HE had to be the one knocked into the water. And of course the water has to be super deep right from the start! Now it's not even funny, as I sprinted towards them, going as fast as I could go. Hating myself for believing that I had more time, time, time is just stupid. Why did I have to go there?

I was gritting my teeth as I finally was right at the edge of the pond, with not a moment to loose I shouted out to the two baffled and frightened looking kids "CALL 911! NOW!", my only option:

Jump in and try to save him.

I jumped right in, trying to swim as fast as I could. Not fast enough, as the burning water was splashing into my eyes, I saw the bobbing head of the frantic kid drop down. No, please don't let this happen, the thought playing in my head, over and over again, like a broken CD player, as I tried to get to the kid in time, the water has a current, and it's moving fast. As something scratched along my arm, instantly making it sting, one other thought manages to escape into my head, maybe this was just stupid, maybe now I am not only putting my own life in danger, but wasting the REAL rescuer's time when they come to try and save him and myself. My arm is throbbing now, burning and stinging, all at the same time, had to be the worst injury I've ever gotten, but that does not matter, I gritted my teeth one last time.

At the moment, my drive has to be to save the kid, that's the only way that I can forgive myself, I HAVE to save him, some how, I just have to. Using up all of my energy that I had left, I forced myself to move faster, patteling the best I can, I braced myself for an agonizing burn, as I submerged myself into the water, I shot my eyes open as soon as possible, instantly feeling the same burn that my arm was feeling now inside of my eyes, a worst burn than before. Looking around in the murky water, my first bet was to try and find any signs of frantic splashing within the water. I looked around, but realizing that it's not going to work due to the already un-organized strong current of the water, I am going to have to figure out a different tactic. The possibilities flow threw my mind for what seems like hours, but must of only taken a couple of seconds, best one was to try and find a big shadow, how big? The kid must have been about 4'4 feet tall, and is about average size in waist, so my eyes began darting back and forth looking for a shadow that size in the murky water.

Beginning to run out of breath, and hope, there he was, in the corner of my vision, from what I can tell, alive, for I see feeble movement from my blurred vision, but barely. Not wanting to loose sight of him, forcing myself not to go up for air, I swim towards him, using every single ounce of my strength to go to him. My now scratched-arm is beginning to feel numb, which is good for it makes it easier to swim without any pain, but pretty darn bad seeing the fact of, what comes next after not feeling it?

I forced myself downward with a quick push of my legs, and grab him with my left hand, trying so very hard to hang on, I swing my right-and-numb arm right around his stomach right next to my left hand, and began kicking as much as I possibly could, upward, to the surface. How much effort I were to have to use just to keep myself up in these waters would be mind-boggling in itself, how much effort to keep myself up and another body in these waters, it's almost impossible. Almost, that's the key word, for that word makes all the difference, it changes fatal to flourishing after a month or so of recuperating, almost is basically what is keeping myself, and this kid alive at the moment alive, and stopping me from just giving up all together. It doesn't have to be a HUGE percentage to keep me going, or even a fair percentage of chance to keep me going, there just has to be the tinniest, molecular chance of making it, and I'll place every ounce of effort into it, to achieve what I have planned.

My lungs feeling as if they might explode, or collapse should I say due to the lack of oxygen I have left in me, though I keep on trudging on, trying to break the current for just a second, so that the kid and I can get a breath, that's really all I need, but the current just keeps on plummeting us deeper and deeper, or at least that's how it feels. Just how it feels. Finally with one huge and sudden burst of energy, I somehow managed to break surface. I gasped for air, breathing in heavy gulps, as I lift the kid up, he was unconscious for that whole time, I just really hope that he's going to live. With newfound energy I am able to hold the kid up so that he could breath in some air, as he began to cough up some water, I begin swimming back to shore, forcing myself to keep going. Not only so that I can live but for him to live also.

Things began to go from slow motion from here. It felt like hours, and hours, as I swam so very slowly to the shore, the other two kids were talking on the phone, 911 I am guessing, worried looks on their faces, I wanted to scream out to them, for them to look our way and realize that there still might be a chance that their friend is alive, maybe even help me with the other kid if one of them were actually able to swim. But honestly, I couldn't, what little energy that I have gained from the air that I was breathing was being put into use for swimming, no doubt dwindling by the second. My eyes were stinging too, they felt as if they were going to fall out of their sockets, and I couldn't help but think how lucky this kid was to be unconscious for the entire time, people don't feel any pain when they are unconscious, do they? Pretty sure not, good thing if he isn't, for his well being.

The shore. It was right in front of me, felt like ages, and ages, but finally! Taking up possibly the last drop of energy, for sure this time, I heaved myself and the boy out of the water, both of us splattering on the ground like fish out of water. I heard the sounds of sirens near by, and getting closer by the second, then Seeing the two boys faces, shocked, thankful, and impressed all wiped across their faces at the same time that they saw us. Finally, I saw the ambulance coming, second time I saw THAT coming for me I realize with a sigh. I took one last glance at the boy who I saved, for a second, and only a second, I saw his eyes flash open. They were a light brown color, deep, and showing a sort of passion(maybe?) I have never seen before in my life. And after that, out of pure exhaustion, everything went blank.

CHAPTER 1

Knocking on the door, 3 men coming through the door, 2 shots ringing out, and a single flame being lit in front of me. All that passed right before my eyes as I closed my eyes for a second to think about that event. That was the very event that seems almost to haunt every year, every month, every week, every day, every hour and every waking second of my life.

"You know as much as I do that you've had quite some traumatic experiences in your life, you must be feeling something right now" she said.

Her name is Ms. Thomas, my counselor that I was assigned to, I must go to her to "vent" and be "assessed" by her twice a year, once right before Christmas day, anytime during the Christmas season would do. And another the day the event happened, June 12th, which is indeed the day school lets out. The day that everyone else is cheering and having fun outside, and I am stuck in here. Which also, low-and-behold, happens to be my birthday, double whammy much? This year, my 16th birthday. Now exactly 4 years from when yet another event happened which resulted in me getting a large ugly scar across my arm, but another life being saved. This scar seems to be a reminder of how close I was to loosing my life, and other's around me.

The other event, exactly 10 years ago, didn't inflict a physical scar on me, but more or less a very emotional scar on me. The death of my adoptive parents, not even my real parents. Those were gone the second I was born. Most people at hearing my thoughts right now, would believe that I am a very depressing person, with a very depressing life, but here's the problem, this is NOT how my thoughts usually run, it's this stinking "meeting" that I always have to go to twice a year that has me so bummed out. I grit my teeth, trying not to be rude n' all and say something about how her counseling tactics are VERY bad and she should drop them all together.

So instead I say "Nope, I have learned to cope with them in my own way". She took a swift glance at the scars along my arms trying to make a "point". Even though I know they aren't the affects of what she thinks happened to my arms, I still shift uncomfortably in the chair I'm sitting at as her analyses is created in her mind, I cross my arms, trying to hide as many as possible, not even trying to hide the longer one in which she knows darn-well where it came from.

"Zoey Aquarius D'Bandit...." she paused for a moment after speaking my whole name.

We have known each other for all too long, I can just see it in her eyes, I know this because some how saying my name "unprofessionally" felt natural to her, until she caught herself that is. "I mean Miss.D'Bandit, we all know that you are obviously not copping with it well. I see that you are still cutting yourself viciously, there must be SOMETHING I can do for you."

It would be nice for her to stop bringing up such horrible memories, why doesn't she realize that "talking" about it all pains me just that much more. It doesn't HELP! Not one bit. But some how she believes it does, she doesn't even realize what I have been doing for five years now that have been causing these scars! Sometimes I have to wonder what goes on inside her mind, if I were to some how magically read her thoughts, would I hear complete and utter silence, or crickets chirping in the background, for there sure isn't any actual thoughts going on in there. I roll my eyes as I blink, so that she won't see the frustration in them, if only she knew what I have REALLY been doing, then maybe I wouldn't be declared emotionally unstable in her eyes, though going to jail is a completely different story...

"Ms.Thomas, I am just fine" I said, trying so very hard not to completely explode on her, she was a nice lady, good intentions and all, just placed in the wrong direction and in the stupidest of ways. I looked up to the little clock that hung over her desk, it read 2:55, great, there is only five more minutes of this left.

To my greater misfortune she caught my eyes drifting to the clock, quickly she said "Miss.D'Bandit, I hope you are not looking at the clock waiting to be let out, for that would mean that I haven't gotten through to you and I would have to apply for you to meet me four times a year instead of only twice a year, hmmm???".

I sighed, I know she's not making false threats, so I move my eyes quickly back to hers, stating, and on my last nerve "No ma'am, just looking to see how much time we have left to talk is all, not begging to be let out or anything". She nodded in approval, though I am pretty darn sure she knew very well that it was most certainly not true. But it's okay, for she really can't claim me for lying to her anyhow, she even seems like she wouldn't even WANT to. Still, good she can't.

She gave up, for today's talk that is, she began shifting through papers, her eyes dropping downwards onto them to asses every single piece of information of my life, a stalker's dream to have such a list for anyone, a counselor is my version of a loop-hole to the privacy acts. "Well Ms.D'Bandit, I believe you are free to go for today, have a nice day and please remember what we talked about" she said, "allowing" me to leave.

"Thanks, you too" I said, as I grabbed my bag from the corner of my chair and left the room.

*   *   *

I looked around at the usual coffee shop that I go to whenever my so-very-lovely(with all the sarcasm in the world!) appointment is done. It smells of coffee beans, and creams, and has the usual buzzing of people laughing and talking floating through the place. This has to be my favorite place in the whole of New York City, it's a nicely designed two-floor area of a fifty five-story building (the two floors being on the very top) with a very nice view of the city below, it's a very popular destination for locals (and a few tourists here and there) due to it being on the very top floor, unmarked n' all, it doesn't see much attraction or appeal to anyone who doesn't KNOW it's here.

I decided to order a mocha-cappuccino with extra coffee added to it for the night ahead, and sat down at a window seat that over-looked the city. I grabbed my laptop out of the bag, all planned and ready to go. Another reason why I love this place so much, it has wifi. I turn on my computer, and waiting for it to load, I take a sip of my beverage and begin thinking about all the info. I have collected so far (not really much, but SOME type of start, right?). One flame, not many crimes happen with one flame, right? Still, not enough evidence. On top of that, maybe a double-hitter, there were 3 men, most crimes, or murders should I say, don't usually happen with more than 2 people, organized crime maybe? Definitely wasn't a robbery for certain, nothing was stolen, just the lost of life. So, revenge. Revenge indeed, but why one might ask? I have no clue, they were police officers but... Still, not every police officer gets killed. Had to be something else. I HAVE to be missing the big picture here, but what?

I grind my teeth, every day I ask myself these questions, but do I get any closer to solving the crime, the answer is NO, in fact, some how I feel as if every day that it goes by unsolved, is another day that the killers are going un-punished! My parents SHOULD get justice, shouldn't they!? I deserve to know the truth too, and I will stop at nothing to achieve this very plan.

After a moment of thoughts with myself, my computer booted up, displaying the average back-round of a single flower being over-showered by the sun. Very nice picture, I always marveled at it, and wondered where the picture was taken, for all I knew, it was possibly photo-shopped into the picture of the sun, though it really didn't seem to have been. Scrolling my mouse over the internet pop-up, I clicked on it which brought up a webpage, the average search engine was ready to be used, so I typed in the word "New York City Police" which got me to a webpage, the original webpage of the NYC police. Five different categories were listed right at the top, I clicked on the one on the very right named "Cases".

In big bold print it read "access denied". I grimaced, by now you'd think the welcome mat would be brought out every time I get on here due to how many times my computer signature has been seen on this webpage. But nope. So I typed in the words "Bandit Flame", which is basically my "password" into the database, out popped up my case. Usually, someone my age would not be given such information, it was actually the situation that brought on me having the password to it. They figured considering the fact that my parents most likely died because the job they were doing, that they should give me the least bit of hope, even though they were only my adoptive parents (which some can argue that it isn't right, not like I was actually related to them or anything). I began scanning over all the information they have managed to collect over the years, not much more than the day the crime even happened.

The words death, lost, and murder all seemed to become one big blur to me. I really shouldn't do this to myself, everyone knows that, but, it just doesn't feel right, giving up on 2 people who were practically my saviors when it comes to trying to have a normal life, that's all gone now, but still. Heat is now beginning to emit out of the computer, I feel it on my hand that is right on top of the keyboard, time almost seemed to have gone by way too quick. It is 5:00 o'clock already, my thoughts have sucked me into their depths, speeding up time to the limit of speed in my world, what was an hour only seemed like a minute, how stupid of myself.

I took one last sip of my drink, realizing that it was now room-temperature, I got up and threw it away in the garbage, making sure not to spill any of it as I did so, it would only be SLIGHTLY embarrassing to spill it all over the floor of a public area. Walking back over to the computer, I sit down and start shutting it down. Waiting for the computer to now shut down, I look outside at the street below. Cars going back and forth along the road, honking, yelling, and slamming on the breaks, basic New York City for ya'. And as I scan the bustling sidewalks, I notice the average hectic of it all, especially seeing that there was a part blocked off, for construction workers to repair a side walk, I think. Mapping out my best route home, I decide that it would probably be best to go to the other side walk and waste a few minutes rather than try to brace myself for a now one-lane two-lane traffic sidewalk. The computer hummed off, and I placed it into my bag, and I left the café.

I opened the door leading to the elevator room and began debating. Elevator, or stairs, one gets crowded and the other, due to how high up this building is, seems to get you tired a little bit. I took a quick glance at the people near the elevator, there had to be like 15 people standing in line for an elevator! That HAS to be the problem with the top floor, it seems as if when ever an elevator comes, it gets intercepted by another group waiting for an elevator on one of the lower floors. That's definitely one of the bugs with these elevators. I roll my eyes, and decide that it would most certainly be best if I just take the stairs. So I opened the door to the stairs, took one last (and hopeful!) look at the elevator, some stupid hope of all the people some how magically disappearing, and went down the stairs.

Walking down stairs, is long, and boring, especially when you are walking down the stairs of a fifty five floor building, from the very top of that building. Though who's to say boring is a bad thing? It WAS indeed taking more time away from sitting at the house doing nothing for me, so I should really not complain. Looking to my right, I start counting the numbers as I go lower and lower, towards my destination (out of here!). 45, 44, 43, 42, 41, 40, 39, 38 ,37, 36.

As I begin to near floor thirty five(only three steps left) I stopped, hearing the loud foot steps coming from somewhere behind me, turning to look to see what it is, my breath was taken away as somebody pushed right into me, knocking me down the last 3 steps and landing me face-first against the cement floor.

"I'm sorry!!" said a familiar voice as I heard the shuffling of him getting up. He handed me his hand so that I too can get up, I grabbed it, got up and brushed the dust off my pants (since the stairs in this building are rarely used except for the occasionally 'me', it collected a good lump-some of dust).

"It's okay" I said, as I glanced over towards him making sure my interpretations were correct. I took a quick look at his eyes first, for that was the one thing I used to identify people. Not by the color, but more or less by the intensity and basic character from the eyes I was able to tell exactly who it is. Weird, I know. Honestly, I don't know why or when I began doing this, but it is just a more easier way to identify someone. And in doing so, I am now most certain that his, he who ran into me, name is William Thomas, my counselor's son. He is only one year younger than me, and I've only met him once, but again, for some reason eyes, anyone's eyes, seems to have a huge impact on me and I am almost 100% sure it's him. Now why he is so clumsy, I have no clue. "What's the rush William?" I asked, throwing the name out as if we were very good friends who hung out together 24/7.

He looked baffled that I remembered him, and that I even cared to act like I did, as I would have guessed. It's sort of funny seeing how people react when I do this to them, they act as if it's the weirdest thing ever, but to me, it's just normal, a part of who I am. "Well, um--" he began stuttering, still baffled at the moment, I gave him a moment to explain himself, so I just continued to brush my pants as if there was still dust on them to give him a little more time, making sure to look down in hard concentration which would equal out to me not needing the answer to my question answered immediately. After a few moments, I looked up at him, he regained himself, good. "Hey Zoey" he said, after a quick second of thinking of my name also, "It's just that my mother told me to catch up to you to give you this" he took something out of his pocket, and in his hand showed me a small rectangular electronic, my phone! Shoot.

"Thanks, it was really nice of her to, um, send it with you" I said, taking it out of his hand and placing it in my pocket. How on Earth did I leave it in the counselor's room anyways?! Thank goodness I didn't leave it anywhere else, that phone cost me a year's worth of saving up from different jobs alone, not to mention the information on it... I kept all of the information I've managed to collect on that phone over the years of the crime, that phone, is basically my life-line, and if lost or somehow stolen, I'd have to go through all that data again from the data base, that's even if it's still there (for the stuff placed online is just old information that I re-look at occasionally to see if I missed any important details, it's only HALF of all the information collected about the crime, for I collected a lot of information myself also in comparison to the actually amount that there is...).

I gritted my teeth as I began realizing that they MIGHT of looked through my phone, and if they did, can lead me into trouble on why I didn't report that information in anyways (top secret information from my point of view, besides, it was collected more than five years after the murder and would be useless to them anyways, for the case was already deemed "cold" at the time and why would they bother re-opening it when hundreds of other new cases are created each year. Even if the case was one of their own.)

I took a quick glance from the pocket in which I put my phone in back to Will, trying to read his face, he seemed to be keeping nothing from me, he was obviously just taking my phone back, but still, I have that uneasy feeling inside my gut that just won't go away.

He grinned, "Don't worry, I didn't look at the text messages or anything, you are all good" he teased, pretty childish if you asked me. He must of saw me gritting my teeth and thought that that's what caused it (though in a way, looking at the contents of my phone was the reason, just not my text messages, which consisted of just messages to my foster mother, a few friends, and foster siblings, which really was not a big deal.), and of course, like most guys around my age, and most guys in general the more that I think about it, immaturity seized him and he decided to prey on it.

"Don't worry, I won't tell anyone that you fell down the stairs either" I winged back at him, with a teasing laugh and roll of my eyes (doesn't hurt to be childish though...), I grabbed my bag that was so very sadly thrown to the corner of the little area of the stairs, making sure to shake it a little to hear for any clinks or signs of my laptop being damaged (thankfully their isn't any), and I began walking away. "Thanks, good bye!" I yelled back, not wanting to linger in their any longer, for I'd rather not be TOO late to my house, late is still not that big of a deal, but I'd rather not push it.

I heard the echo of "Bye" and the gentle opening and closing of one of the doors. As if he didn't want me to hear him bluffing out of a walk down the stairs! Laughing to myself at how ridiculous William is, I began speeding up my pace down the stairs to a gentle jog. After a little bit, I began counting the floors again, until, finally I hit floor one and left the stairs to go outside into the city. I took in a big breath of air of the city in front of me, the honking of the horns, the flashing of the lights, all of it I seemed to love. This was where I grew up. My favorite city on Earth. I began walking across the street as a pedestrian walking sign lit up. Taking my easy-route was going to be, well, easy.

*   *   *

I looked around as I walked yet another cross-walk and finally to my home, I took out my key, and unlocked the door to the little apartment and walked in. The sound of the T.V in the living room ringing through the house as usual as I un-sling my book bag from my shoulder and hooked it on one of the hooks in the hallway. Going to the bathroom, I went to the sink and washed my hands. Right after I walked to the kitchen and began preparing the kitchen table. Forks, butter-knives, plates, napkins and cups, all being set up on the kitchen table. Tonight we are having pasta, and like usual the water is already boiling on the stove, all I have to do is add the pasta to the mix. I open up one of the very-worn out cupboards and bring out a box of pasta, pouring it into my hands, breaking and dropping it all into the water, I listened for the sizzling sound that I usually hear as it hit's the water.

I look at the clock on the stove that now read 6:00 o'clock and began walking across the hall way to the living room. Another girl and 2 boys sat in the living room watching the Television intently, reminding myself that sometime this week I should take them to the park so that they could enjoy outside, I said "Guys, get ready for dinner". Summer was the first to get up, she was 7 years old and possibly the most helpful out of the three, she nodded and with a quick smile went to the bathroom to begin washing her hands. Casting my gaze over to the other two, who seemed very well-aware of me but otherwise completely ignored me. A 6 year old and a twelve year old were hard business indeed, what made them even more harder is the fact that they were brothers! I say it again, this time, walking in front of them while I do and changing my strategies "Get ready for dinner, you want to eat, don't you?"

That got them. "Okay, okay already" Scott, the twelve year-old said most bitterly. I didn't take it to heart, we both know that he hates me and the fact that I'm the only one in the way of him being the oldest in the house hold and being in charge of everything, and quite frankly, that I too wasn't very fond of him either, something I am not too proud of since he is only twelve but I have a pretty good reason to after the day we first met, which resulted in spit in my face, an extra bruise on my arm, and a good slap in his face (which again, an action that I am very un-proud of, but sooooo well deserved.).

Tim, the 6 year old, looked up at me and said “Do I HAVE to leave the T.V, can’t I just eat in here?”. His question was of innocence and wanting more than anything. Most people would probably have given in, especially seeing that Tim has possibly the most sweetest face in the whole universe, but still, the rules are rules and not of my creating either.

“Sorry Tim, can’t let you, you know the rules all too well” I said, giving a light grin to try and lighten the mood and not seem like such an enemy in the little kid’s mind.

“Okay” he said, getting up from where he sat on the couch and walking towards the bathroom. I picked up the controller and clicked the Television off, then placing the controller on a small little brown side-table, I walked back over to the kitchen to take the pasta out of the boiling water. I grabbed a strainer and placed it in the sink, then, after turning off the stove, I grabbed a hold of the handles of the container and poured the steaming water into the strainer. I took the pasta and placed it into a semi-decent (and possibly the best) bowl. Walking over to the pantry, I pulled out a can of sauce and I poured the sauce into the pasta bowl as I heard the scuffling of feet, and the pulling of chairs, I turned around to see all the kids sitting down, ready to eat.

Only two chairs at the table weren't taken at the moment, myn, and my foster mother Ms.Smith's(as she'd like to be called by her oldest foster-kid). She isn't necessarily what most would call a "nurturing" foster-parent. She usually sleeps all day and then leaves at night, living off of worker's comp in which she got about 10 years ago, supposedly from falling at work and harming her back (though she seems just fine to me). The reason she leaves at night is to go to a bar, and after that, she sleeps off her hang over during the day, only to do the same thing the next night. You'd think by now she learned from her mistakes, that every time she drinks too much she harms herself the next day, but no. She either is too ignorant to see the mistake, or could care less about it. Above all she has no impact on our lives what-so-ever, and the only reason why I haven't reported her is because this place is the only place that the two brothers could stay together, and I wouldn't want to be the reason why they were separated.

Even without her here, she still manages to have her "rules" in the house that I'm forced to abide to for she does know my weakness and would most certainly exploit it if angered in any way (those rules including the no eating in front of the Television, which isn't really a bad thing but the whole 'rules' reason is more so because she is control-hungry more than anything, and that weakness being the fact that I DON'T want to split the two brothers up in which she could easily decide to "return" us all.). Though she's not all bad, I mean, without her we'd probably all be in the orphanage or something like that. Also, I definitely would not be able to go out at night if I had a more "protective" foster parent.

Walking over to the table, and I sat down, making sure that everything was on the table, then I said "Okay, Dinner is served", and they began filling their plates with the delicious(if I say so myself) looking food, I glanced over to Scott and added "Thanks again Scott for starting the water, I might just have to get you that game you want anyways".

He grinned, even though he and I butt heads sometimes, scratch that off, MOST of the time, Scott was no hater of a complement, ESPECIALLY when that complement lead to a promise of a gift. "Awesome", he said, trying to hide the grin and trying to place a bit of sarcasm into his voice, wasn't really working, but I ignored it anyhow. After everyone else filled their plates and started eating, I began scooping some pasta onto my plate too, making sure to give myself only a little bit for I'm not that hungry at the moment. Eating the pasta, I began listening to Summer talk about all the arts and crafts she made today in school (for the Elementary students get out of school later than the High school students, due to the fact that we have regents and they don't. Reminding myself that I have the test tomorrow and should probably go out earlier tonight and get back here earlier also so that I can get some sleep before the test, I tried to get back into the conversation with Summer). The other two looked like they were listening, but I am pretty sure that they weren't due to the glazed look in their eyes as they ate. At least they had the decency not to tell Summer that they didn't care and everything, that would definitely have me lecturing to them about being respectful to others for a half an hour, and then them being sent to bed for the night.

"Well, I am done" Scott said, breaking my train-of-thought, he got up, and began scrapping his plate of the food into the garbage. He drew his gaze over to his younger brother, signaling for him to finish up too. They seem to have a sort of brotherly-connection that I will never understand. They do that every night, one would finish before the other, and then would signal the other one to finish also (by now, you'd think that they would automatically follow each other, but they still need to signal each other.) Tim got up, walked over to the garbage and began clearing his plate also.

After they left, Summer got up, grabbing her plate and because she didn't have any food left on her plate, she placed it into the dishwasher. I too got up and began clearing the table, when she chimed in "I'll help also", Summer looked up at me with sparkling light brown eyes, as if she was volunteering to go on an amusement park ride. I laughed at her expression.

"If you WANT to" I snorted, joking around with her I added "Afterwards you mind if you clean the boy's room too?", she grinned in reply.

*　　　　　　　　*　　　　　　　　*

I hummed a little bit to myself as I booted up my laptop on top of my bed and sat there waiting for it to finish. Following the tidying up of the kitchen, I headed straight towards my room after grabbing my computer to check on some things. This room being Summer's too, I made sure before I went up here to check and see if Summer was alright with watching a little bit of television. She joyfully said yes, it being a better time than cleaning up the kitchen, she ran right towards the living room and plunked herself right on the couch. Unquestionably thrilled that the other two were upstairs so she had the whole living room to herself, to watch whatever she pleased.

Just as my computer turned on all the way, a pop-up appeared in the corner of the screen. On it said "Message from Sam123NYC", huge coincidence that he messaged me the second I logged on. I clicked the window and out popped my chat-screen. The message said "Hey, you there, Water-Bringer?". I scowled at the screen for a moment. He KNEW that nick-name annoyed me greatly. Anyone else would have gotten a for-sure kick in the face for calling me that, but since he is possibly my best friend, I'll let it slide. Though that nickname agitates me so very much, that nickname derived from my middle name "Aquarius" which is a constellation which means water-bringer, why I was given that middle name, I have no clue. But it just gave people material to annoy me with greatly (Most don't realize it at first, they just make that connection and bingo, you got me annoyed. Thankfully I have just enough self-control to not actually kick them in the face, to begin with).

I grind my teeth for a few minutes, gnawing over at how I should reply, when out popped another message reading "Hey, you there :P", that emotion-type-thing signaled to me that he was TRYING to get on my nerve in a teasing sort of way, so I basically decided to get him back by calling him by his nickname that he doesn't like so much either, though, no one cannot possibly get annoyed as much as I could at my nickname with their nickname, it's unheard of. "hey, Samuel Adam's beer!", I typed. His real name is Samuel Adam Bear, which is very close to the alcoholic beverage known as Samuel Adam's Beer, oddly enough. Why his parents (or rather parent, his mother abandoned him when he was born and left him with his dad before she even named him) named him such a name like that is beyond me.

Another message came in reading "Ha-Ha, you know that joke was so funny that I forgot to laugh. Anyways, where were you? I've been online for nearly an hour trying to get a hold of you!"

I rolled my eyes, I looked towards the corner of his log-in time and it read just 5 minutes before I got on, quickly I typed back "O'rlly now? Cause your log-in time is saying something different", there was a semi-lengthy pause, then another message was sent. It read "Well, my computer booted me off for a second... Anyways, when is the next time we can meet up, there is something that I REALLY have to show you".

I rolled my eyes once more, now he is just trying to get off topic, I replied back "Well done .... regents Exam tomorrow, meet up after that?". Way too soon after I hit sent, I got another message from him, it read "K". Really, what is that?! "K" is hardly a reply, much less a complete answer. Rapidly I typed back "K? Um, is there a problem?".

Another message was sent, "No, there isn't. I hve got to go, dad is telling me to get offF, he doesn't like the fact that Ive been on for so long", almost as if he knew what I was going to type back, another message was sent soon after and before I had time to reply "And YES I have been on for an xtreme about of time already, get over it.". I snorted, why did it matter to his dad if he was online anyhow? I mean, his dad is all right and all, he is indeed a police officer himself, which is actually the reason why Sam and I bonded so well, having a similarity like that meant a lot. Though I've never actually MET his dad face-to-face,

I've heard pretty good stories about him from Sam n' all. But it just seems as if he has a real problem with me, and I can't seem to put a finger on why he would. Just the little things keep on adding up, it just doesn't make sense. Like the fact that Sam and I have been really good friends since we were 9, and yet his father still dictates when and when not we can hang out, and for how long. It never made sense to me and probably never will.

I Must have been thinking for a bit too long cause then another message flashed up onto my screen "Hello....?". I rolled my eyes yet again, really? Quickly (so as not to keep princess bear from waiting), I typed back "Kk, meet at a park?". Basic place in which we can hang out at as long as I tell Sam where it is, and where I did my routine of jogging around. It is a government place, and happens to be the place in which I gained a light pink long scar(which still has a stinging sensation from time-to-time) across my arm from trying to save a nine year old boy from a pond a while back. "No" he typed back, waiting for more of an explanation, I looked at my watch to see what time it was, it was already 7:45, which means I should probably start getting ready in fifteen minutes...

"Best if we met in the coffe shop?" he typed back, odd. Most of the times he is sure to not state that place as a meet up, the only time we meet up there is when we are talking about "The Bandit Files" (which is the name I call anything that has to do with my parent's case and all, which includes any details from that night, and details that I've collected from all the other night outs. Sam is the only one who knows about it all in my life, and I would like to keep it that way. In fact, the only reason why I told him is so that he wouldn't have to question the scars and everything, and so that if I some how wind up dead in a street mostly known for dealing drugs, he would be able to tell everyone that I wasn't trying to do drugs!). Choosing my words carefully, I typed in "Fine... but you are paying :P". To try and ease the most clear tension in the conversation. Replying back only took him a short moment, "Yeah, oK". Sarcasm, a sure sign of everything being alright. "K, 12:30 pm, bye" I typed back, and that was the end. I logged out, and turned off my now heating up laptop.

Shutting off, I closed it shut and placed it on my desk in the corner of the room and began charging it. The desk was carefully placed in the corner, far away from any windows, three years ago for a reason. When I first bought the desk(with my hard-earned money from my job), I had to make sure that it was away from any windows, the reason was for my laptop. Before then, I had my laptop most stupidly placed right under a window to be charged. And of course, I forgot to shut the window before I left for school. Out of all the days, it was that day that it began raining. So, my nice newer computer got fried to my greater discontent. So, I had to spend a whole two hundred dollars to fix the stupid thing, getting all the water out of it, not the first thing one would have in mind to spend some of her savings on. Yet another life-lesson I have learned from my out-most stupidity.

Walking over to my closet, I pulled out a T-shirt, and a pair of sweat pants (both being the color black), and a pair of white sneakers(now a pair of white-ish sneakers due to um, usual wear-and-tear?). I walked over to the bathroom, and turned on the light switch. Setting my clothes down on what little counter-space in the room there was, I took out a hair thing and began putting my hair up into a quick(and quite sloppy) ponytail. In the mirror I examined myself for a moment, looking at my nose, making sure it wasn't scathed from my run-in with William earlier today. Thankfully it wasn't, though it had a very dim, purplish color to it that told me it didn't go TOTALLY unharmed from the event. My hazel(mostly green) eyes bore into me as I analyzed my nose, maybe a bit too much, for after a few minutes I had to drop my gaze from the mirror. Grabbing my shirt, I quickly slipped off my bright pink shirt(very florescent, my favorite color), and threw on my black t-shirt. I began to debate whether-or-not I would be just fine wearing plain shorts instead of a black pair of sweats. Deciding against it due to the lack of protection shorts brought to my increasingly vulnerable legs during "battle", I took off the shorts and threw on the pair of sweats. Slipping on the pair of sneakers, I looked at myself in the mirror to see if I missed anything.

I ran off the list of things in my head, Shirt…. Pants… Shoes…. Hair…. Jewelry! I almost forgot! I moved my hands to my neck and unlatched the necklace apart. On the chain stood a Cross (Which stands for faith), an anchor(which stands for hope) and a Heart (which stands for love), it's a very symbolic chain in which I hold near and dear, it would have been a shame to have lost it…. ESPECIALLY seeing that it was the gift I got from my parents(adoptee, but still the same to me) on my 6th birthday. One gift that I will surely never forget. Carefully, I took the chain from my hand, and placed it in a small little wooden-chest on a shelf in the closest, and I gently pushed the top of the wooden-chest shut. I then grabbed my black bag out of the closest, and double-checked the supplies in it.

Most people would call this irresponsible, leaving a 12 year old alone with a 7 and 6 year old every night in a small apartment in New York City. Also, most people would think that a 12 year old is not fit to baby sit 2 kids that age in a huge city like this. But believe it or not, Scott is actually quite good at baby-sitting both of them. Not that he has much time to baby-sit, they fall asleep in like 30 minutes after I leave, and on top of that, not to sound possibly the most selfish and ignorant person in the whole universe, but how is it my job to baby-sit them anyways? I act like this now, but honestly if I really didn't think Scott could handle it, I would probably stay here every night. Besides, it probably simmers down the electrifying hate that Scott and I have between each other just a bit, by giving Scott some sort of control.

Gathering up my clothes, I walked over to the laundry basket and placed them in, reminding myself to do laundry tomorrow for it's beginning to look quite full. Then I walked over to the boys room, and knocked on the door twice. Scott came to answer(and like usual, as if he was answering to the door of his own house, rather than a room in which he shared with his little brother), "Yes?" he said, most curtly.

I tried not to roll my eyes at this when I said "Listen, I am leaving, you have things under control here right?".

Before I could say more, he rather bluntly said "Where do you go, every night?", his eyes scored my face, looking for answers. I know all too well that they automatically thought that I went to my job or a friends house every night, but they never actually ASKED where I went. Not that they had any need to, they have only been here for two years now, and Summer five years (before then, I had much more older, and trouble-making foster siblings, who didn't care what-so-ever where I went off to. Plus, I always made sure that at that time little Summer had a baby-sitter because of this.) I have planned this out already, every single last detail and question that he would ask.

"To a friend's house..." I said, adding before he had time to say anything more(skill sub-consciously learned from Sam, though I haven't really "mastered" it as much as he did), "Sam and I are going to hang out tonight, ya' know, go to an awesome movie that just came out.".

"But where do you go EVERY night, you can't just be hanging out with Sam twenty-four-seven?!" Scott said, very un-convinced. Suddenly I felt as if the reason why they leave dinner every night wasn't just because they had a brotherly bond, but because they were talking about me? I swear, if they start telling people about them being alone every night, they are the ones who are digging their own hole separating themselves apart.

"Work" I said, using the same curt tone that he used with me, adding as his mouth opened up trying to add yet another question "GOOD-night".

"Fine, don't speak up." Scott said, as I began walking away, he shut the door(with no anger at all, just frustration), and I heard him talking to Tim "She is probably out doing drugs or something!". Wow, as I predicted people were to make those accusations, amazing how I am sooooo right about that. Good thing I did tell Sam about it all...

As I walked pass the living room I said to Summer "Good night Summer, make sure to get to bed in a half-an-hour or so. Remember, you still have school tomorrow". Summer just looked over towards me, and nodded with a smile in reply.

Then she added "Here" and held out a hand containing a card,

“Happy Birthday!”, she yelled out, her eyes shining like crazy.

I grabbed the card with a smile, it was nice of her to remember. On the card written on it was “happy birthday“ (in the best way a seven year old could, she spelt birthday with two “t”s). I opened up the card and she drew a picture of two balloons(with huge smiley faces drawn on them), and then in huge letters, the words “From Summer”(all words there were spelled correctly that time). I smiled in return “Ahhhh thank you Summer, this is beautiful, it was so nice of you to remember my birthday!”. She grinned in return, as I added “and this drawing is so well drawn, that I think I just might have to keep this card for the rest of my life so that when you are a famous artist, I can tell everyone that I have your first original picture all for myself!”.

Her eyes glowed with warmth and appraisal at what I just said, as she added “Well, good night!”. I waved good night and that was it, placing the card neatly on a side table, reminding myself to make sure to pick it up later.

CHAPTER 2

As I shut the door behind me, a cold gust of wind seemed to have swept me off my feet as I walked outside into the open streets of New York City. The sun hasn't set yet, but still it felt really cold(especially for a summer night!). A quick chill ran down my back as I debated which way I should go tonight(personally, it really wasn't something that mattered, for the crime seemed to magnetize to me where ever I go, unless maybe it's just the fact that New York City in general has a high crime rate?). Choosing to go right, I started to head off in the general direction as far away from the apartment as possiblc(so as not to create any suspicion as usual.) I jogged briskly(but not too fast for curiosity of neighbors were never good, I tried to make it seem as if I was just going for a usual jog).

Taking no turns off of my general direction as usually, I kept this pace for awhile, just waiting for the sun to go down so that I could REALLY start what I was planning for(going out early would have worked if there was a good amount of dark-time before I went out on other days, but of course, my plan failed seeing as in actuality, I cut it short the second the sun is down and I go right out. So in other words, I am just wasting my time now.).

Suddenly, I began to welcome the coolness of the night, as exhaustion began to creep up on me. Now just begging for the sun to start setting as soon as possible. As the last spark of natural light left my eyes, I know it's time. Immediately I stopped jogging and began walking, relishing the darkness of the night to act as my cover(for now, there is only one or two street lights every block or so.). Keeping myself calm and steady, I listened for any abnormal sounds from the night. Trying to subtract all the other sounds from the equation(like the honking of cars in the distance from the more populated areas of New York City, and the hovering of helicopters in the distance), I listened carefully, trying not to breath heavy so as not to disturb what I was doing. A scamper of feet and the faint outline of a shadow against a brick wall told me that there was a rat in my presence, allowing for a quick shudder to go down my back even though I lived in New York City my whole life, I still haven't gotten used to the usual presence of rats.

The sound of glass crashing caught my ear. I listened carefully for any more signs of distress. Angry voices caught my ear, yet I couldn't exactly decipher what they were saying. It was all happening at a distance. Cautiously, I began to sprint, trying to figure out where it all was coming from. The sound of my heart roared inside my ears, making it even more hard to try and concentrate to see exactly where it was coming from. Building upon building, street upon street, no matter how much I ran, I seemed to have gotten no closer or no further. I am definitely not running in circles, I know for a fact, yet the sound just stayed the same level of intensity, and I cannot decipher why. Is it all in my head, or is there actually something going on? Am I forgetting where I am going? I take a side-glance towards the nearest street sign, Clay Pitts road. Nope, definitely know where I am going. Then WHAT is it!?

Suddenly it hit me like a rock, as I was about to turn a corner, I stopped suddenly. Maybe they knew I was here, maybe they heard some sort of disturbance from me, and have been getting QUIETER as I neared, making it almost sound like I wasn't making any progress. I listened again, and yet the third chill crept down my back again, only this one seemed to have more of a lasting effect on me. They were right around the corner! How could I be so dumb!? I should of saw this coming or something! This is WAY too close to be able to devise a plan without a huge chance of getting noticed! Slowly I poked my head around the corner, almost making my heart stop as I saw how many there were. Four people, possibly the most amount of people I ever had to deal with in my life! And of course there has to be that many people the day I made a mistake. I quickly shot my head back as one of them shot a glance in my general direction. But before I did that, I managed to pick up two things from the situation. First, the guy who is getting beaten up right now(and chances are murdered), seems to have so many injuries, that he probably is going to get knocked unconscious any minute now, so I have very little time to spare. Secondly, based on how they are going about doing it, with their fists and all, leads me to believe that it's an enraged crime more than a robbery(though I do believe I saw one of them take a bill out of the guy's wallet), which means they are dangerous and no joke.

I begin gritting my teeth once again, gnawing over different ideas on how to go about this as fast as I could. Tonight, I am for sure going to get a scar from this encounter no questions asked, these guys know someone is coming, they almost seem to be sensing my presence. For two of them are punching the guy with fast but uneasy punches and two of them stopped all together, and now are beginning to look around, almost stupidly looking towards the back of the enclosed alley(yet another hindrance in tonight's "battle") as if someone was going to appear out of nowhere with no exit or entrance and start smacking them silly, though they most certainly deserve to be smacked silly. But at least intellect is one upper hand that I have.

Now was my chance, it was time for me to save this guy's life. Quickly, I sprinted as fast as I could towards one of the guys who were checking the back of the alleyway. Immediately I was spotted by the other two men who were punching their victim, they spoke a quick warning to their friends as they came hurtling towards me. But it was too late, as I launched myself up, and jumped right on top of the guy, using the force of gravity to my advantage, I grabbed a hold of his head to brace myself(as he tried pushing me away with his hands), and he fell face-first into the ground, I made sure to bonk his head against the ground, knocking him unconscious, one down, three more to go. Above my great judgment not to do so, I took a swift glance at the guy who was getting beaten up to make sure he was still alive. He laid still, but I saw his chest painfully rise up and down, he was unconscious, but still alive, for now.

Just then, the air got knocked out of my lungs as I was pushed to the ground by one of the men. Bad IDEA, Bad IDEA, those words echoed in my head as I tried scrambling away from his hits. Two blows from his fists managed to land their aim on my head, my hands tried to scramble for a hit. I think I managed to gain a hit on him when suddenly he got up, I looked to see why, and noticed that they were all blocking the only exit. I gulped. This wasn't good at all. Blood streamed down my forehead and into my left eye as I got up and looked to see what is going to happen next.

"Well, well, well, it looks like it's just a little girl" one of them said, his voice filled with hatred, and annoyance, but he knew he had the upper hand at the moment as he said this. He stood in the middle of the other two, obviously the "leader" of them all.

The one to his right chuckled the most twisted chuckle I ever heard, it made my stomach twist in disgust. "Trying to be a hero I see?" he inquired, grinning a devilish grin.

I kept my gaze solid as a rock, trying to devise my plan out. They were all arrogant, so I know I wouldn't have to worry about them also trying to devise their own plan, they probably think they already won, and that I was already dead, that all they actually had to do was make that fact into a reality. Best bet, was to wait for their first move towards me, and go right from there.

My hands tightened up into fists, getting ready for their first aggressive step towards me, that's all that it would take for me to slam their faces into the concrete. Better run now when you guys have the upper hand, for tides do change, I thought, deciding against sharing my thoughts with them, even though it was very tempting. "Why not call 911?" the other one on the left said, mocking me, "You'd have to be so brainless to come up to four guys by yourself and expect to have the SLIGHTEST chance of winning". Which was true, I was pretty brainless when I came up with the idea, but not for the reason they think. The reason why I was so brainless is that they took me by so much surprise, that I actually did forget to call 911 before I came to fight like I usually do when I am dealing with more than two people. Other than that, my plan didn't fall through ENTIRELY. I'm still going to try to save our lives, and hopefully succeed, whether they think I am going to is a different story.

In reply I wiped some blood off my forehead so it wouldn't eventually get into my eye. I'm pretty sure I have two abrasions on my head(how severe, I really don't know), and multiple scratches on my arms and legs. All in all, today really wasn't the best on me, but I have seen worse.

Unlike the criminals one would see on television shows and movies, the ones I deal with, are actually real (Of course), so they don't stay on the topic of how much I lost or anything(good thing too, for I'd get VERY bored), they just get to the point. If one would've blinked, they would have for sure missed the exchange the three shared. It was a small exchange, almost a curt-nod, but that's all that I needed to know that they were going to attack like sharks in a feeding frenzy. I braced myself for my counter attack, I am now more ready than I ever was.

Quickly, they all ran towards me, the one on the left's hands stretched out, almost the designated one to hold me down, for the other two had their fists out. Sharply and with precision, I took one side-ways glance towards my right and there was a balcony-type thing a floor up, and so, without anymore thinking, running over as fast as I could to the other side of the alley, and without hesitation I jumped up, and gripped on to the balcony, dangling I swung myself back quickly, and then shot myself forward in the air. Landing with a hard thud now behind all three of them, I reminded myself that the smart thing to do was probably run away and call 911, most certainly giving all of them time to escape but ensuring my safety all the same, now that was the smart thing to do, now of course to my greater-satisfaction, I am not very smart.

So I spun around and ran straight towards the one on the now left side(he was the one on the right side before), they didn't have time to turn around as I most keenly took a different approach then last time, I jumped on top of him, starting to make him fall, and kicked off, doing a once-in-my-lifetime flip. Landing most clumsily on my feet, and using my hands for balance, I stood right back up(in time to see the guy fall right down, hitting his head on the ground thankfully, knocking himself out). Now the other two had time to turn towards me, now charging the short distance towards me like enraged bulls. I ducked right down in just enough time, for I heard the swish of a fist flying right above my head, just skimming my hair and making a gusty breeze blow into my face.

As I did this, I swung my right arm backwards, and hooked my aggressor right in the stomach, making a thumping noise as I hit the flesh. With no time to spare, I used my left hand to grab a hold of an ankle(by catching a fast glance at his face I was able to determine it's the leader's ankle), I pulled forward, making him fall right then and there, as two other hands came right towards me. With no hands free, I used the only option left possible, and butted my head right against his in defense. My head began ringing the second it happened, it was like ramming your head into a brick wall!!! Still, it worked like magic, as he yelled out in pain(like a GIRL!) and stumbled back a few feet holding his head in his hand, obviously trying to dull the pain, but of course that sort of thing doesn't work! So seeing my chance, I leapt up onto my feet and charged right at him, and I pushed him against the side of a building, grabbing a hold of him, and then I pushed him right towards the ground before he had the chance to react. Knocked unconscious.

I took a sigh of relief, then was stunned to see the "leader" coming straight towards me, his eyes burning with the sort of anger one would only be able to imagine that would come from the devil himself, without really thinking, I ducked down, and he was running so fast, that he couldn't have had anytime to be able to stop himself, and with a crack and thud, I heard him run into the wall. Covering my head, he fell right on top of me. Trying not to completely loose the contents of my stomach, I shoved him off of me, taking a good amount of my energy from me. He felt like a thousand pounds for Pete's sake! Blood rolled off of my head, not my blood, but his blood, as I did so. Finally he was off of me and laying right on the ground, blood coming out of his head at a slow enough pace to say that he wasn't in any danger right now.

My hands now sticky with blood, I wiped them on the ground next to me(dodging the bodies), smearing the blood across the ground, as I tried to think about where I should start. Believe it or not, my first priority is most certainly not to clean up, for the things I am going to have to do after that would ruin it all. Noticing that I don't have my bag with me anymore, that it must of fell during the little scramble, I got up, and looked around for my bag, scanning the whole area, I found it sitting in a shadow right near the balcony. It had to have fallen when I did that little jump, I'm very surprised that I didn't realize that before. Walking over to it, I began assessing my injuries. The ones on my legs were just minor cuts and bruises mostly from getting pushed over, the ones on my arms, just the same. Of course it had to be my head that had the worst injury, I felt some blood dripping out of a cut on the top of my forehead, which could probably be covered up by my hair. Though the one on my cheek would probably have to be covered up by some make up or something. As for the healing purposes, some ointment should probably do the trick as it usually does and time would do the rest.

I bent down to pick up my back pack and began scrummaging through it. Out came a junky looking cell phone, not my main one that cost me a pretty penny to buy it and then to service it, but one of the 40 dollar pay-as-you-go cell phones that really are decent when you first get them, but when it comes to myself, gets pretty junky looking after a month or so of carelessly dropping it at the weirdest of times. I bought this phone so that when I call 911, the police can't track it in anyway back to me so I don't get caught. I placed it on the ground, ready to dial straight away the second I need it. Then, I took out a paper and pen and quickly(and messily) began writing:

4 guys dressed in black were attacking victim...

I took a side ways glance at the victim and what he was wearing, looked like a white t-shirt? Really couldn't tell the EXACT color under all the blood, but I was pretty darn sure it was white before the blood.

dressed in a white shirt, for who knows what exactly the reason was other than being mad. One with head badly banged up seems to be the "leader" fyi.

I finished off with my usual "B" signature and then I took the paper and placed it in plain view in front of the crime scene. Then I picked up a lone rock that I managed to find and dropped it on top of the piece of paper so that the paper didn't fly away due to the gathering wind(The wind was picking up faster and faster every second now). After that, I turned back to my bag and pulled out a rope. Deciding against dragging them all together and saving a little bit of extra rope, I thought that it would be better to save my energy than just twenty dollars worth of string(at most!). I wrapped it around one guy's left hand, then another's right, then another's left, and then another's right, until finally, I got it all knotted up around every one of their hands. I did this more or less for a precaution just in case they woke up a little bit sooner than I expected and got away with this crime. Of course I didn't wrap the victim's limbs up, but those and my own were the only ones not wrapped up with another by now. I allowed myself a quick laugh at how foolish and odd it looked, a bunch of men tied up together by rope. It is plausible that there could be a better way of restraining them but.... It's just too funny of a joke to pass up, besides, why spend an extra 100 dollars per night and burn a hole in my wallet just so that criminals can feel comfortable when they are knocked out unconscious. If they wanted to feel comfortable, they shouldn't have messed with anyone in the first place(most particularly anyone within a five mile radius of my house.).

Using my elbow to wipe a little blood out of my eye yet again(the cut was beginning to slow down, but hasn't stopped all the way), I walked back to my bag and placed the white-rope back into it. Then I looked around and thought about whether or not there was something I was forgetting. I glanced over at the victim, narrowing my eyes just a bit to focus in on him, I saw the small rise and fall of his chest as his body fought against the lack of blood, I wanted to help him, but I am no doctor and I'm pretty sure I'd harm him even more by trying to help with what little knowledge I have. Even though I have been doing this for some five years now, I never really did get any knowledge what-so-ever of taking care of the victims. It's not necessarily that I don't WANT to, but more or less that I really don't have TIME to learn different ways to help stop the blood without harming the person you are working with(for everyone knows that if you press down too hard, you will bruise them and harm their vital organs even more, if you press down too light, you would just get blood on you and it just won't do anything. I'd rather not take any chances, especially when there is still time until he is in any immediate danger.).

I yawned a huge yawn as I turned the other direction back to the phone. I guess it is probably time to call 911, with everything done now... I clicked 911 and pressed send. I spoke into the phone without waiting for the answerer to begin her/his usual "911 what's your emergency?", I spoke fast, and quietly so that the operator couldn't pick up the various pitches my voice has, as usual, and couldn't somehow trace it back to me, yet again. "SEND POLICE cars, and ambulances to the street address I am at right now, I have no clue where I am so start tracking it", I knew exactly where I was but I'd have to stay on line longer to say it if I did "There has been a major crime here, and a victim is dieing, bye". I heard replies of "WAIT, Don't hang up!" over and over again, I let it go for some twenty or so seconds so that they did have time to track it, then I hung up. I snapped the phone shut, and turned it off quickly, then I shot it right into my backpack.

I swung my bag over my left shoulder, and walked over to the edge of the alley in wait. There were cameras everywhere in New York City, I know this for a fact. And the police are most certainly going to check them after tonight also, that's a fact too. But see the thing that is false, is the fact that these cameras can pick up crisp and clear images of everything. In fact, these cameras merely shows just figures during the day, and even worse images at night. So why have cameras, one may ask? Well they are merely so that the Government can tell the public that they have cameras out to help stop crime, when in fact they do indeed have cameras and can't be scorned whats-so-ever for lieing to the public in order for them to feel secured, they didn't exactly LIE, they just didn't tell the whole TRUTH. The Government has a pretty crafty way of doing things if you ask me, but I do indeed gain from this. For now I don't have to worry about them trying to track me down(not that they were to care or anything, but just in case), so basically, it sort of back-fires on them. It is kind of funny how karma is a pain in the butt to some, yet a really nice weapon to others.

I stood there waiting, I want to make sure that they were able to track it down correctly and that the victim would be able to be in medical attention very soon. I leaned up against one of the walls of a building and darted my eyes back and forth, looking for any signs of one of the first arrival vehicles. For before they actually send out the real vehicles, the police and fire department always has one of the patrolling police vehicles check it out for a number of reasons at night. First reason, and possibly the most obvious on of them all, is to make sure it's not a prank or anything. They HATE it when that sort of thing happens and it stops them from doing what is really needed of them from doing, and personally, I'd be very ticked if some sixteen year old kid thought it was so funny to claim that there was a serious crime happening, thus wasting my time, none or less getting me worried out of my mind just for a stupid prank.

Secondly, there is the whole fact that it could still be dangerous, and they'd rather not have a bunch of civilians(quite nosy ones actually) coming over to see what's going on and end up being injured or killed because of it. It would harm the people, and I'm pretty sure the department would have a pretty lawsuit on their hands because of it costing them millions of dollars for some stupid-civilian's mistake. It's amazing, the things people would do just to get money! More or less even the fact of blaming someone for their negligence when in fact that one person was trying to HELP them. People really aren't the brightest, are they?

I got way too lost in thought, for before long I saw the

headlights of one of their patrol cars turning off suddenly as it spot me. I felt my body froze in an instance, quickly jotting down the question run, or stay to see what happens. Not in a good situation. I glanced to see how far the car was, maybe a block or two away, enough time to run? I took the chance, and darted away, as fast as I could. Because this car was coming from the direction my apartment is, I decided(or rather HAD) to go the opposite way it is and then swing back. As I ran I realized for the first time tonight that my breath was uneven and erratic, something that REALLY said bad things. Ignoring that thought(more so for my Emotional health then my Physiological health), I concentrated on running as fast as I could, while figuring out my route home.

It really isn't that hard, I know these streets from inside-out, I know every turn, every street light, and every sign there is. All thanks to five years of going out here at night, I can practically figure out ten different ways back to my apartment from here, blind-folded. So running it NOT blind-folded, has to be a piece of cake for me, even if that piece of cake is covered in the grotesque and bugging discomfort of blood and dirt, plus the possibility of several scratches getting infected by the moment. Now of course that one "easy" thing for me, has to come with some difficulties.

One problem was staying quiet, I don't know if it's just the way I walk or the types of shoes I buy or something, but when ever I walk/run/jog, I some how manage to be REALLY loud, and when I say really, I mean REALLY. For as I'm running, I some how manage to wake people up out of their beds enough for them to turn on the light in their room and shut the window and blinds(why they have their windows open at night in the middle of New York City is almost a complete mystery to me. Alarm systems maybe? Still, I wouldn't exactly take the chances...).

Second, the ability to tolerate ANY sort of pain. I, like most people, am not a fan of it. But unlike most people, you will KNOW when I am in pain. Not something that I consciously do, but for some odd reason, my eyes always seem to tear up the way they are right now when ever I feel the stinging and have enough time to think about it. And when I'm running a mile by myself in the middle of a vacant summer(still spring, but feels like summer for summer is coming really soon!) with dirt in all my scratches, I most certainly do have MORE than enough time to think about it. And NO, I am NOT making myself tear up, again, it just happens naturally almost. So, running with tears blurring up my vision isn't my FAVORITE thing to do, but of course there has been worse.

To my amazement, I made it to my apartment safe and sound(trying to ignore the scratches n' all). Taking out my key from my bag, and silently placing it in the key hole, unlocking the door, I slowly opened the door, trying so very hard not to make a sound and wake up the kids. Thankfully the squeaky door did not squeak the tiniest bit as I closed the door behind me.

Unlike that one awful time about a year ago when I went so slow, and I took so much of my time not to disturb them all, then suddenly out of no where it made the largest squeak I ever heard! It was literally as if that door had some sort of vengeance with me! I mean honestly, it was so quiet and then bam, it squeaked up a storm. That night lead me with reading Summer a bed-time story five times over again for a whole hour, and then me being kept up by the two boys when they said how they really did deserve to watch television after I woke them up(when in actuality I could see it in their faces that they were watching television right before I got in and quickly ran upstairs when they heard me coming in. So in fact, they were just trouble-making liars, and yes, even little Tim is a trouble maker, but it's not like Scott doesn't have anything to do with it).

I looked at the clock, checking the time(duh), which read 3:00 o'clock in the morning. Yet like usual, I was wide-awake somehow, almost energized(maybe?) from the fight some how. Definitely kept me awake when I was jogging, the fact of getting caught still lingers in my head from time to time. I began walking towards the bathroom, careful not to step on any creaky boards, and really careful as not to stomp so loud(walking slow takes me a long time of course, because it's walking SLOW, but when you add in the fact that I have to keep my feet silent, that's when slow gets a new definition in the dictionary as not the least fastest in the book, but the second least fastest thing in the book, right after the name "Zoey Aquarius D'Bandit" and the words "While trying to walk silently".) I wasted more time than needed walking to a bathroom that was less than ten feet away, but still always worth the extra precaution.

Once I got into the bathroom, I shut the door behind me(silently), before I turned on the light so as to let as little light into the eyes of sleeping children as possible. Then I went to the closet in the bathroom, opened the door, and took out a whole new set of pajamas that I kept stored underneath some towels(replenished almost every morning). Those pajamas, were basically a t-shirt and pair of sweats, so the only reason why I always have to change from my former outfit at night is because of sweat, blood and dirt. I placed the things on top of the counter by the sink and began running some hot water for the shower. The sound of water is possibly the only thing that NEVER wakes up the others, ever. It's indeed a strange blessing, but one that I really do appreciate. So I really don't have to worry about how loud the water is running in the house hold unless for some reason I'd rather not hear it running myself(which would probably create a problem seeing that I am a sixteen year old girl who shouldn't have the immaturity level of a three year-old or the lack-of-patience for things in life of an eighty year old woman.).

I took a look at myself in the mirror, dirt and blood was smeared all over my face like I was almost swimming in it. The only adjective that I can really clearly describe it as was the word: gross. So first things first, wash my face before I start tending to the cuts on it. So I turned on the sink and began splashing water into my face, scrubbing real hard. Reaching my left hand from the water and to the open closet, I pulled out a towel at which I began rubbing across my face to dry as I turned off the water with my other hand. After that I looked into the mirror once again, now I can see the actual cuts in which the blood was coming from(the one on my cheek and the one on my forehead), now that I can see them without any blood blocking the way(for the cuts also stopped bleeding), they didn't look AS BAD as I thought they were. They just hurt real bad, which I guess is something I can deal with as long as I don't really think about them for any long period of time. My eyes looked tired though, they really needed sleep and bad. The hazel color to them, actually now had red streaks in them, signaling the fact that a bit too many blood vessels were popped. I looked away from the mirror once again due to the same reason, the appearance of my eyes, yet a different appearance. From that scary look that I can see why people turn away when ever I give them eye-contact to the disgusting blood-shot look that probably happens to my eyes ATLEAST thirty times a year. Still, I don't get use to it, either of them actually.

So after all of that, I took a shower, and I went to bed.

CHAPTER 3

My morning went something like this. I woke up to the honking of cars and NOT the ring of my alarm clock. Of course I forgot to set my alarm clock, and so I was late for the regents. I had to quickly get ready, throwing my hair up in a pony tail, and rush to the kitchen to grab a granola bar to go. I was half way out of the door, when I realized that I forgot my bag, SO of course I had to rush back up the steps and into the apartment and grab my bag, trying so very hard not to fall over all the junk on the floor(and reminding myself to either clean it up later, or have the others clean it up for it sure wasn't my stuff on the floor.). Because of the fact that I was indeed VERY late, I didn't have the option what-so-ever to walk to the school like I usually do, so I had to take a taxi(thankfully, the one I called was nearby).

Well, that sure didn't go well. Taxi drivers in New York City, are no joke in any way, usually, locals get used to it, and why not, seeing as they have to ride one everyday. Not I, I hated taxi drivers when I was a kid, I hate them now, and I will probably always hate them for as long as I live. Taxi drivers are just way too fast and unsafe for me, and they swear up a storm with how much road rage they have. The drives make me queasy, and very uncomfortable, so one could only imagine how over-joyed I was when I found out that I HAD to take a taxi cab right before my regents. Great. Lovely. Just the best thing in the entire world! I swear, if I EVER had to take another taxi again.... Well, lets just leave it at THAT.

Thankfully, I had enough time to regain myself, and run right into the test-taking room right before they were about to shut the doors(gaining myself some nasty glares from students and teachers alike). The test was decent, definitely not easy, but not hard either. Although there was a mishap in which I accidentally skipped one bubble and then filling in the rest wrong, didn't realize it until I was like forty questions through the test. It was a MAJOR setback, and it agitated me so greatly, but I managed to work with it.

Finally, when the bad luck began to dwindle, I managed to get to the coffee shop in one piece. Ordering myself an Iced-cappuccino(iced because, I am honestly not sure whether or not the bad luck finally wore off, or if it's just hiding in the shadows waiting to pounce on me like a jaguar when I least expect it), I sat down at a table in plain view, but off to the side slightly and I began browsing on the internet on my computer(that booted up rather quickly this time). Nothing really interested me, sports, clothes, movies, nothing that I actually cared about to look into more, so I just settled with some online racing game against some stranger to distract myself with as I waited for Sam. The game was one of those annoying games when the person is so good, that you know for a fact that they spend their lives online, trying to perfect their skills so that they can beat someone at the game. Plausibly(and very certainly) a guy with no life, no family and definitely no girlfriend. One is really not supposed to judge, but it's kind of hard when we are playing a kid's game and yet I can't seem to get ahead of him for even the slightest of moments, no matter how-hard I try(I love competition, and competition seems to be equally attracted to me as well. So basically, I really do TRY HARD), he always seems to beat me.

I was about to rage quit when suddenly my screen went black and on the screen it read "User logged off". I grinned with an immature-satisfaction. Good to know that I wouldn't look like the child logging off,. Though it probably wasn't the fact that the competition was too good for him, but more or less the fact that the competition was too lame for him, still, it makes me feel THAT much better.

"Wow, you are quite immature, water-bringer" Sam said, his voice interrupting my thoughts. I rolled my eyes in annoyance at him.

"Good to see you too, Bear" I said, being so polite in using the average less-offending nickname I had for him. That nickname has soooo much history to it, to make a long-story short, that's the name that I called him due to his last name, merely as a joke when we first met, but it kind of grew on me, so I began using it often, and now here we are.

He gave a half-grin, his dark blue eyes brimming with a sort of intensity, most certainly the more clearer set of eyes I've ever seen. He is one of those "pure" type of people. He says what's on his mind, but it never really isn't all that bad. I mean, yeah, he thinks it's quite funny using the nickname like nails on a chalkboard against me, but that's kind of just because we are friends. I mean, he is always straight out in saying things, for example, if he wasn't too fond of you, you would know all too well. He sat down at the other chair at my table, and closed my computer.

"Yeah, help yourself, there is plenty of computers to close here at the café" I muttered, not very serious, but not very happy in the way he just shut my most expensive computer like it was just some piece of junk.

"I need your FULL attention when I am talking to you right now Zoey, please, this really is important" Sam said, as he held out a New York City newspaper and showed it too me.

I grabbed the newspaper from his hand as I said "What's this?". I began flipping through the newspaper with really no interest at all, though a spark of curiosity of why he was showing it to me was there also. He grabbed the newspaper back from me, without saying a word, and began flipping through it, possibly trying to find the article that has him so worked up at the moment? I blew a strand of hair out of my face, ignoring how rude Sam was being at the moment, and I looked out towards the streets below. They finally seemed to have fixed the streetlight and was beginning to put everything away. I wonder if it would be all taken care of by the time this little "meeting" with Sam was finished.

I felt a quick gust of air blow right past me, signaling that Sam must of found the article he was looking for and placed it in front of me. I took a quick glance at the newspaper, nothing caught my eye except one of the articles(actually, the biggest one on the page, which was smack in the middle). The headline was "The Bandit". My eyes narrowed, as I began skimming through the article(for I'm not much of a fan for reading myself). Bandit, night, criminals, New York City, wanted, those were basically the words I managed to pick up from the reading, even then I had a pretty good idea as to what it was about. I glanced back up to Sam, inquiring whether or not it was what I thought it was about with a look in my eyes. He nodded, proving my thoughts rights. "But how?" I asked, I've done it for five years now, and the media is JUST beginning to care about me doing it.

"Look at the one that wrote it" he said, pointing to a little box in the corner of the article. It said that it was written by the police!? Why on Earth...!?

"Okay, now why would the police care now?" I asked, I can almost feel my heart rate increasing by the moment, this is not good at all!? It doesn't make sense what-so-ever, why they'd suddenly care! After all these years too! You'd think I would be making their lives a lot easier. And what's with the semi-ironic name they gave me, the Bandit? Very interesting name, is that the only word that they could think of that started with the letter b? No imaginations in any way.

"My guess, they always cared, and they always wanted to know who it was" Sam said, taking a sip of his coffee(which I haven't noticed before now strangely enough), and then he went on "they've probably been trying to catch you ever since you were doing it for over a month, and after failing more than enough times, I think they are putting it into the public's hands".

I snorted with even greater displeasure. "Pretty lame idea if you ask me" I said, rolling my eyes in huge annoyance. Honestly, this is when I start treading dangerous waters, which is not good in any way imaginable(hence the word "Dangerous".).

"YOU better watch yourself now, trust me, it isn't good for you to be doing that in the first place, and as soon as the F.B.I or something gets wrapped up in this case, it's game over for you" Sam said. And it probably WOULD be game over for me, people don't like it when you get into their business, even if it is trying to help stop crime(or rather bring it to justice), I'm pretty sure I'd get fined with a pretty hefty bill if I got caught, even(HUGE chance) go to jail. "You should probably stop Zoey, I mean it, it's not safe for you anymore, and quite honestly it is only sooner or later when you start getting some REAL injuries" he took a side-ways glance at the newer scratches on my face for a moment, then looked away.

"I'm not going to stop, you do realize that, right?" I said, rather bluntly, but basically to drive the point across. I really do owe it to the people of New York City to help them in ways that the security system has not. People DESERVE justice, and without me doing the things that I do at night, all those criminals would have been just marching along the streets, ruining more people's lives without punishment. Harassment in any shape or form to others is what needs to be stopped. When someone is hurt, that is the case that the police should try to tackle as fast as possible, not cases that involved drugs or things like that! I mean honestly, SOMEONE has to be looking out for the victims, the people.

"You should, really Zoey." Sam said, trying to convince me, but he knew that the battle was over before it even began, I made up my mind.

"No, Sam, honestly, it is alright, I can figure out a way not to be caught, trust me on this when I say that I haven't been caught before, now how will I be caught now, with even more knowledge on all of this?!" I said, realizing that now we both were speaking in a whisper for some reason. Oh, right, shouldn't be heard by anyone else.

"Fine, I suppose there is no use in trying to persuade you anymore. Just please, don't get too arrogant of yourself" Sam said, as he took a glance out the window towards the street below. Me, arrogant!? Wow, he should be talking now. One flaw in Sam has to be the fact that he is the KING of arrogance, and I mean it. I've never met anyone more arrogant in my life than Sam(hopefully I won't, for that would just be way too arrogant). What Sam doesn't realize is probably the fact that he is arrogant himself. I never understood how someone can be so arrogant and not realize it. I don't think I've ever heard Sam say something like "I'm going to loose" or even ask "Do I look alright today?". Nope, the words that comes out of his mouth are more like "WHEN I win this game against you, what else would you like to do?" or "Wow, I definitely look good today, and everyday actually…"(when he says that, he's kind of getting in touch with his more feminine side, and it kind of scares me, just a smidge.).

Of course when you first meet him, arrogant is not the first word that comes to mind, but it is the first word that comes to mind once you get to know him. So, why he was calling me arrogant is above me?!

"Yeah, fine, I won't be ArroGaNT" I said, saying the last word with such sarcasm, that I had to roll my eyes.

"Yeah, whatever Zoey. Lets just leave it at that then. Anyways..." Sam said, leading into a huge discussion about his regents that he has to take, and how for sure he was going to pass it, he felt pretty sure of himself(the arrogance showing there), then he asked me how I thought I did on the regents, I just said fine and asked him what he and his dad was doing over the summer. Then, he got into a long discussion with me about how they were going to go camping next week, and it is going to stink for it's just him and his father, and the big open wilderness. But he also admitted to the fact that he was sort of siked about finally getting to use his fishing license that he got a couple years ago(for who knows why, he's in the middle of New York City, where there is only lakes in random places that are way too crowded to actually enjoy fishing without having the fish getting scared away by a passing boat every ten minutes.). I asked him where he was going as the thought of camping there would just be way too stupid, and he told me, some place in upstate New York, on lake Ontario. I told him it sounds like fun, and to make sure not to get eaten by a bear or anything cause that would REALLY be ironic and something to laugh at. Sam didn't think it was too funny, so he countered with telling me that he wished that I can come along cause he is really going to need someone to bring his water. My reply was a quick stab on his toes with my foot, and that was the end of THAT discussion.

Amazingly though, he still seemed a bit too smug that he came up with such a good joke, so I told him that it's pretty sad when he is the only fan of his own jokes, in which he replied to me, at least he had a fan, compared to someone who isn't even a fan of her own jokes. Which really didn't make sense, but being the good friend that I am, I allowed it to slide. Then we got up, and left the coffee shop.

Taking the stairs, Sam began talking again and said "So anyways, I've noticed that you don't seem to like the word that they tacked you with in the newspaper. So my question would have to be, which one do you hate the most, The Bandit, or Water-Bringer?". That one was possibly a very hard one to answer, both of them were annoying and lame but in their own ways. Mauling over it for a few minutes, we managed to go down a couple floors before I finally replied back.

"I definitely hate The Bandit name more, but both are pretty stupid names, so it's surprisingly a close one" I looked at the next floor marker that now read floor 45.

"Oh, that's interesting, Bandit" he said the last word like ice. A chill ran down my back.

"Oh no" I said, my eyes looking towards him in disbelief, I am officially the stupidest person alive, right after those criminals that I messed with last night. Why is it that I am such an idiot, not realizing what he was hinting towards before this!? Ug, if this is what friendship is about, I'm glad I only have one friend that I hang out with as much as I do with Sam, even that, I can probably deal without.

"Oh, YES" Sam grinned a huge wide grin, Sam isn't the only one who likes messing with my intolerance for nicknames, but he is the one who likes it the most! "So, watcha' wanna do next, Bandit?", that wasn't a real question, it's just so that he can use that awful nickname now!

So trying not to give him the reaction he wants, I curtly said "Your grammar is incorrect, the words 'Watcha'', and 'Wanna' should be 'What do you' and 'Want to' ."

Sam rolled his eyes, "Don't act like you don't LOVE the name Bandit." he said, his grin seeming to double in size every second, now he's beginning to look like a less-dramatized grinning Cheshire cat.

"Ok, Samuel Adam Beer" I said, trying to snap the joke back to him.

"Bandit" he replied back. We went back and forth about ten times, until finally he added most smugly "I'm not going to stop calling you Bandit, and that name doesn't effect me anymore, so you mine as well save your breath and leave it be.", he clunked me on the head with an open hand, then began running ahead down the stairs like an immature child.

I sighed, as I looked towards the next floor marker that read level twenty, I decided to give him a head start. 10, 9, 8, I began counting down to zero in my head, 3, 2, 1. Then I began running down the stairs at such a high speed, that I knew for a fact that I was going to win. The rabbit and the turtle race thing only works in books, not in the real race. Especially when this "rabbit" trains every night with the worse of competitors the world can bring. So within moments, I managed to catch up to him, his eyes widened in shock as he slowed down to a walk again.

We were now on floor fifteen. I grinned, years of running most certainly paid off. And I can see it puts a damper on Sam's ego, for he is in track and running is sort of his thing, especially when getting beaten by someone who is in no sports what-so-ever.

"Ahh, don't worry, I really do run pretty fast Sam" I said, making sure that he is just fine with the fact that he just got beaten at his own game "Remember the fact as to what I do at night, don't forget, I think I'd be dead by now if I COULDN'T run that fast", not that Sam really needed ALL of his arrogance reinforced, but still.

Sam grinned, "Oh yeah, I forgot who you were for a second there Bandit", he said. Sam found his opportunity, and managed to pounce on it. Last time I EVER try to cheer him up.

I huffed "Last time I ever try to cheer you up Samuel Adam Bear!" I said, making sure to smack him in the back of the head when I had the chance.

"Wow, at first I thought a little five year old smacked me at the back of the head, then I realized that a five year old has more force than that, and so it must have been little old Bandit" Sam laughed. He earned himself another smack in the back of the head for that last one, twice as hard this time. Sam rolled his eyes "Still didn't hurt, but nice try, I love the enthusiasm you demonstrated right there". Okay, now he's just taunting me now. So instead of replying back to that, like I so very wanted to, I just kept on walking down the steps in silence. Sam seemed to have gotten into an even BETTER mood, really? Is this seriously happening right now? Sam is now whistling an annoying melody as we walk, its sound waves echoing off the stair wall, I felt like I was being bombarded by a thousand song-birds! Only if it was actual birds, instead of Sam's, lovely(with all the sarcasm in the universe now), melody, I would've found some way to really enjoy it. But of course my patience wearing down, I crumbled under the pressure.

"OKAY already, you can call me any name you want, just STOP with the whistling already!" I said, laughing uneasily.

Just right then he stopped "Okay" a long pause (possibly fifteen seconds afterwards) "BANDIT", he grinned yet again.

I rolled my eyes, "Sometimes, you are such a kid".

"And you're the one whose only friend is a 'kid'" Sam chimed back, completely unaffected by the poison in my words. I swear, sometimes it seems like he knows every little word I'm going to speak before I even THINK them.

I rolled my eyes, letting the conversation drop, as we began to reach the 11th floor. Counting the floors in my head as we went by them seemed to have lengthened the time, so by the time we got to the 5th floor, I just stopped counting all together. Finally, Sam spoke up once again.

"So, where to next?" he said those words quite serious, I looked at my watch to see what time it was. It was three o' three already! Wow, time fly's by sooo fast. It's a shame that I have work in an hour.

"Home, for me. I have to go to work at four o'clock and I need enough time to get there and get ready. Sorry" I said, apologetic.

"Can't I come with? I mean, you work at a clothing store don't you? As a cashier to be exact. I'm sure you'd have enough time to spare to just TALK to me, even then I can just look through the clothing when you are busy" Sam said, acting all clingy right now, something is up.

Out front I said "What, can't take much of your dad?" somehow, I knew this was the cause, but I laughed a bit at the end to lighten the mood of the question so as not to offend him.

"Sadly, yes. He's planning on going bait-shopping for the trip" he said, and as I opened my mouth to say that's not that bad, he cut me off "After that, he's planning on taking me to go see the movie "Fish", a documentary on, you wouldn't believe it, the history of fishing.". Sam almost seemed to hang his head in failure.

"Oh, well, that DOES sound bad..." I said, imagining how awful of a movie it must be. Who in their sane-mind would want to watch a documentary about the history of fishing?

"Yeah, it is. So basically my idea is, if I'm not around him long enough to do those events before going camping, then I will not have to see such a RIDICULOUS movie." Sam said, glancing over to me he added "So, are you going to let me come, or let me suffer the most intolerable fate anyone can have?".

"Fine, but don't go crying to me when your dad ends up charging into the store with several of his police buddies claiming that I kidnapped you, cause it won't be pretty for EITHER sides alike" I said, finally we were now standing right in front of the 1st floor exit.

* * *

Never has working a boring and semi-long shift(four to close) felt so short as it did when Sam was there. We really didn't talk about anything in particular but gosh does it help when a friend is there. I have never had so much fun working in my life as I did with Sam. Basically, it was all his obnoxious(and rude) in-a-good-way comments/actions to the more ruder of customers that made it SO FUNNY! Usually when people talk to me as if they are some how "higher" than me, I manage to stick it with them, and end up getting the tables turned on them. But since I am an employee and I was working, my usual approach would not work unless I'd like to see myself get fired. So, I kind of just basically kept my mouth shut when a customer was being rude to me. But Sam seemed to catch on all too well and decided to take matters into his own hands.

When ever a customer was acting quite superior to me, Sam would figure out his own way to get them back. Like, how one of the customers were ordering(yes, ordering me) to get her the exact sized t-shirt she wanted when I clearly(and rather politely) said that we were all out, and I'd be happy to find her another shirt just like it in the size that she wanted(which was an XXXL by the way). She began exploding off the walls and saying basically how I was discriminating against larger people because some reason I don't like them and then, she told me that I had to get the shirt unless I wanted to be fired for discriminating against larger people. When all this was happening, Sam managed to slip out of view, and came back with something in his hand.

Before I knew it, Sam "Accidentally" tripped over a clothes rack, and fell right over, spilling then, what I finally found out was water, all over the lady. He quickly got up, putting on a real good act he said "Oh my gosh, I am so sorry miss!" and then literally walked away as if nothing even happened, the lady was so stunned that she didn't even have time to say anything to Sam until he was too far gone. I was trying ever so hardly not to laugh at what just happened, but really, that was the most funniest thing I have ever seen! Though the lady wasn't so happy herself, but thankfully she just walked away mumbling something about how the world is against her, playing the fiddle for herself once again. So depressing knowing that there are people out there, just like that. I almost pity them, that they cannot live life to the full extent that Sam or myself might of. But not enough to say that I want them ruining my day either. Things like that happened throughout my working-shift, of course not as huge or funny as that one, but still kept me very entertained.

VERY glad that Sam came with me now. So now, as we both walk back to my apartment together, I made sure to ask him something before I forgot "Can I have that newspaper by any chance?" I asked, knowing that there was something that I managed to read just enough to know that it is important, but oddly not enough to even remember what it is.

"Just after you pay me five dollars for it" Sam said, I could tell he was trying to make sure NOT to make eye contact with me, for it would ruin his supposedly "Funny" joke. We took a left onto the same road that my apartment was on, as the last bits of sunlight began to poke through the buildings in front of us.

"Haha, very funny. What? Is there a 4 dollars and twenty five cents fee, for last I knew newspaper should only cost about seventy five cents AT THE MOST around here, and that's if you are cheap enough to re-sell it to a friend after you clearly read through it more than enough times that you probably have MEMORIZED every single WORD in there", I said, proving my last statement with a quick sharp-point towards the winkled newspaper in his hand, I laughed and rolled my eyes. "Fine, you are just not allowed to use me as a reason why you stayed out so late Mr.", I skipped triumphantly in front of him, not looking back in the slightest bit.

He quickly caught up to me and off-balanced me just slightly mid-skip as he shoved me disapprovingly to the side. Catching my balanced I huffed "HEY, what was that for?".

"Not my fault you have bad balance skills little water-bringing Bandit." he said curtly, throwing in the most unexplainably, unfathomably, intolerable nicknames(of course now because of the lovely public, the word "nickname" is now plural) to boot. Things like this get really old, fast.

"Ha-ha, very funny, so can I have that newspaper, please?" I asked, throwing in the "please" just to sugar-coat it with Sam, even though any other time with each other it REALLY doesn't matter if we use the usual "polite" words when speaking.

"Yeah, of course." he handed the newspaper to me, I took it with gratitude, "Why do ya' need it anyways?" he added, honestly curious as to why I even wanted it.

And so to reward him for being semi-serious for a whole thirty seconds since we began walking to my apartment, I answered his question "I don't exactly know what I missed in that article, but I know it's something pretty big. So I want to go over it again and see if I can figure out what I managed to miss.".

He nodded his head, deep in thought. "Well, do me a favor and tell me if you do find out what it is, I'd like to have a little bit of knowledge to chew on seeing as I was the one who brought you this intriguing newspaper myself, hmm?", he said, the last part being more of a joke than serious more than anything, but still, he really did want to know the one thing I was trying to unravel, so the least I can do is tell him what happens AFTER I unravel it.

"Fair enough" I said, as we got to my front door and I pulled out a key to unlock the apartment door.

Sam's phone began to buzz in his pocket as I was just about to open the door, his eyebrows scrunched up as he looked at the caller, then he said "I've got to go, it's my dad. Didn't really tell him where I was going or anything, so I'm guessing he isn't in the most happiest of moods…".

"Wow, nice call Einstein, you couldn't have honestly thought that your dad would be okay with you going out without telling him, even if you are sixteen years old. I even know that!" I scowled at him in a joking manor then said "Well, see you later then".

Sam laughed, saying "Yeah, see you later also, maybe even in the newspaper, hmmm Bandit?". I rolled my eyes in reply and then he left. Opening the door silently I came into the apartment, thankfully seeing that Scott did in fact listened to me and got everyone in bed even though there was no one supervising them(sometimes Scott pushes it a little more later than he should, instead of 8 o'clock, he'd push it to 9 o'clock, not too happy when that happens). Setting down my set of keys, I walked over to the kitchen to grab something to eat before I get ready for my little night out. I picked an apple and bit into it, using the light that filtered in from the streets through the window to guide myself along the kitchen to get a glass of water. Quietly I sat down at the table and began going through different things in my head.

I always wanted to know who my REAL parents were, but not to the extent that drove me insane due to the fact that I had a loving adopted set of parents to fill in that gap. Now after they were brutally murdered, I had no one. Still, that feeling of wanting to know who my real parents were didn't increase in size or anything, even though that void now was completely empty and now scarred. Yet a lot lately, I have been wondering who they really were for some reason, I really can't put my finger on it. It's not like something of real significance in my life happened or anything, at least not that I know of. And it's most certainly not the fact that seeing Sam's relationship with his father makes me want some type of relationship with my birth parents, cause that would be pretty sad for his father wouldn't exactly be considered for "Father of the year", at least not in my eyes. So, why on Earth would I care what-so-ever now, when in fact during this time parents seem to be the least needed? Then I began thinking about that day.

Those eyes still burn at the back of my head, they were a cold set of dark-grey eyes that will never go away. The way they looked at me with such menace made me shiver in disbelief that day. How could eyes look so cold? Those were the eyes of a murderer. Those were the eyes of someone who didn't honestly think that I was going to remember, for he left me there, not injured or anything, just watching. I was six years old, how could I NOT have remembered that? His eyes were the only ones I managed to see during that whole time, the two others I never really caught. But truthfully, somewhere inside of me, tells me that his were the only ones that mattered. Him, and him alone was the REAL reason why they were killed. He might of just watched as the other two did the dirty work for him, using their own guns, but somehow, he has to be the REAL killer. He is the true murderer. That one lone flame he lit, I just know there was a reason behind it, almost symbolic(in a very horrid way), but WHAT?

I sighed a big sigh, trying to push back the thoughts for another time when I wasn't alone in the dark with no one to stop me from completely balling my eyes out. Trying to take my mind off of it, I glance at the newspaper that I still held in my other hand and opened it up right to the page of the article. I then went over to the garbage and threw away what was left of the apple and sat down once again. I took out my phone to light the page, outside wasn't light enough for reading for there is only small fragments of light now coming through the window. I then began reading it, word by word, line by line, paragraph by paragraph, until finally I stopped on the words that I was looking for. They read "It is still unknown as to who exactly he is...", that's it! I KNEW there was some type of major importance to this article other than the fact that it signified that they were catching on to me. This article SHOWS just how little they know. They somehow thinks it is a guy, so the cameras really don't pick up much as I thought they would, at all! I didn't even think the cameras picked up much, but now I know that they picked up so very little! The police are just GUESSING that it's a male, who knows how much more they are just GUESSING at too. This buys me some time, actually, a lot of time. There are so many people in the city, that even when they know my age and my gender, it would still take MONTHS to track down me. Yet they don't even know my gender, let alone my age! This is possibly the best miss-lead article in the newspaper that I have ever read.

Such a small little detail is going to make all of the difference. It kind of does make sense why they think that it's a male, cause the nickname "The Bandit" has no feminine touch what-so-ever, so it's good to know that the people of New York City aren't THAT stupid. Also, the fact that I'm pretty sure most females wouldn't do what I do even if they got paid a billion dollars, much less for nothing at all. Then again, there is probably no one in the exact same set of circumstances that I am in, good thing too for I wouldn't exactly "wish" it on anyone no matter how bad of a person they are.

I flipped over my phone and looked at the time. It is now nine forty five, time to go out, I thought with a slight grin to myself. I took the glass of water, and chugged the rest of the water in it down my throat, then I placed it into the dishwasher. I went to the bathroom to get changed, making sure to still be as silent as possible, and still being as slow as ever too. Once I got in there, I changed into my other set of clothes for tonight, and reminded myself once again to do laundry. I will have to do it tomorrow, I threw my other set of clothes in the basket. Then I went over to the mirror and placed my hair up in a pony tail once again, double-glancing at the mirror I realized that those scratches I managed to get yesterday night are indeed not the prettiest scratches I have ever gotten(not that scratches are EVER pretty), but were thankfully healing up quite nicely for the blood was already dried at the opening, stopping anymore blood from bubbling up.

They didn't SEEM infected, so I didn't bother trying to put antiseptic ointment on them or anything. I turned off the light in the bathroom, and opened the door afterwards, making my way to the door I stopped quickly to glance at the clock on the wall that now read ten o'clock, and I left the house, now I can actually walk faster than 2 miles per hour for now I don't have to worry about being quiet.

I then began jogging away from the house. The weather outside is exceptionally warmer from the other night, possibly by fifteen degrees. Interesting how the weather changes so drastically like that. After a little bit of jogging, I finally passed the road that I stopped at last time and kept going. After a few moments, I heard the crashing of glass and the whimpering of a kid. Someone shouted, as if struggling with something(or someone!) for his words were un-clear to the point that I couldn't quite decipher what they were to the slightest bit, my eyes widened, please tell me it isn't what I think it is, please, please, please. That thought rolled through my head some fifty times as I made my way to where the sound was the strongest. When the sound of it all was now pretty loud, I was pretty sure that the corner in front of me would lead to the scene that was unfolding. I really could've cared less at this point about a plan, for I already knew that I would ignore it the second I saw what was unfolding, so instead of just wasting time, I just cut-to-the-chase and bolted right around the corner and saw the most sure-scene I knew was taking place. A kidnapping.

A man was bent over a little girl(possibly five, MAYBE six years old, definitely younger than little Summer), and was placing a washcloth in her mouth to muffle the noise. This scene was most certainly that of a kidnapping, somehow I am still thankful due to the other thing that can be happening to her right now... I really did had to act quick, people like him usually had a get-away-car to hop into once they get the kid-nappies. Hopefully, his "backup" isn't much of a fan of him to come to his rescue after I am done with him. Running over as fast as I could, I jumped up with all the force in the world, and landed a blow up against the back of his head, quickly I made sure to grab a hold of his head, and I pulled back so he wouldn't land on the girl. Instantly I felt the kick of his leg against my stomach as he tried to break free of his attacker. This kick was well-aimed, and seeing as he didn't get a chance to have a good look at me, I think he thought I was much taller and definitely of a different gender, still, it hurt like crazy, enough for me to loosen my grip for just a millisecond. But that was all he needed to break free and turn himself around, ready to punch me in the face he swung back.

Seeing this coming I ducked quickly and dropped to my hands and knees, and using my entire body, I rammed myself against his legs to make his legs buckle out, he fell head-over-heels right above me and to the other side of me. Quickly, I got up and turned around, ready to punch him in the face so very hard. But he was faster, suddenly I got this awful feeling that he was a "professional" at this, he was right in front of me standing up high with his hands balled up in fists, and he swung back, pushing me to the ground, just inches away from the crying girl. My hands felt the wraith of the ground raking across them as I tried to most dumbly save myself with them. They felt like someone was lighting a match against them, but before I had anytime to worry about them in anyway shape-or-form, I was quickly whacked again by a well-aimed smack in the face. Trying to regain myself, I shot myself back up and almost blindly swung my fists in the air as I did so, still trying to shake off the surprise of the last blow. I know that one of them did land on the target because before I knew it I heard a huge thud on the ground, obviously it either was some-how a well-aimed punch, or I am just lucky and he is just a very weak man. Either way, I'm just glad that now I have the upper hand. I walked up to him, he was laying flat on the ground, trying to regain himself, but somehow couldn't. I looked down at him, not an ounce of mercy in my eyes for I know for a FACT that a little girl can't possibly have done ANYTHING to deserve it.

The only reason why I'm not so enraged when it is some adult is possibly the fact that I KNOW all little kids are innocent, there isn't a single thing that they could do to deserve it(even though most of the time when ANYONE gets kidnapped they really didn't deserve it). I mean, the victim last night, I really couldn't tell why he was getting beaten up. For all I knew, he was a criminal himself and stole from those four guys or something, I just don't know. Of course I wouldn't give him the chance to get beaten to death or anything like that just because of a small suspicion that he supposedly "deserved it", but yes, it does give me a different view on things when I KNOW it's out of pure "evilness" when someone is acting on a crime.

Quickly, I bent down to his level on the ground and I shot a punch right to his face, knocking him out. I might actually have a little bit of mercy in me due to the fact that I made the process of him becoming unconscious fast, not slow and painful, in which he very well deserves. Of course I wasn't going to kill him, that just means that I have stooped to his level and am just as bad as the rest of them. I got up, wiped the blood off my hands, and walked over to the whimpering girl. She saw all that was happening, poor little girl. Carefully, I walked over to her and removed the washcloth from her mouth and threw it to the side. Her eyes were now watering up as she looked me into the eyes, I wiped away a tear from her face with my hand, whispering "You okay?", she nodded.

"You, you saved me" she said, her eyes full of confusion, sadness, and gratitude. I felt a jab of pain, right inside my heart, did she honestly think that the world is so awful that she wasn't going to be helped, much less missed.

"Don't worry, you are alright now" I replied back, not really answering to what she said. Looking towards my book bag, that was still miraculously hanging from my shoulder, I took out my "working" phone, and dialed 911. This time, I allowed it to just ring for a quick second, be picked up, and then I just listened, making sure that the lady was going to send someone. She was, afraid that something really was happening. I then clicked the phone, and took another glance towards the little girl. "Listen" I started, a little rushed "I will stay here with you until the police come to help you out" I was going to stay, for I couldn't leave a little girl alone like this, it almost seemed WRONG, "Only then will I leave. Now, can you keep a secret and NOT tell anyone that I was here..." I paused, thinking up a plan in my mind, I thought that wouldn't happen, so briskly I said "Actually, if, WHEN they ask, just tell them that the Bandit saved you, and that is all, don't give off any information. Don't tell them that I'm a girl, my age, my eye color, nothing, understood?", I looked right into her eyes, seeing if she got anything, she nodded her head in response.

"Good" I said, then with a smile to try and lessen the pain of the situation for her I added "It will be our little secret", she laughed lightly, giving off a small little grin. Her eyes were a pretty light green color.

"So does that mean we are friends now?" she asked, a spark of hope shining in her eyes.

Part of what she just asked made me somewhat uneasy, I don't know why because she is only acting like most little kids, wanting to make friends with everyone they meet. So instead of saying my first reaction/thought which was laughing uneasily and then saying "NO", then leaving it at that, I decided the more correct and nicer way to be towards a little kid her age by saying "Of course, I already gave you my name, what's yours?", I hinted towards the fact that my name is The Bandit with her, she really didn't need to know my real name or anything, even though that nickname is such a stupid one...

"Willow" she said, her eyes shining even more at the thought of having a new friend. I grinned at that, for surprisingly she does look like a Willow to me, I then listened for the sounds of tires over the road in the background. Suddenly I saw the flashing of bright lights coming through into the alley, they were getting brighter and brighter as the car got closer and closer to the corner of the alley. I placed my finger across my lips in a shushing way, making sure she remembered to be quiet about me, and she did the same with a little grin. "Bye" she said, I replied back with a nod.

Realizing that it was far too late to be able to sneak out of the alley the front way, I began running towards the back, hoping that the plan in my head was going to work out. To my greater happiness, I saw what I was looking for. One of those basic ladders hanging from a balcony, quickly I grabbed a hold of the ladder and hoisted myself up, then I leapt towards another, more higher balcony. Regaining my balance, I took a swift glance over to where Willow was, who was now getting confronted by a worried looking cop, to make sure she was alright. She was, and so I got up on top of the small little side-wall on the balcony, and leapt from there on top of the roof of the other balcony(thankfully making it to my surprise) which was slightly higher than the base of the one I was on. From there, I leapt onto the roof of the balcony I was just on, finally I was at the highest point I could be without being on the roof. So I hoisted myself right up onto the roof, and that was that. All I had to do now was get home, using the roofs of some twenty buildings, so I don't get caught by the passing of police cars below, sounds simple enough(NOT!).

Balancing on the roofs was pretty much my strong point during the whole thing, my weak point in the plan has to be the fact that every building isn't the same height as the next! Some ranged from only a few feet or so, something I can learn to DEAL with, but most of them(lucky me) ranged(only on average) ten feet or so. So not only did I have to leap from building to building, but I had to so carefully plan it so that I can get onto a 3 by 3 foot balcony without falling! With the buildings that I had to go down on the other hand, I had to free-fall straight down onto the roof of the next building, trying so very hard not to fall onto my face.

Lovely. Thankfully, I am in New York City, so it was only about 20 percent of the buildings I had to cross that had a huge gap in between them, still, not my cup of tea.

If I'm calculating correctly, I think I took more time traveling home, then I did traveling there, AND helping the little girl out COMBINED! This managed to take a toll on my throbbing stomach by the time I got to the top of my building. My stomach felt like an Elephant sat on it more than an overly-messed-up-in-the-mind man punched me there. But I guess, all the same, right?

I took a moment to catch my breath as I sat down on the roof of my building. My hands were still burning from that one fall during the little, "fight", and not to mention the fact that my head was pounding, and yet I was more happy now, in this very moment, than most people ever feel in their entire lives.

CHAPTER 4

My eyes began watering as Sam began pouring the anti-bacterial healing-liquid stuff on to my hands. Squirming a bit, I pulled away slightly as the pain began to be unbearable. "Hold still" Sam said with a laugh as he kept on pouring it on my hands and then stopped to check out the work. It was twelve o'clock in the afternoon, and I already managed to get everything in the house cleaned and neatly placed together including the laundry. Even Ms.Smith seemed pleased with the work I did with the household when she got home, right before she passed out in her bedroom from exhaustion(happy to have her out of my hair for the day, I closed the door silently). And now, right now what Sam and I were doing at the very moment, was basically fixing my mistake. Last night, I was so tired that I forgot to clean my hands before I went to bed. It was a horrible and stupid mistake, for those lovely cuts I managed to get raked across my hands from last night, must have been filled with thousands of bacteria.

So, because of that mistake, my hands began to feel literally like they were on fire a hundred times over after I was just about to get ready for lunch. No joke at all. Luckily, Sam decided to drop by for a visit, which is now why he was helping me with those, injuries.

I rolled my eyes, "Sorry, didn't know I was bothering you with my screaming in pain, I won't let that happen ever again" I said sarcastically, exaggerating my small huffs(maybe?) and turning them into "screams".

"Just don't let it happen again" Sam said, as plainly as if it was all true, Sam had to be the best actor I know BY FAR! Sam grinned as if he was studying a work of art that he just finished "Perfect, it looks like your cuts will be just fine, lay off the Bandit business for a couple days until your hands heal up a little more" Sam said, as if he was a doctor.

I snorted, "Nice try Dr.Bear, but no" I said, catching on to what he was trying to force on me, won't happen so he should just give up.

He shrugged "At least I tried, and you've got to admit, I am a pretty darn good doctor", I rolled my eyes, not replying to his arrogant behavior, though it was quite funny, but I'd probably would have been fed up with it by now if it were anyone else but him. “Now explain to me what you found out about the newspaper, I know you, you wouldn’t have been sitting around like this when there was something that you KNEW you had to do, so spit it out or Dr.Bear is going to leave and buy himself a nice ice cappuccino without you. Which would be a shame for it’s really hot out today, and lets face facts, your day would not be complete without hanging out with me”.

I laughed at this remark, “Yeah, OKAY.” I said, walking away from the kitchen sink and sitting down at the table. “It really wasn’t anything TOO big, but big enough to honestly say that you really don’t have to waste any efforts on trying to talk me out of going out every night-” he broke me off.

“Yeah, yeah, just get to the point, the crowd is growing tired and I think I just heard a cricket stop chirping somewhere in here” Sam said with a huge laugh and grin as he sat down at the table also.

“Hey! I listen to you when ever you have something to say, MR.!” I said, smacking the table lightly with my hand, annoyed.

"Hey, you KNOW that's not what I meant by that, I'd just really like to find out this hunk of information before I'm middle-aged." Sam said, tapping his hand lightly against the table almost as to prove a point.

"Fine, it's just that I was able to find out, that basically, they have ZIP information on me what-so-ever, they don't even have the gender correctly, and they automatically guessed that it's a male, so it probably means they guessed at a lot of more things than just that also!" I said, happy to let Sam know.

"Well that's great, so I guess that means that they will NEVER be able to find you and you can go on your merry way" Sam said, sarcastically, he then added "Zoey, you do realize that they are going to find out sooner or later, and it's NOT going to be good when they do, so I recommend not deluding the problem to make it seem less then it actually is. Who knows HOW they would punish you when they find out what you've been doing for the past 5 and some years!? Think about it, they are definitely not going to reward you with the Nobel Peace Prize for messing with so many different cases in New York City, and yes, I am talking about drug cases that you've most certainly messed with when aggressing towards some of the population's fights. None or less, these people, don't like it when people show them off in their jobs, they don't take it lightly. YOU make them seem like they are doing their jobs incorrectly, which makes the police department, and any other government officials look like the bad guys. Not good Zoey, at ALL".

I was stunned, just the way he said it made a huge chill go down my back. Some how I do know this, deep within my heart, but quite honestly, I'd rather not think like that, not with SO much on the line. Thinking before I said anything, I chose my words wisely as I said "Sam, you do realize that right now, I think I've already dug myself into a pretty big hole, and either way the rain is going to come pouring down on me whether or not I stop. The difference is, I can either keep on going, digging myself deeper and deeper, maybe even discovering some gems along the way, or I can just stop now and let my efforts be wasted. Cause either way, that rain is going to fill up that hole, now whether or not I am going to be digging it while it fills up, getting every last ounce of gems I possibly can get, is a different story.".

Sam looked at me, just looked at me for a moment, keeping all of his emotions locked inside of him, telling me nothing of what will happen next what-so-ever. "I get your point, I suppose..." Sam said, trailing off. I can tell that he did seem to get my point, he didn't like it in any way, but does got it. We sat in silence for a couple of minutes, recollecting our thoughts, Sam was first to break the silence "So, anyways, I got ya' something." he said, gaining up his confidence as he went into it. Based on the tone of voice Sam was using, I can already tell that it wasn't going to be a 'nice' present but more so a joke. Sam went on, as he began taking something out of his pocket, "Found it at the grocery store, I thought it was real comical considering the circumstances" he held it out in his hand, and said what it was with a grin as I began analyzing it "It is a dog collar, with the name 'Bandit' right on it! It reminded me of you so much, I just had to pick it up for you. This was the REAL reason why I came here, not to help disinfect your hands or to argue over something so stupid, it was for this lovely joke", Sam laughed with a grin. It was indeed a dog collar, typical of Sam to find such a thing. Only I highly doubt he just walked across it, no, Sam's warped-reason in life is to mess with me in anyway possible, he definitely went looking for it. For I think we all knew that I was aware of that word being a common name for a dog, no questions asked.

"Haha, very funny, just to let you know the nick name is "THE Bandit" not "Bandit". It is so funny, that I think we should invite a bunch of friends over to talk about it, over some Samuel Adam Beer, huh?" I said, making sure to add the Samuel Adam Beer thing just to get him back even more.

"Wow, I think you should probably bring some water to the party too, you should also get more material Zoey, if I do say so myself." Sam said, rolling his eyes at how I just walked myself into that one. I practically left myself wide-open for yet another joke.

I got up, and began putting away the anti-bacterial junk, then I grabbed a wash-cloth from the drawer, and began drying off the counter tops that were slightly damp due to the splashing of the anti-bacterial stuff. I walked over to the basket and threw the rag into it. Then I walked back over to Sam, "Well as much as that was indeed the BEST time I ever had, I really have to go" I said, pushing in my chair.

"Where?" Sam asked, raising an inquiring eyebrow, that had to be the first. Weird. "I can most certainly come along with you and keep you company again, you KNOW you want to say yes" he grinned a wide grin.

"On a ten mile run?" I asked, he might be in track, but there was no way he was going to last that long, I don't care how much they run on a tread mill everyday, and the track meets that they have every week, he only runs outside with all the pressure of the hot sun beaming down on him probably UP TO five miles A WEEK(the track and field coach has a sort-of weird policy in which when they practice for track, they only practice inside on treadmills, that way there is a less of a chance of someone getting injured compared to running outside. I never really got the sense of it all, for they run outside during track meets, so why don't they get USED to running outside during practice too!?). Plus, that's only when track is in session, right now, track is NOT in session.

"Yeah of course! I'm in track, of course I can keep up if THAT'S what you think! In fact, it might be YOU who needs to be able to keep up with me" Sam said, as he was walking over to the counter-top and began leaning up against it so that he was at eye-level with myself who was standing at the moment.

"Whoa, don't get full of yourself too much there, besides, I didn't say that you couldn't keep up, I was just asking! None or less, you do realize I have ran that much four days a week, for five years now, so the chance of me somehow not being able to run it today is VERY slim, so I wouldn't count me out in any way there. And if you want to come along, come along, no one is stopping you. Though of course you'd need your running wear if you were to come with" I said, looking him up in down at the attire he was wearing, a pair of flip-flops, Capri's, and a button down t-shirt would NOT due(weird Sam-style).

"Fine, just give me about thirty minutes to run home and go change, and then we shall run, together, don't worry, I will slow down for you" he said, adding that last part meant he completely ignored what I said before then, typical Sam. Before even waiting for a reply, he went over to the front door, and left. So I guess unless I'd like to be extremely rude like my friend Sam was over there, I'd HAVE TO wait for him and go on a jog with him today. Great. It's not that I DON'T want him to come along, but more-so that I will NOT be able to concentrate correctly with his goofy-self being there. We'd probably end up running for a mile or two, and then walking while talking the rest of the way. I can almost picture myself re-doing this run tomorrow(one of my off days) instead. Lucky me. I looked towards the table where the dog collar still was, really Sam, really? He left the dumb thing still laying on my table, what am I going to do with it? The joke was funny and now it's over. It is almost as if he wants the joke to still linger in my mind even after he left. Very funny Sam.

I rolled my eyes, leaving the collar on the table I head towards my room to gather my clothing. Like usual, I planned on taking it to the bathroom to get changed. It's kind of out of habit since I have to change in the bathroom when Summer is here anyways, so mine as well keep it as a habit a hundred percent of the time. I quickly grabbed a white t-shirt, a pair of black shorts, and a pair of running shoes along with some socks(for I too had on a pair of flip-flops). All the while making sure not to grip on to anything with too much force because my hands still felt pretty bad from the infections(of course, infections don't just leave the second you put medicine on them, they take a bit to get rid of). Other than those infections I managed to get on the palms of my hands, the only other injury I gained from last night had to be a light bruise on my stomach for getting kicked and punched a thousand times there(VERY surprised that it wasn't any worse), that's all thankfully.

I walked over to the bathroom and shut the door behind me. Getting changed was a pretty fast process due to the fact that I didn't have to worry about waking anyone up(Ms.Smith was sleeping, but with a hang-over, no worry at all) so I didn't have to watch out about making too much noise. The longest step had to be getting my necklace off(the same one that I was given for my birthday some years ago), and that wasn't even that long(took only about five seconds more and that was because of the hurting in my hands made them slightly more clumsier, so I fumbled for the latch slightly). After getting changed, along with getting my hair in a pony tail, I went back to the kitchen to get something to eat. I knew I had time for so far only ten minutes or so has passed since Sam left, which means I have about twenty minutes to eat lunch. I'm pretty sure that Sam was smart enough to eat lunch, and not dumb enough to eat a huge lunch so I don't have to call him up right now to remind him of it, hopefully...

Casting that thought away, I went over to the fridge and pulled out a thing of hard-boiled eggs that I boiled the other day for such an occasion(along with being packed for Summer's lunch, she loves hard-boiled eggs, the other two, not a fan so I just bought pudding cups to replace the snack for them). I took 2 of the 6 eggs that were left, then placed the carton of eggs back into the fridge, shutting the door. I then walked over to the closet, and pulled out a paper plate, I placed the two eggs on it. Went over to the garbage, and began peeling the shell off of them(along with a little bit of egg due to my bad egg-peeling 'skills').

I couldn't help but think back to what I said just some twenty minutes ago, about the fact that either way there is no escaping my known fate of being found out by the police. It sort of scares me. Really scares me, it seems to almost echo inside my heart, that knowledge. It really does seem inevitable to me. I guess I should just hope that I go out like an exploding volcano in comparison to an oozing volcano, that way, it won't be slow.

I sat down with the eggs on the plate, and then I began eating one of them. Surprisingly the door opened up wide open as I was eating and in came Sam dressed properly in running-attire. Wow, he was fast. I laughed, placing down the half eaten egg, "Hey, come on in why don't you!?" I said as he walked over and grabbed the other egg and popped it into his mouth, "And help yourself to that egg while you are at it too", I said sarcastically.

We laughed in unison, me eager to get off the subject of my thoughts and onto a more happier type of subject, as Sam said "Hey, I need to be paid in SOME way for offering you my company for this run. You should feel graced with my presence.".

"Graced wouldn't be the first word that comes to mind when I think of your presence. I believe it starts with an 'un' and ends with a 'lucky'." I said, getting up and throwing out the rest of my egg, my appetite no longer there.

"Okay, so where do you usually go to jog, the park, the woods, or what?" Sam said, as he added "I can call a taxi cab for both of us to ride in, THIS ride will be on me". Just now, I've realized that I must of never really talked to Sam about where I jogged or anything. I guess I never really THOUGHT about giving away such mild details like that anyways. Interesting.

"Try down the street and to a Government site, without taking a taxi" I said, looking out the window for a quick moment then turning back to Sam. His jaw dropped open. "Problem...?" I asked, as he looked at me as if what was on his mind should be as clear as day. Of course it wasn't!

"Are you serious?" Sam said, adding "Or are you just trying to joke with me here, because honestly, I'd think you are lacking something if you did not just realized the irony of it all.".

"Sam, unlike most people you manage to meet, I can not tell what is on your mind, spill it" I said sarcastically, trying so very hard to guess what he was thinking, going over the words I said to him in the past five minutes a couple of times in my mind before Sam finally spoke up again.

"Zoey, you can't honestly think that you weren't painting a huge target across your face doing your daily routine around a GOVERNMENT-owned piece of land. It's like you are drawing a huge arrow to yourself, telling them to pay attention to you" Sam said, beginning to rub his chin, thinking. "Now, I want you to tell me how long you have been doing this".

"Five years...." I said, hesitating. I know there is a huge point in all of this, but for some reason, unlike usual I wasn't finding it too quickly.

Sam swung his hand across his face in agitation, making a huge 'clapping' type of noise, as he shook his head and dropped his hand down, he said "You do realize how EXTREMELY bad this is, right. Never mind, I'd rather not know the response to that question. You see, if you have been doing your little routine for five years, and 'The Bandit' has been out for five years also, this means, that anyone with the resources can easily put two and two together, and finally connect you with the Bandit, Zoey." Sam paused, giving me a moment to absorb it all in. I most certainly understood the second he began speaking each and every word of it. I now know, that I am treading on VERY dangerous waters, and now am certain, that there is no turning back, the end is when I finally give up.

"This, this isn't good" is all I could say at the moment, and really, that's all Sam actually needed for a reply. Ingenious, I know, I find out that basically my whole life is going to for sure end in ruins, and all I manage to say is that it isn't "good".

Sam nodded slowly, "Now is when I start ORDERING you to try and restrain yourself from 'Bandit-business' until we can figure out just how bad of a rut you truly have managed to get into. And PLEASE tell me you will, for this is serious Zoey, plus there is a fact that how can you help out the people of New York City when you are six-feet under" I winced at that really harsh-ironic statement, but he ignored it and went on "or behind bars for life? So think of you staying away from the um, 'streets' as a way to help protect them, not harm them.".

I sighed, really thinking this through, I finally said(after five minutes... maybe?) “You’re right, for now...” suddenly the fire inside of my hands began to really burn, making itself known inside my conscious-state, and I’m pretty sure it was just my imagination acting up but the first time in a while, that lovely scar I gained some 4 years ago or so, felt as if it too was burning, something that hasn’t happened as bad since about 6 months after I got it. I swallowed hard as I added “Then I think I will probably catch up on other things tonight then...”.

Sam seemed content with that answer “Good, do you want to still jog then, keep up your endurance for when you get back to it all so you aren’t huffing and puffing like a middle-aged man on crouches, trying to go up stairs while eating a donut?!”. Where Sam gets these similes from, the world will probably never know. What goes on inside of Sam’s mind, the world will never WANT to know.

“Yeah, of course.” I said, glancing out of the window once again, this time uneasily.

“Great. Cab, or walk to the park?” Sam replied. Of course I said walk, considering my greater-hate(Yeah, NOT fear) of cabs and their more-stupid drivers. And then we were off.

It felt really good to run, and surprisingly, Sam DID manage to keep up and I congratulated him for it(though I made sure to tell him I slowed down my pace a bit more to make sure he would be able to keep up). That mistake lead Sam to drop his foot out in front of me, tripping me(Should of known that Sam would take it the wrong way somehow). We even managed to go a couple more miles than my usual ten also(Stress and anger does tend to push people to their maximum.). Suddenly, after some twelve or so miles, Sam stopped. I stopped and turned around to look at him, with a questioning look on my face I'm sure.

"Show me this government piece of land" Sam said, and always one more step ahead of me, he added to answer my oncoming question "You've have already been there for hundreds of times, I'm SURE going there once more isn't going to do much.".

"Okay" I said, trying to catch my breath a bit. "This way" I said, beginning to run towards the property.

Once we got there, Sam began looking the whole area up and down as if he were some type of detective. "What cha' looking for?" I said, my eyes trying to follow his.

"Cameras" Sam said quickly, and very bluntly, then he asked "Now Zoey.." still looking around, he went on "Have you done anything, um, different around here that were-to draw even bigger attention onto you like tripping over something, but instead of falling to your face you caught yourself like a trained professional with your hands and shot right back up.".

I laughed at this one "You do realize anyone can do that with the right needs, right? It really doesn't take much practice..." I thought back to the one time I did trip over something(a stupid loose-stone which I know for a fact was never there before!), and did manage to catch myself like that, but that's besides the point anyhow.

"You know what I mean" Sam said, keeping it serious.

"Well, there WAS that one time..." I said, hesitating. I don't believe I ever told Sam about the time when I took a dive for a kid in the

Government land. He was gone that week, to some type of family reunion, and I really didn't think anything of it. It just never really came up, he just automatically assumed that the huge scar across my arm was from a huge mess-up during my nightly raids(I was still very new to it all, and it wouldn't be too far-fetched for that to happen to me). And because he was out of town, the brief footage of information on it that got on the news(Why they didn't have anything else better to cover is a mystery) wasn't still on by the time that Sam came back. Sam looked towards me, waiting for me to go on.

"Well, long-story short, I think I just might of saved someone's life on that very same piece of property you see gaited up with a chained-link fence and signs saying 'No trespassing'.".

Sam sighed, "I don't even want to know the whole story, do I? Let me guess, you swam in the water without any hesitation, as if you were used to risking your life for a complete stranger. And don't even ask HOW I managed to come up with the idea that it was all in water, because quite frankly, I know you all too well to basically GUESS at every little event in your life with a ninety percent chance of being correct.".

"You are correct" I said, though based on all of that, I am pretty darn sure he needed me to say that. I looked up towards the sky, thinking. I then added "So, since you are obviously the whole brains of the operation, what do you suppose I should do?".

"We" Sam said, correcting me for some unknown reason, and then leaving it at that.

"Um, excuse me?" I said, confused, we, we what!?

"You said the word 'I', last time I checked, WE do this together, we are a team, remember that? I'm probably the reason you are still alive." Sam said, beginning to bring out his comical personality now. Good, cause quite frankly, I've never been a HUGE fan of Sam's serious side, which is sort of good since it's usually his funny side that comes out.

"Okay then, what should WE do?" I said, rolling my eyes as I said the word 'we'.

"That's better. Anyhow, there really isn't much more we can do then just wait and see how it plays out. Like I said, you do have to lay off the 'Banditing' junk for now." Sam said, completely ignoring the scowl I gave him when he used the word 'junk' to define what I do at night. Then Sam added "It's sort of funny, because one thing they did help us out with has to be the new word to call your little nightly outings. It was kind of getting old trying to find a good word to describe it, this seems pretty decent and well-thought-out, an eves dropper would never be able to figure out what we are talking about unless they truly know what the Bandit means to us. And even if they do have what the words "The Bandit" was stamped on, what are they going to do? ASK you if you go around saving random people's lives at night for no TRUE reason at all, they would sound completely nuts if it weren't true, so they'd stay away from that." I took an uneasy glance at the camera that was shinning its lens right on us, slightly unnerving about the fact that I never noticed it until now, a shiver went down my spine at the thought. "Ah, don't worry, I don't think it picks up sound. I believe they can get into major law-suits when it comes to privacy acts and everything", Sam must of seen the look on my face.

"Yeah, lets just get out of here" I said, not liking at all being here with the threat of what I now know lingering right behind the fence.

Sam laughed a huge, and heavy laugh "What, the great BANDIT is getting scared now!? Ah, I see, someone who can't control her own emotions on things like fear can most certainly help protect the city against all things evil.", Sam stuck his tongue slightly out for a quick moment like a child, rolling his eyes he said "Fine, we can go I suppose.".

"Good" I said, smug that I got my way with Sam for once.

"Now, have you taken all of your regents yet?" Sam asked, as we began walking away from the place. We then got into a long discussion about anything regents-related. I told him that I haven't, and how I needed to take one more in a couple days, and that it had to be my worse subject, Economics that was last(out of only two regents, but still). Sam like so many people(maybe?) would have, caught on to the fact that I only had two regents to take! So there weren't that great of chances anyways, and besides that fact, I shouldn't have been complaining, I only had two regents to take while Sam had to take four. I strictly told him that I wasn't complaining(didn't get across him entirely because he was too busy laughing at his own joke to hear or even care about listening to me). To shut him up, I told him that it was only because I managed to get a lot of my classes done in Summer school, to help bar the weight of everything during my actual schooling time. That way, I was able to take the other regents during the Winter time, so I didn't have to take them during the Summer time. Well, that really didn't shut him up, what actually did had to be the smug grin I placed right on my face just to annoy him, so that got him on a different topic about how I was WAY to arrogant and everything. It amused me more than annoyed me at how SERIUOS Sam was when saying this. It was five o'clock by the time we got back to my place.

Unlocking the door, Sam went right inside, not even bothering to ask if he could come in(would have said yes anyhow, but it is the POINT). "SO, what's for dinner? I'm feeling like pizza myself, but anything is good with me." Sam said with a grin as he hopped onto the couch, making himself comfortable. It's indeed a good thing for him that we are really close like this, for with anyone else, I'd probably leave the room, leaving them alone until it gets so awkward, that they had to leave.

"You're not having dinner at your place suddenly?" I said, as I began looking into the fridge to actually see what might be suitable for dinner.

"My dad is working late tonight, and there is the fact that I am not a fan of cooking" Sam said, I began to cut him off.

"Nor' buying your own food?" I asked, sarcastically with humor. He laughed, and rolled his eyes.

"What ever you'd like to call me, if I end up leaving here with something in my stomach, I'm the winner anyhow" Sam grabbed the television remote and began flipping the channels. I looked around the apartment for any of them, it's quite weird that the television went un-touched before we got here. Nothing. I listened, the boys were talking in their room, my curiosity wanted to see what on Earth they were talking about, but decided against it, and it seemed as if Summer must have been drawing or something. Cause in the room I heard the closing and opening of drawers(she kept her drawing supplies in my desk, I told her that she could, as long as she always made sure to put them away. Easy way to get a kid to clean up after herself.). I breathed a sigh of relief. Nothing has happened, good.

Ignoring the last comment Sam said, I looked towards him and said "Well, we can either have take-out pizza, or we can have hotdogs, your choice I suppose" I already knew what he was going to say. As one would have realized, Sam said he wanted pizza! He didn't just say some type of weird clues that one could pick up on. Sometimes, I wonder who is the better friend? But I reassure myself due to the fact that if Sam wasn't too fond of me, he would have already just left. Besides, he cares enough to NOT say happy birthday on my birthday due to bringing up bad memories, good friend. Way off topic, how I go from food to friendships, is a huge mystery.

"Hotdogs of course" Sam said with sarcasm, as he finally settled on boxing to watch, "Why would you ever think I'd want Pizza!? You silly girl.".

I rolled my eyes, "Fine. Pizza it is, would you like beer with that too?". Sam ignored me as he began watching the boxing match. Good idea, I thought with that happening, for honestly, I KNOW he'd come up with a better come back, so why do I even bother?

I grabbed my phone from the counter space where it charged, and began dialing the pizza place's number. Memorized by heart, due to the fact that it makes a lot of dinners easier that way. Healthier, of course not, but most certainly easier. I ordered two large pizzas and two dozen wings, a lot for five people, I know, but I decided that it would be nice to have some leftovers. I skipped the pop, decided that it would be better for my pocket(and our health) if we just stuck with what we got(juice with pizza, anyone?).

Closing my phone shut, I began taking out some plates and setting them along the table, making sure to add an extra spot for Sam. Silverware and cups were placed along the table next. And then, everything was done. I walked over to Sam who was laying on the couch as if he owned the place. "Really Sam?" I said, he was laid out across the couch, and looked exhausted "if I knew that jog was going to take so much energy out of you, I would have stopped you from coming." I added.

"Not really, I'm just not used to so much running, I'll get a hang of it" Sam said, adding a grin.

"Did I invite you to the next run, hmmm?" I said, Sam drew his eyes from the television towards me.

"You did now. I'm going whether you like it or not. I need

something to do during the summer ahead, and it's definitely not going to be applying for a job. I have enough of that when I come with you to your job" Sam laughed, as he turned his gaze back to the television screen, still listening, but I'm pretty sure just barely, seemed like the match just got back on after the rookie just got done breaking the pro's nose. Didn't look good for the pro at this stage.

"Sorry I'm not that exciting when I work, I'll try harder next time to make the experience better, would you like me to get a clown, or have a party with some of your friends? Your choice." I laughed, then added "But seriously, why run with me? Don't you have better things to do then run for no reason?".

"Don't you? You realize now you have no reason to run, other than the fact that you MIGHT get back to your Nightly Banditing in the DISTANT future and you'd need to keep in shape for that. But that is a small possibility you see, you are probably wasting your time" Sam said, not even drawing his eyes from the television set for one second to look at me when he said this. Yep, the television has to be the number one most annoying thing to have on when talking to someone.

"Wow, that's harsh" I said, trying to push away such thoughts. I HOPE that that isn't how it's going to happen, for I know for a fact that it would all lead up to me being in jail or something. Not cool, at all. Plus, I'd rather not think about the fact of how many more criminals would get away or how many more people would die because of that. I gulped, really got to stop these thoughts. "Thank you Samuel Adam Bear for the optimistic ideas you just gave me, I believe they just brightened my world THAT much more" I added, for it's indeed true on the sarcastic side.

Sam turned down the volume and looked up from where he was laying "Well it's true. But that's not the point, the point is, I AM going to start running with you. And quite frankly, why WOULDN'T you want to run with me?". He flashed a quick grin, then went back to his, no, THE television. Pretty sad when that television suddenly becomes his television in my mind. Gosh, I now REALLY have to take the three kids and now Sam out to the park sometime. Not that Sam hasn't been there say, fifteen minutes ago, but still, television seems to be the mind killer. On second thought, just the kids.

"It would be my dream come true" I said with as much sarcasm as possible in my voice, the door bell rang, must be the pizza guy. I walked over to the door and opened it up, holding out my wallet, I took out a fifty dollar bill, "Here" I said, grabbing the pizza and wings from the pizza guy's hands, trying to repress my laughing at the fact that his name tag read 'hello, my name is Samuel', such a very interesting and ironic name.

"Thanks" he said with a quick grin, I gave him a ten dollar tip, the type of tip I most certainly would have wanted if I worked delivering pizzas. The guy left, and I shut the door behind him. The smell of the pizza must of wafered through the house, because by the time I turned to place the pizza on the counter, all three kids were busy in the bathroom washing their hands(I knew this due to the splashing noise they made as they fought for the first one to get their hands washed.). I casted a glance at a very bemused looking Sam, who's boxing match obviously was finished for now he was sitting on top of the arm of the chair. He then got up and walked over to the pizza box, and took out a slice of pizza and plopped it on his plate.

"You don't wash your hands now?" I said with a laugh, Sam never really was a clean-freak what-so-ever, so I sort of expected this from him, just not entirely.

"Nope" he replied back, as he bit into the pizza. I rolled my eyes at this, when all three of the kids came running in and began grabbing their shares of the pizza. I walked to the bathroom, and began washing my hands. Reminding myself to have them clean up the mess after they are done eating dinner.

I walked over to the kitchen, grabbed a slice of pizza and sat down. Grabbing a couple of chicken wings from the carton, Scott asked "Why is HE here again?". Something that Scott asked far too often, and I gave the same reply every time.

"Because he wants to be" I said curtly, taking a bite of my slice of pizza.

Sam laughed, already on his second piece of pizza, he went over to the sheet of pizza and took another slice "because I knew that I'd just make your day with my lovely presence if I did come here", he grinned a sly grin, then began eating his next piece of pizza. Scott rolled his eyes, obviously not amused to the slightest bit, don't really blame him, seeing Sam did go too overboard sometimes, but it was more Scott's sour attitude that is causing his annoyance at the moment then Sam's way of joking. Sam just kept on eating, even though he clearly saw the rolling of the eyes from Scott.

After everyone was done with their dinner(the boys being out of the kitchen), I began to clear away the plates and put away the pizza(Summer helped too). As I was doing this, Sam said "So, I was personally thinking about going out for ice cream or something right now. I am sure that Summer would LOVE a nice ice cream, wouldn't ya' Summer?" Sam grinned, he took a quick glance towards me, then Summer, and then withdrew his wallet. He then began counting the money inside of it. He was obviously trying to get on SOMEONE'S good side.

Summer smiled a huge grin after she placed the chicken wings in the fridge "That sounds GREAT!" she said, her eyes sparkling with pure joy. I laughed.

Sam turned towards me "What, jealous that I am skilled when it comes to making kids happy, unlike you?" he said, with sarcasm. Didn't he realize that he managed to get on a twelve year old kid's bad side pretty fast, right? Not that I didn't manage that one either or anything, but still.

"Yeah, always. Summer can you go get the other two?" I said.

* * *

Above all, Sam did manage to get on EVERYONE'S good side, and yes, even Scott to my amazement. Though, on how far Sam went, there were limits. Like the fact that I think just to mess with the kids, he told them only to get one topping each, then he went around and got himself about ten different toppings on his ice cream, honestly, it was QUITE a joke. I tried so very hard not to laugh at that one, but a little laugh managed to come out, and so in apologies to the kids I bought a box of chocolate covered bananas for them to eat another time.

We were just beginning to finish up, when Sam looked at his phone and said "Hold on, it's my dad calling me..." he left the ice cream parlor for a quick second, then came back. "Okay, so, my father called just to say he was going to stay at work later tonight, something about a major meeting of some sort, and that he recommends hanging out with friends now, for tomorrow night, we are going to that movie thing, sadly. ANYHOW, so I told him that I was going to be hanging out at your place helping baby-sit the kids tonight and that I won't be done until later tonight, so I mine as well stay the night, if it's all right with you that is?".

"Yep, of course it is Sam. Still like sleeping on the couch?" I said.

"You bet" Sam said, with lots of sarcasm, but I could tell he doesn't really mind, after all, he IS the one who wants to stay over in the first place. And judging by how long we have already spent together in the past couple of days, I can already tell that I am going to get sick of Sam by the end of this summer, especially seeing the fact that he is going to be bored(except for the camping trip) and I am going to have a very uneventful summer too(BECAUSE of the fact that I won't be able to go out at night anymore...). We began walking out of the ice cream parlor, and onto the side walk. Scott and Tim walked in front of us, and Summer walked right next to us, she began chatting to Sam about her different pictures she was drawing and that she COULD sell one to Sam if he'd really want one.

Sam laughed, “As long as you buy one of my pieces of artwork, they are truly the best anyone has created” he said.

“How much is it? Myn are twenty five cents each!” Summer said.

“Well, myn is slightly more expensive” Sam said, not saying any more.

“Are they? How much?” I said, curious to know just how ‘valuable’ Sam thought his ‘imaginary’ pieces of artwork would be.

“Twenty five hundred dollars” Sam said, as he kept on walking. Summer laughed at this one, she knew Sam’s humor all too well.

“Yeah right! RIGHT after I spend that much on spending more time with Scott” Summer began laughing even more like crazy.

“HEY!” Scott said, turning around and giving the younger girl a glare, he then swooped down his hand, and swung off Summer’s pink baseball cap, “Now we are even” he said as it landed on the side walk, he turned back to Tim and continued walking.

"I should of warned you Summer" I said with a laugh, as she picked up her baseball cap, almost running into another pedestrian along the way. I definitely would have tried picking it up if my hands weren't stinging so much still! They keep on going on and off when it comes to the pain, it really stinks.

"Nah, it was sort of a double-diss for both of them, so I don't regret it at all" she said, brushing off a little dirt from the cap then she placed it right back on her head.

"And that's when I officially say that I am now on Scott's side." Sam said, as he began to speed up his pace and went in front with the other two, almost making a point.

I laughed, "Looks like it is girls vs. boys now tonight" I said to Summer, meaning to speak it loud enough for the other three to hear. Sam just waved his hand back towards me as if I was just some annoying bug that he could shoo off.

After taking a couple of turns and everything, we managed to make it back to the house at eight o'clock. I looked towards the three kids, who seemed eager to do something. "Okay, you guys can stay up a bit later tonight to hang out with Sam and me, but, I want you to get your pajamas on right now and brush your teeth, that way, when I say it's time for bed, I do mean it. I don't want you guys going to school half asleep tomorrow.".

They all nodded, Summer and Tim zoomed off into their bedrooms, but Scott lingered for a moment. "Don't you have somewhere to go?" he asked, narrowing his eyes, it was either out of curiosity, or pure suspicion why he asked that question, and right now I really can't seem to tell.

"Uh, no, I don't have work tonight, and Sam is right here" I said, trying to play it off the best way I can. And now that I think about it, this 'taking off' is going to cause a lot more problems then I first thought...

Scott did not seem convinced, but left without another word. "Great" I mumbled to Sam "Any more problems going to surface?", he nodded his head in agreement, as we walked over to a box in the corner of the room, where I stored the games. I took out checkers and cards, leaving the chess board by itself. Way too complicated of a game for Tim and Summer still.

"So, what are you doing tomorrow?" Sam asked, taking the games from my hands as I handed them to him.

I blew a piece of hair out of my face quickly, then replied "Work. Opening to close.", I got up and sat on the couch as Sam took the game boards over to the kitchen table and setting them down, he turned back to me.

"Sounds like fun. Spending your whole day in a hot-sweaty department store with a bunch of jerky customers who look down on you like you are just another door mat to step on, and to top it all off, you only get paid minimum wage. YAY!" Sam said, making the job sound a lot, no, lets not exaggerate that too much, a LITTLE bit worse than it actually is. The department store has air conditioning, so it's not TOO hot there.

"Wow, you are really making me have second thoughts on working now Sam. Congratulations." I said, getting up and going over to the kitchen, and sitting down at the table. I began taking the cards out of the little box, shuffling them idly as I waited for Sam's response and to come up with a game that we ALL could play.

"Oh, and to make it worse, I won't be able to come with you this time. Remember, father-and-son day, yippee for me too" Sam said.

"THAT, I can live with" I said, deciding the best game would be go-fish, I began shooting the cards out into five different piles of seven. One, two, three, four, five, six, seven..... And so on, and so on.

"You only WISH you could bear to stand not seeing me for a whole day. But we all know that I am too much of a likeable person for that" Sam grabbed a random pile that I had already done(two more piles left to go), and began looking through the cards to see if he had any matches(I think?). After a few moments, he managed to pull out three pairs of cards, leaving him only with one left. How is he THAT lucky!? I mean, seriously!

Sam grinned, seeing how baffled I was at him getting such a good hand "I have skill" he said, pretty bluntly.

We were then interrupted by Summer, who sat down at the seat across from me, she, being very used to the ways of the game, grabbed herself a pile, and began looking through hers too. "Two matches!" she said, grinning, only until she looked towards Sam's pile and saw three matches, "Wow, Zoey, what did you do, CHEAT for him or something?" she said, her eyes glancing back and forth between Sam's hand that held only one card, her hand that held three, back to Sam's pile that held three matches, and back to her own pile that held two.

"No, Sam's power in this world is to try and make anyone else playing a game with him, enjoy the game as little as possible. Did I ever tell you that?" I said, still pretty stunned myself also. Summer laughed, and then dropped the discussion as the two boys came in. Scott grabbed two piles, one in each hand, and then gave one to Tim, keeping one for himself, he too began sorting through his pile. I picked up my pile, and managed to pick up one match in it. Looking over to Tim and Scott, I noticed that Scott also had only one match too(and didn't really look too please of it either), and Tim had two matches. So basically, Sam started off with a pretty high advantage with just pure luck on his side.

"So, lets have it be so that who ever has the most matches gets to go first, hmm?" Sam said grinning, and as if to bump up the act a little more, he looked around the table at everyone else's hands, then back at his, he then said(putting a pretty good 'surprised' look on his face) "So, it looks like I get to go first! And then Summer can go next, Tim after that, Scott, and then you Zoey.", somehow I get to thinking that putting me last wasn't by accident for Sam. Nice one Sam, it won't stop me from getting him back, but nice one.

Summer smiled, "Okay, go then!" she said, as she folded her cards right onto the table face-down, probably to stop anyone from 'accidentally' glancing at her cards and using their new-found knowledge to their advantage(and by anyone, I mean Sam, because he is the only one who is allowed to actually call from her hands due to the order we are playing in, and I wouldn't really put it past Sam to do such a thing).

"Do you have an..." Sam paused, as if he had much to choose from "Ace?". Summer shook her head pretty smugly, and Sam picked up an extra card from the pile. Somehow, I was thinking with his luck he'd end up picking up a match from the pile, then ruining the game for the kids, but it didn't happen luckily(For basically anyone but Sam, or seeing that he'd have three angry kids on his hands, it might be lucky for him anyways).

Summer looked towards Tim, "Hey Tim!" she said, snapping her fingers, Tim's gaze was wandering off a bit, he quickly shot back to her, waiting for no reply Summer said "Do you have an eight? Hmmm?".

"Nope, GO-FISH!" he said, hitting the table with his knuckle two times happily. And out of the corner of my right eye, I saw Sam grin. Someone obviously has an eight, I wished Summer good luck, for she has no clue what's going to happen to one of her precious cards, but really, I couldn't do anything.

"King" Tim said. In reply, Scott scowled, and threw his card toward his little brother, Tim grabbed it and matched it with his own card. "Seven", Scott shook his head and Tim 'fished' for another card.

"Zoey, do you have a three?" Scott said, tapping his fingers along the table in anticipation.

"Here you go" I said, giving Scott the card. Scott took the card, and then held up his fingers, reading four. "Go fish dude, you have just pushed your luck" I laughed. Then I looked towards Sam, he mouthed the words 'Good LUCK!'. I rolled my eyes, yeah, to him, I thought, brushing my gaze along one of my cards, before I said its name "Do you have an eight?" I grinned as Sam's jaw dropped. "Hand it over" I said, holding my hand out towards him, he dropped the card in my hand with a grimace, Sam doesn't like the thought of losing as much as I do. "Jack?" I said, not really expecting him to have one. Sam shook his head smugly. Then he pointed towards the card pile.

"GO FISH!!!!!" He said, grinning a wide grin right now. I picked up a card from the rapidly depleting pile(there is MAYBE about ten cards there). I picked up a four. Hopefully Scott doesn't end up retrying for the four-card again.

I must of zoned out, thinking about who knows what, because before I knew it Scott was telling me "ZOEY! DO YOU HAVE A NINE!?" quite loudly, and in an agitated voice. I Must have been zoning out long enough for this not to have been the first time Scott asked this question.

I stuttered, glancing at my cards real fast I said "No, Go Fish.". Sam huffed out an agitated breath as he "fished" for his card. He then quickly grinned, "Okay, fished my wish, now do you have a two?", I stubbornly handed over the card, "How about a Queen?".

"Nope, you can go fish now" I said, deeply hoping that he isn't going to find that card he wanted, for I really don't know how much longer I can keep on giving my cards away.

"Okay, your turn" Scott said, I turned to Sam.

"Do you have a Jack?" I said.

We had to have played that game five different times, and yet I didn't win one game. The kids each won a game(Scott miraculously won the first one, probably because of my bad luck with card games), and Sam won two. He joked about the fact that it must be in our friendship that he has all of the gaming skills. I didn't laugh at that one, but he had a pretty good crowd from the two youngest ones(Scott really didn't seem to care for the joke, but he wasn't really eager to stand up in my defense either.). All-in-all, they were pretty short games, seeing that it was eight fifty five by the time we got done(Sam's gloating didn't stop until a whole five minutes, when it was time for his audience to go to bed).

"Can I hang out here with you two tonight?" Scott asked, not looking tired at all.

I mauled this over for a couple moments, he WAS exceptionally older than the other two, I can see why he'd want to stay up later. But quite frankly, I'm not that sure what time a kid his age should go to bed at(Due to the fact that I really didn't have an average night like any other twelve year old kid, well, unless you called going outside in the middle of the night to save random people being an AVERAGE thing, then, definitely not average). Finally, Sam must of seen my problem and took the decision on for himself and said "Until ten o'clock, after that, I think it would be best for you to get some sleep" by now, Summer and Tim were in their rooms, and by the sound of nothingness coming from that general direction, were fast asleep. I made sure to read the emotion on Scott's face for future references, he seemed satisfied.

"Sounds good enough to me" Scott said with a shrug. Both of them walked over to the couch and sat down next to each other. Sam was in the middle, good. But he managed to claim control of the remote, so what was on was boxing, yet again. Both of them seemed to like it, so I made no effort to have Sam change It, for I guess as long as they are both happy, I am happy. Zoning out(for I have no interest in Boxing in any way at all), I began thinking about the case. The case that has went about ten years, unsolved. It's amazing how little information I have managed to collect over the years, kind of sad if you ask me. But does that really matter? No, well, not as much as the cases that just keep on getting made now. And now, because of people getting the wrong idea, yet another case is going to go unsolved. For everyday I'm not out there, another person's life is going to get ruined, and for what? Simply because of misleading information. This just isn't right, at all. I mean, I guess I've always told myself that I just went out there just to figure out MY case, and that was all that really mattered to me. But come to think of it, it's not. It IS the reason why I came to this, but in actuality, I really can't think about so many people's lives being ruined, while I just sit inside all night feeling scared for my own life, that's really not how I think.

Now, the question is, what job path would I choose? Obviously I am never going to be able to go out at night, doing the things I have done in the past ever again. But does it stop right there, do I start NOT caring in anyway about people, or do I go into a career field dedicated to helping people. Definitely the second idea, but what job is there that I can possibly do, that can help people? Lots of them I suppose, but what would I be ABLE to do? I've thought about Doctor ten times over, but every time, the same problem comes to mind: the amount of years. It take like eight years of schooling or something like that before someone can even get out there and start "doctoring". What a waste of time. One can only think about how many people's lives are getting destroyed for that whole amount of time(not ruined, destroyed, cause in this case, it's a for-sure death). I've thought about becoming a cop, perfect choice right? I love protecting people, and I am willing to put my own life below someone else's just for a chance of them living. But no, not the perfect choice, at ALL.

As one would very well know, as a cop, you have to do what's BEST for the over-all department, they can't just go out on a limb and arrest someone because they KNOW that that person did it, there is something called evidence. Evidence, is the one thing that I always manage to leave out. I couldn't find much evidence while I worked on a case for ten years, in which I was standing right there when it happened. Evidence, who needs evidence when you have the ability to memorize anyone's eyes after just looking at them for a split second? Problem, you have to see that person again, which happened to fail with my adoptive-parent's case, because if I did see that person again, I'd probably be charged with murder. Which, is again, another reason why I wouldn't be fit for the bill, my emotions run everything, a cop always has to keep their emotions from every case, to stop them from doing anything rash. Rash seems to be my middle name(if the word Aquarius is another word for Rash that is, but still.). So, what other options are there? Nothing, I'm sure of it. People keep on saying, that there is still time to think about it, well that time is sure to run out sooner or later. I am going to be a junior next year, and then a senior the year after that. College comes later, but if I don't KNOW what I am going to do, I'd probably end up just skipping the college all together, because it would be a waste of money just to get the college in if I don't even know what job I'd be interested in. So, where does that leave ME? Well, stuck in the shadows just like most everything in life.

CHAPTER 5

I had an awful, long, and frustrating night. After three hours of boxing, both Sam and I decided to go to bed. Only, when I went to my room, I couldn't sleep. Zip. Nothing at all. I felt like I had all of the energy in the world, and I'm pretty sure it was because I was used to using up all of it on my nightly runs. So basically, I just sat in my bed the entire night thinking, which isn't a good thing at all. For when ever I think for too long, alone by myself, anxiety seems to build up, along with some minor depression. Stupid idea, but yes, I did it. After some five hours of just breaking myself apart, piece by piece, I did manage to get some sleep(maybe like an hour or two) for after that, I woke up to the sound of my alarm clock. Summer got so used to it, that she doesn't even so much as make a SOUND when the alarm clock goes off. Quite frankly, even though I managed to waste so much time NOT sleeping that night, I still felt pretty well-energized surprisingly. Good thing also, due to the fact that I have a long work-day ahead of me.

I walked down the hall and into the living room to see if Sam was still here, he wasn't. Must of gotten up early and decided to leave. One less person I'd have to worry about waking up, so it's a good thing. I then went to the kitchen to get something to eat. I looked into the fridge, and the first thing I saw in their was pancake mix. So I whipped up myself some pancakes(quietly, of course), I was just about done, when I heard the beeping of alarm clocks, very glad that I decided to make some extra for the kids, I placed the pancakes onto a plate, when Scott came out, his eyes were dreary with sleep. "Can I have some by any chance?" he asked, his voice thick with sleep. I nodded my head.

"Take as much as you want, there is plenty for everyone." I said, grabbing myself a pancake and I sat down. I poured some syrup and began eating my pancake as Scott sat down.

He looked at me for a second, as if he was going to say something. But as if he decided against it or something, he dropped his gaze and began eating his pancakes, such an odd kid... "Hey, can WE have pancakes?" Summer asked, some how she was already dressed and seemed pretty ready for the day, Tim was still in his pajamas unlike Summer, but he still seemed way more awake than Scott. Interesting...

"Of course, help yourselves" I said, pointing to the plate of pancakes. Tim rushed over, grabbed some plates for him and Summer, and quickly grabbed himself a pancake, and before even sitting down, he took a quick bite out of it. "Woah, slow yourself there Tim, sit down" I said, laughing at how amusing it was, he must have been pretty hungry based on how fast he took a bite out of it, it's kind of funny because I bet that he is ALWAYS like that in the morning, I'm just usually not staying around long enough to see it. Tim smiled a shy smile, obviously slightly embarrassed from what he did and being called out on it, he sat down, and began devouring the pancake again, this time without me stopping him. Summer, being a little more mature, walked over to the pancakes, picked out two, grabbed a fork, and then sat down. Only THEN did she start eating. There is, and probably always will be a huge maturity difference between males and females in my opinion.

Just then, the door swung wide open, and in came Ms.Smith, the smell of alcohol clearly on her breath, like usual. "Hello, I am just going to go to bed now" Ms.Smith said, almost loosing her balance as she hung onto the coat racks for support. She definitely has been out way too long last night, not that any other night isn't the same. She was also, purely drunk. Her eyes were clouded up due to years of drinking alcohol, and if I were to have an alcohol seminar to try and persuade kids to NOT drink alcohol, she'd definitely be the first person that would come to mind that I'd want to be the guest "speaker", only she wouldn't be able to due to most of the time she is pure drunk, and then she'd REALLY prove something. I looked towards the other three, pretty sad when they don't seem startled at all, as if used to it. I fear for the younger two, for their thoughts are still developing and this all might whack out their minds into thinking it is semi-normal, but seeing as the fact that I pounded into them that it is NOT normal, it is NOT how someone should be, they should be fine. Actually, the more I think about it, the one I feel worried for the most has to be Scott. Pure hatred shown through his narrowed eyes as he looked right at Ms.Smith. I really don't like just

HOW MUCH hatred shown in them, it unnerved me, by a lot. Seeing such anger, displeasure, in a young kid's eyes, truly does worry me.

Quickly I shot up out of my seat, sort of out of reflex of trying to help people all these years, but before I could warn myself not to, Ms.Smith turned right towards me, her eyes flaming in anger "I can help MYSELF now ZOEY. Do I LOOK like I need help, hmmm?", she said(More like 'slurred' due to the alcohol's effects on her) it was the sourest, most witch-like tone I have ever heard(besides any other time she snaps at me).

"No. You don't" I said, grinding my teeth. I should really give her my all, not hold back on her what-so-ever. SO much bad language, that on T.V, you'd hear the beeping sound every five seconds, that's the BEST case scenario, for her that is. Worst, I'd end up attacking her and getting into a full-out fist fight with her(Winning would be on my side, hopefully). She'd probably wouldn't live from that outcome. But it was as if we were a divorced couple, trying not to cause any problems for the kids. Only one parent is trying not to cause any problems for the kid's sake, the other, is trying to make a problem(pretty sure no one needs explaining as to who each "parent" is) Though, I'm sure no one in their right mind would ever THINK about marrying her, let alone having KIDS with her. A shudder went down my back as I had some very nasty, grotesque images crossing my mind. Those are going to leave a mental-scar. "Just thought that I would get up to make sure" I said, coldly.

She made a devilish grin, she isn't oblivious to how much it kills me to say such false things. "Good" she said, only it sounded more like "Goo-th" then "good" due to the slurring, but I pretty much got the point. She stumbled out of the door-way area and went towards her room, saying no more, but you see, she KNOWS that that type of ending gets to me. So right now, her 'spirit' is thriving due to the knowledge of me sulking in annoyance because of her. I can almost picture her twisted mind grinning in pleasure. So ANY type of niceness I managed to find in her a few days ago, is demolished. There really isn't ANY goodness in her what-so-ever, I keep on finding that out, and re-doing the same mistake in my head by trying to find SOME type of purity in her, and it keeps on getting destroyed within another confutation with her. I really need to learn.

Scott looked at me, his eyes reading it all. He was yet again disappointed in the way I handled it, he really doesn't understand why I handle it the way I do. Sometimes I want to scream out 'It is for YOU both! Don't you see, if she has the means to do it, she WILL have you and your brother split up!', but I hold myself from doing that. Somehow, some part of me feels like he just wouldn't care, and some how he would persuade me that it really doesn't matter. I couldn't do that to Tim. Not when he isn't old enough to TRULY understand the bond of family. So, anguish is now the emotion I now carry with me before work. This is the type of emotion NO ONE wants to carry when going to work, it just destroys your day. So, the question has to be, how does one fix it? Easy, well, maybe not SO easy, but there is an idea that has a seventy percent chance of working(in my mind, of course I can't ACTUALLY have a real percentage, that would be completely impossible and pretty ludicrous, point taken though?). Just try and cheer them up, and my spirit will lift also.

"So anyways..." I started off, thinking as I went on "I was thinking about maybe after you guys are done with school, we can all go to the park for a day and have some fun" I thought for a second, trying so very hard not to look at their expressions so that I can save it until I'm done telling them all the fun things that are going to happen, so that if they don't seem thrilled, at least I know I tried my best. "We can have a picnic, get some ice cream and play some type of ball game, probably soccer cause I know how much you guys LOVE playing it.", now I looked to see the expressions on their faces. Summer and Tim's eyes were lit up like Christmas trees, I KNOW I already sold them. I turned to Scott, he looked pretty content. Not really EXSTATIC, but not annoyed either. That is a job well-done. So, like usual, my spirits managed to rise at the sight of them being so happy. It felt good to see HAPPY faces compared to flustered and enraged looking faces.

"Good" I said, glancing at the clock, I realized that I had to get ready for work, so I grabbed my plate, placed it in the dishwasher(along with all the other dirty dishes needed to make the pancakes) and then I placed some dishwashing soap into the dishwasher, "Turn it on when you guys are done please, Okay?" I said, looking mostly towards Scott due to his older age. He just nodded. So I left towards my room to get my stuff ready.

*   *   *

Work was long(of course), and boring. It was a slow day, and unlike most people who seem to LOVE having a slow work day, because they DON'T like working, I thrive on a busy day, and hate such nothingness as a slow-day. I had AT THE MOST about one customer come up to me with either help or getting checked out per fifteen minutes. So a good amount of my time was spent just zoning out. Though, having that little amount of people did have its advantages(actual, advantage, with NO 's'). The fact of having less people, lead to the fact that there were less rude customers, something that I'd like to have more often(only about three or so people were considered rude through out the day in my eyes). It felt so NICE not to have the pain of all those nasty customers breathing down my back like a bunch of savages.

And finally, it was time to leave. I dropped by a coffee shop(which closes exactly an hour after my shift ends and isn't THE coffee shop that I usually go to due to it not being on my way from the store, though it would due), and got myself a delicious iced-coffee to drink on my way back home. Walking on the side walk I thought about how NICE it was going to be to relax (it's relax because I am not 'allowed' to go out at night anymore due to Sam... well Sam and the government combined.... of course). I guess I can finally catch up on my own life and hobbies(though what they are, I'm not quite sure...). Sam will definitely not be there(I feel somewhat happy due to the fact of us spending a bit too much time together, it's nice to have some space) because of his little 'bonding time' with his father. Very amusing thought, Sam having bonding time with his father. Especially when I know exactly what they will be doing(boring movie anyone?).

Turning down around my house's corner, I walked a few paces, and turned right to my house. Taking a quick sip of my coffee, I grab my house keys out of my purse and opened the door, silently as I usually do(slowly too!). Walking in, felt almost weird, knowing that I won't be walking out again today. Strange has to be the word I feel right now, STRANGE. I looked at the clock that read nine thirty. I walked towards my room as quietly as I could, knowing that I would probably wake Summer up if I walk even the slightest bit heavy, Summer is a very light sleeper. I walked over to the desk, and picked up my laptop, then I walked right out and towards the living room. There, I sat down, and began turning on my computer. Lazily, I looked around the room, thinking about anything that I should catch up on. I thought email and instant messaging for a hot second, but quickly dropped those ideas due to the fact that I have such a small social life, that the only person on my contacts is only Sam(this boosted Sam's arrogance up even more when he snuck onto my account one day and found out about this). I typed in the password, as I thought some more. I'm not really a television watcher, so you can disregard that option too. Sleeping is off the list, my energy level is pretty high, especially after the fact that I had about eight ounces of coffee so far(the coffee is a ten ounce, so two more ounces to go!).

I thought to myself, then decided looking over some more information on the case wouldn't harm anything, could it? I clicked on the internet browser, then typed in the usual. And I typed in the password to that too, realizing the resemblance between the password they assigned me, "Bandit Flame", and THE name "Bandit". Personally, I really hope it is just a coincidence, not the fact that it is a warning that "they are on to me!". This time, I decided to go back to the crime scene photos. I always look at these photos, and feel as if I am MISSING something. Kind of like the way that I felt when I was missing something with the whole newspaper thing, but sadly, after SO MANY years, I have come down with nothing. I scan the one photo I felt this feeling with, spec by spec, trying so very hard not to miss anything, while also trying not to cry(not full-blown cry, but sometimes I have started to tear up in the past by simply looking at the photos, but who wouldn't?). Yet again, my wants were unanswered. I sighed, it felt like I have been doing this forever, when I glanced over to the clock, it read nine forty three. How did I just spend only thirteen minutes on ALL of this TOGETHER!? I began involuntarily grinding my teeth. I thought about other things to do besides this. That maybe God doesn't WANT me to be doing this right now, but wants me to be ENJOYING myself or something like that. But I came back with nothing, at all. I really do have no life, do I?

I sighed. The choice was so OBVIOUS in my head, I keep on trying to shove it down, to stop the temptation of it all. But lets face facts, it is no use. No matter how many consequences I am going to have to deal with after this, I HAVE to do it. I have to honestly to it. I must do, what I have to do. That is, I have to go outside, and risk everything, just so that I can help someone. That HAS to be what God wants, right?

I grabbed a hold of my necklace, praying, that this is the right choice. I shut my computer(not really bothering to shut it down properly, but at the moment it really doesn't matter to me), and placed it on the coffee table in front of the couch. Then I went to the bathroom to start changing. I took off my necklace(wincing for a quick moment, the necklace must of struck the more damaged tissue on my hand). Then I began getting changed. I grabbed my night-bag(stashed in the usual hiding place), and slung it over my arm. After that was done, I walked(still VERY quietly) to the front door. I took in a deep breath, whispering under my breath "PLEASE let this be the right choice". Then I opened the door, and left the house. After shutting the door behind me, I broke into a quick jog, with the sun just peeking across the horizon, and dropping down by the moment, I knew I was safe from nosy and curious eyes, but it just felt natural to do my usual little jog before 'battle'. After a few moments, I slowed down my pace to a simple walk. I listened.

The breath knocked out of me, I felt someone push me to the ground. And before I had time to react, I felt the metal piece of something jabbed against my forehead, my eyes closed from the impact, I opened them up to see who my attacker was. His breath hot on my face, I squinted my eyes to try and see who it was. "Don't MOVE, or you will get tazed." he muttered, spitting the words out like venom. I looked up slightly to see a tazer gun aiming right on my forehead. This is not a good situation. I have a bad feeling about this... Hand-to-hand combat I can deal with and win like I usually do, tazers, are a different story. I gulped, trying to look for his eyes. I KNOW this voice is familiar to me, in some way. I just can NEVER figure out who someone is just by a voice, I NEED to see their eyes. "I'm warning you" he started, jabbing the tazer into my forehead even more to a point that it hurt just a bit. "Stop snooping around if you know what is better for you" he said, his breath just beginning to catch up to him finally as he said that. His voice now definitely is a younger person's voice, I know that for certain.

"Snooping around, with WHAT?" I asked, couldn't really help it, but I had to ask. Maybe there is a CHANCE that it isn't what I think it is, but who am I really kidding?

"You know what. That case is not meant to be solved, so deal with it. I am doing this for you! Don't you see, I don't want you to get hurt, you don't DESERVE to get hurt, but you must stop it if you value your life." my attacker said, making it sound like he was doing me a favor. He was almost pleading, but why? I squint my eyes even more, trying to make out his eyes. I looked as hard as I could, until I finally saw what I needed to see, only it didn't help me at all. SUNGLASSES!? He was wearing sunglasses to protect his eyes!? This CAN'T be happening? How did he know...? It really doesn't make sense, how anyone in the world, somehow found out about my photographic memory of eyes. The only way I can TRULY remember a person. That is messed up, I'm sorry, but who have I ever told about that? Maybe if I can knock the Glasses off, maybe then can I see who it is that knows such a thing about me.

As quickly as possible I try to fling my arms up to knock over the glasses, instead I felt air for a brief(very brief) second, and I felt the electrifying pulse of the tazer go through me. It felt like thousands of bees stung me at once, I felt my muscles instantly lock, I wanted to cry out in pain, to have SOMEONE come and try to help, even call the police. But I knew that was risky, who knows how much information this person really has? "STOP IT" he hissed in a very agitated voice "I DON'T want to hurt you, but you just left me with no choice" he said, as I tried to regain the feel in my limbs, regained, but so much STINGING. Then a different tone of voice seemed to surface, a more creepier tone of voice "Like the shades, huh? You see, I bought these, just for this meeting of you and me, once I found out about your 'special' little ability of course. That ability did manage to come with a down-side, didn't it? YOU can't even remember my voice, can you? I bet you are wondering how I found out, or even WHO gave you up, well, I can't really tell you, I am sorry about that, BANDIT". He grimaced, which made me wince at that. This really isn't good, is it?

Suddenly something on the tazer caught my eye. A badge number. I gulped, couldn't read it, but I just KNOW it is a badge number. "A police tazer?" I said, trying to add two and two together, did he steal it, or was he a policeman...

"Oh wow, you ARE as quick-witted in this field as they said you would be. Just please, Zoey" he said, using my name surprisingly, which I guess it shouldn't be THAT surprising seeing the fact that he knows just about everything else about me, but him using it as if he truly KNEW me, kind of scared me, not going to lie. "PROMISE me that you will stop snooping around. For your own sake, please.", his voice is going back to the pleading tone again. I really don't know why he even cares.

"And if I DON'T stop 'snooping' around, then what? Are you going to kill me?" I said, adding as much poison to the words as possible, as I looked him straight in the eye glass, though I know for a fact that I caught exactly where his eyes were.

He winced, why on EARTH would he care!? It really doesn't make sense. "No, I would never kill you, even if I had to, but someone will. And if that someone doesn't, you would wish that he did, honestly Zoey. If you keep on snooping around, you are going to ruin your life. You don't know what you are looking for. This rain that you are looking for to help end the drought, is going to end up being more of a life-destroying storm than the rain of life. You are going to have more than you ask for if you keep going. I SUGGEST you stop, I really do.", wow, I ALWAYS trust some guy who uses a metaphor to warn me of the destruction of my life. Though, this really doesn't sound good(better term, it sounds horrific)

"GET OFF OF ME!" Was all that I said, I glared right at him.

"Just, please." my attacker said, and he got off of me, and quickly ran as fast as he could away. By the time I got myself up, he was gone. So many questions. No answers. For the first time in my life, I truly feel lost and hopeless. It just seems like problems keep on getting stacked up more and more, yet none of them are ever going to get resolved, not a single one has so far anyways. I can feel the burning feeling right on my forehead where he tazered me, definitely left a mark. I looked towards the last spot where I saw him, at the corner of the street, and just stared. Thinking. He knows everything about me, I know nothing about him. How can someone learn so much about me, when only a small percentage I told to people, and that was only one person, and it was Sam. I trust him too much to ever think that he would have told this, this, JERK(not the word I would have usually used, but right now, the shock of the tazer is still messing with the way I am thinking right now) all of that information! And even at that, lets just say Sam did tell someone about such secrets, lets say Sam turned out to be a back-stabber some how. It still doesn't make sense how the person would find out about the whole eye-thing and me! I NEVER told Sam about that, ever. Most people would A, not believe me, or B, prey on my weak point(though I do memorize Sam's voice, and a few other people that I am around very often.). There is also that fact that it really doesn't matter, but in this case, it does. Because that little down-fall just ended up stopping me from knowing possibly the most important information that I ever needed!

My head felt like it was going to explode at how AWFUL it felt. Tazers, possibly the worst thing man has ever created. I sighed. Grabbed out the track phone and dialed Sam's number. This is truly an emergency and I needed him now. A couple seconds of it ringing, Sam picked up, his voice sounding quite confused "Hello?".

"It's me, Zoey" I said, casting cautious glances around me, now the city that I loved so much, has became a stranger to me.

Sam, being, well, Sam, skipped to the point and asked a question

"Why are you using a track phone?" he said, even more confusion in his voice now.

"Because I went, out..." I said, confessing, but before he could say anything, I quickly added "Listen, can you by any chance meet me at that place, it is an EMERGENCY.".

"Okay, I'll be there as soon as possible" Sam said, good thing he realizes what I mean and isn't asking all sorts of questions.

"Thanks" I said, about to shut the phone.

"Zoey, are you hurt?" Sam asked, wearily, he must not like where all of the clues are possibly leading up to.

".... I'll explain when you are there, okay?" I said, and I shut the phone. No need for more words. He should come with just that knowledge, he KNOWS what the place is, and how to get there. If he really cared to know what will happen next, he'd show up. And I am SURE he will. I began to walk. Walk into the same direction that my attacker disappeared through. But only because that is the direction that the place is. This place, is the place that Sam and I found shortly after Sam found out about my 'nightly missions'. The use of this place was all Sam's idea. He wanted a place in which we could meet up at to discuss anything important together about my 'Banditing trips', where no one could eavesdrop at. We never really used it actually. It being an abandoned building, we had really no impulse what-so-ever to go there too often. Though we do indeed manage to go there once a month or so, mostly to talk about nothing in particular, but today, it is going to be used the way we wanted to use it from day one.

Walking the whole two mile trek, felt long and lonely. I never have walked so slow in my life, but I have been driven to exhaustion(Mostly mentally, though physically the tazer did take a pretty good toll out of me), and really couldn't walk much faster. Shadows seemed to have followed my every move, almost whispering to me that I am in danger. A shudder ran down my back, how could this all have happened? Is this really how my life is going to end, in fear of the world? The world truly does seem as if it wants to destroy me. I sighed. I took one more right, and there it was. A small little building that was so small that it looked like it was going to be eaten by the two other buildings(who weren't so large themselves, only four stories high, not that high compared to the rest of New York City, yet pretty average in this part). I glanced around myself, making sure that no one was watching me. I looked the whole area around me twice, I can FEEL someone watching me, but I can't SEE anyone. Maybe I am being just paranoid. Maybe...

I walked over to the building, and pushed my hands up against the glass of a push-in window, it glided in smoothly(the now slight pain in my hands seem to have ebbed away due to the even worst excruciating pain on my forehead). I throw in my back pack, and then I climbed right through the window. I quickly shut the window, and then walked over into one of the empty rooms. In a corner were some paper, and pens, something Sam and I put in here a couple years ago so that we could jot down ideas, or just doodle on them when we got bored. Also, in the middle of the room was a desk and two office chairs, all things we managed to savage from the whole building. This building used to have been an office building(the purpose, I'm not sure), some 8 years ago, it was foreclosed, the owners were in way too much debt than they could handle, so basically it belonged to the bank. The bank couldn't sell it no matter what they tried. No one wanted to have such crappy space such as this building. And the bank can't knock it down due to the building being way too close to the other two buildings so they'd end up spending more money due to damages to the other two houses then the land was actually worth. So basically the bank just keeps it as abandoned I suppose. I walked over to the desk and sat down.

I reached over towards the lantern to the side of the desk(A battery-powered lantern) and turned it on. It emitted a small light, but enough to see more than just shadows and sketches of images in the room. I began to stare out into space. Nothing was going right for me. Nothing at all. Is there even a way to save myself from all of this, destruction. No, the answer has to be no. If one problem doesn't get me, the other problem is going to end up eating me alive. There really is no end to it all, is there? I listened to the opening of the window, and then footsteps coming in, I turned to see Sam. The expression on his face was stunned. "Tell me what happened" he said.

So I told him every bit of information on what happened. From being tazered, to the fact that I actually knew who it was, I just couldn't seem to identify him. The whole time, Sam looked towards me with a blank expression, he seemed very deep in thought, I'm pretty sure that I don't like it either. But maybe he is coming up with a plan in his head at the very moment, maybe he knows exactly what to do, for I sure don't.

After I gave him every piece of information, he got up suddenly and grabbed some of the paper and a pen, then sat down, he began writing. I couldn't really see what, but I know there has to be a reason other than the fact that he felt like doodling, so curiosity getting the best of me I asked "What are you writing?", he looked up from his paper for a split second and held up his index finger to have me give him a moment. Then he went back to the paper. With a fast movement, he showed me the paper, passing it over to me. There were three columns, each with a heading. One said Scott, the other said Government/Police, and the last one said Unknown attacker. I grimaced realizing what this list stood for. Those out to destroy me in some way or another, without intentions of destroying me or with the worst of intentions of destroying me. Great.

"I'm guessing you know what this list is already" Sam said, with an obvious forced laugh, and then he went on. "And incase you haven't figured it out yet, this is a list of those who are going to get in your way in some shape or form. Most people have one or two people they have to watch out for in their entire lives, AT THE MOST. You are not doing so good having so many people after you like this all at one time. Now, as far as you go, you have a nosy twelve year old boy who doesn't SEEM like that much of a threat, and compared to the others he really isn't actually." Sam took in a deep breath, and then he went on "You have a whole fleet of Governmental officials chasing after you with guns, skills and don't forget lots of money to blow. They definitely want you Zoey, I hope you know that, cause that is a fact that they will stop at nothing to find you" Sam gave me a quick glance filled with silence as I opened my mouth to speak and ask him how he can be so sure "I'll get back to that after I identify the last threat, at least I hope it's the last threat, you aren't keeping anymore from me, right?" I nodded in reply, not that I would ever want to keep something like that from Sam, but, I really shouldn't be obligated to tell him everything, I suppose I will let that one order slide due to the fact that Sam IS trying to help me. "Okay, good. Now this last threat is probably more than one person like the threat before this one. This is probably the threat you want to watch out for the most, because it is a for sure death, and judging by how you told me about this threat, you aren't going to back down like they want you to, are you?".

"No Sam, you know me all too well" I said, forcing a small laugh also. Really didn't seem right in the situation we are in right now, but it does take off a bit of steam from the situation.

Sam shook his head, and with a sigh, he went on "that's what I thought". Then he went on "Okay, so yeah this threat is definitely out to kill you, and so, I suggest watching your back seeing they seem to have way more information about you, then you have ever told, ANYONE.".

I stopped him right there with a quick flick of my hand, "Okay, I get it, I have a huge target drawn right onto my face right now, and I should watch out. Now tell me how you KNOW that the police are resilient to find me. My guess your dad, but isn't that sort of stuff confidential?" I said, very curious as to what he was going to say.

"Right. You caught me, my dad tells me almost EVERYTHING that is going on at his work." Sam said, with the first semi-real grin I've seen since we met up here. "And, you are basically the most wanted person in...." Sam paused, acting like he was trying to memorize something, but I know he wasn't "The NYPD, The FBI, and a bunch of other little organizations that I don't think would really ring a bell to you, all have you on their most wanted lists, I'm amazed that they haven't caught you yet! Honestly, the one thing that is helping you so much has to be the fact that there aren't any cameras around your house what-so-ever so they can't trace you back to your house exactly. HERE" Sam placed something on the desk, I believe it is a newspaper...

"What's this?" I asked, pretty sure I know what it is though, but hey, you never know?

"Read the front page" Sam said, sliding the newspaper over to me, and then pointing at it with his index finger. I grimaced at what the front lines said "The Bandit: Savior or con?". I felt my stomach curl at the words. "Yeah, it has gotten to that point. And as you can read in the heading alone, they are having troubles interpreting you. They are not to sure whether it is an actual good citizen trying to help out their city, or a hoax. From what my dad said, most of the police department believes it is just a hoax and that the actual criminals are getting away when in fact their victims are getting tied up. He doesn't know about the FBI, but he said, knowing the FBI, they probably WANT it to be a huge criminal that way THEY can look like heroes when they find the guy who is doing this. And based on how my dad said 'the guy' my guess, they don't even know the gender still as you said before, so you are good right now... ".

"Anything else I should know?" I asked, casting a glance around the ratty-wallpapered room. This place is in decent condition seeing as how long it went without use, especially there is the fact that many abandoned places in New York City would have been over-ran by drug thugs and homeless people, but not this place. I thought back to the way it looked outside, maybe the place doesn't even look abandoned? Realizing that even in a time as peril as this, I still seem to wander off with my thoughts, I whip my thoughts back onto Sam, as he finally began speaking again.

"Yeah.... There is a lot more actually. Now, against the aching thoughts of NOT wanting you to put yourself in danger, I'd have to say that you should go about your regular nights roaming the streets as you would have before. Because I realized that if you stop now, even more suspicion will increase. They will then believe that you are afraid of being caught, then signifying the fact that you think that you were to be punished, meaning you did something wrong. They WILL attack you like a pack of hounds if they do manage to catch you. Which is why I'm saying this, be careful. My dad didn't say anything about this, but I'm guessing that they will be increasing patrols out at night where 'The Bandit' has been 'spotted', kind of like Bigfoot only without all the mystery" Sam laughed at the end of this one, I was not amused, but he kept speaking after that quick outburst, I mean, at least he feels that it is an okay enough situation to start cracking a wise-joke, even though that joke was pretty darn cheesy, even for Sam. "It's like a huge race to see whoever can capture 'The Bandit' first. You are causing a lot of things to stir up. You are basically affecting everyone's lives in New York City to such an extent, that one literally can't walk a few feet in a semi-populated area, without hearing talks of 'The Bandit', it is astonishing how much they think about you. Whether it is good or bad, they keep on talking up a storm about it all".

"Oh really now, Sam, you do realize that I'm not completely cut-off from the outside world, right? I've been to a lot of places and I haven't heard a single word about it all, you are definitely trying to mess with me on that one" I said, rolling my eyes. Honestly, how stupid does he think I am, I haven't heard a single WORD about it all.

"Well, that must be because you don't LISTEN, I saw you ignore almost every single person around you as we went to get ice cream the other day. YOU shut yourself off from the world, I can very well tell that you are just watching out from where you are going, not exactly using all of your senses to the full extent that they should be used. LISTEN, I'm sure you'd finally be able to hear it all Zoey. Truthfully, with how much you zone the rest of the world out, I'm not too surprised that your little friend managed to sneak up on you like that when you were out this night. Okay, so you said you had regents tomorrow, just before you get into the school, listen and see what you hear. I can GURANTEE you that they WILL be talking about 'The Bandit'. Now, off of that topic, and back onto the main idea I wanted to get across to you. You really do have to watch out, stop getting so many injuries when you are out at night, those injuries are practically labeling you as suspicious." Sam said, looking towards me for a brief second, and pausing.

I laughed "Yes, because I MEAN to get injuries. Don't worry, I'll STOP asking the criminals to push me to the ground trying to kill me. I know exactly how to stop them too, I'll be very polite and use my manors, I will say please and thank you and even offer them some confiscation in return. How does giving them a hundred dollars each sound to you?" I said, liking the fact that the sarcasm sort of just came to me, instead of me forcing myself to have such a care-free type of attitude while talking. Good, maybe this situation might not be so dire after all.

Sam laughed, then he grinned and said "Yeah, yeah, I get the point.

What I mean is just try to be more careful, don't think as rash as you usually do is all. Make more than a five-second plan before you go up against them is all.". Sam yawned, "What time is it anyways? It can't possibly be any earlier than midnight.". I suddenly just noticed how truly tired Sam looked. His eyes were blood-shot and they were semi-closed, as if he was just struggling to keep them open. Poor Sam, he really does do a lot for me.

I grabbed the track phone out of my bag. I flipped it open, and as Sam predicted, it was indeed passed midnight. "Wow, you're right, for once" I said, grinning, then I added "It's two o'clock in the morning. I hope I didn't keep you from your beauty sleep too long", Sam rolled his eyes.

"Yeah, but I can now see the reason why you look the way you do with the small amount of sleep you get" Sam said keenly, as if he was planning those words all along. I really walked into that one, didn't I?

"Very funny Bear, I dId NOT see that one coming. You'll get your just-desserts, you'll see" I said, putting my phone away and then getting up, while grabbing the newspaper and placing it inside my bag. I began to stretch out my arms a little bit. I most certainly would not have had a good-night's sleep if it weren't for Sam calming me down the way he does. Now, maybe I will be able to get SOME type of sleep before my big test tomorrow.

"And I keep on watching yet nothing happens" Sam said, getting up also. He turned off the lantern. "So, the regents you are taking, is that in the morning, or during the day.".

I began rubbing my forehead that was still stinging a bit. Thinking. "Morning, I believe" I said, after listening to Sam's increasingly groggy-sounding voice. He is definitely an early sleeper, not a night person in any way, he's a bit too use to going to bed early.

"Cool, I have it in the morning also, meet up after it? We can go jogging, or we can go to the coffee house. I recommend both, because you need some exercise, and I'm definitely going to need more caffeine" Sam said, using the most serious voice I have ever heard, he STILL managed to slip in a joke right there.

"HA-HA, that joke was so funny I forgot to laugh" I said, rolling my eyes. Right now, because of the darkness of the room due to the fact that Sam turned off the lantern, I only saw a shadow in front of me, so I felt like I was kind of talking to myself in a weird sort of way.

"What JOKE?" Sam said, he gained himself a quick jab in the gut. "Kidding, kidding!" he said, with an aggravated whine to his voice, might of hurt him a little bit, but not enough for an apology. "But really" Sam said, still trying to regain himself(I reminded myself never to take Sam with me at night, he is not too durable) "We can meet up at your place like usual, go for a quick jog, my preference would be under five miles for my legs are still aching from last time, and no that does not give you any room to comment, then we can go get some coffee and meet up here to talk about it some more. I'm sure there will be PLENTY of more news by the end of the day that I will be able to share with you. Besides, I'm going to be gone next week and I rather get sick of you before I leave, which shouldn't be hard" Sam laughed, I ignored it, then he went on "that way the trip is more bearable with the thought of not wanting to hang with ya' the whole trip".

"Sounds good to me though there is one problem, you can NEVER get sick of me." I said, as we began to make our way out of the building. Sam laughed. When we got to the window, Sam pushed it opened(really didn't matter which way you pushed the stupid thing, it is junk anyways), and then jumped right through like a professional(which is good, because this is our usual route in and out of the building due to the door being boarded up to such an extent, that there is no way that someone can possibly get it open without bringing a bunch of huge tools to get the boards off. Which is sure not to go unnoticed, getting some unwanted attention pointed right here). Then, after Sam got out of the way, I jumped right through the window also. I grabbed the window and I closed it. "Thanks again Sam" I said, trying to make sure Sam knew how much I appreciated him coming here for me, he really didn't have to, and I know he knows that I wouldn't have gotten mad if he decided to blow me off, so it really does mean something to me.

"Shouldn't I be thanking you for protecting our city, Bandit?" Sam said, with so much taunt in his voice.

"Okay, lets just walk this road home in silence, I see you can't possibly be serious if it were to save your life" I said, beginning to walk away. Sam followed.

"Sounds good to me, that way I don't have to hear your awful voice" Sam said. Even though I wasn't looking at him, I can just PICTURE the Cheshire cat grin across his face. I ignored that comment, more so for Sam's sake then myn and kept on walking. Every few buildings or so, a yawn managed to erupt from Sam. He was indeed VERY tired. Finally, I broke the silence again.

"You are welcomed to sleep at my place on the couch again if you are too tired to go home." I said, waiting for some flash of a comeback, a crack of a wise joke.

"Ahh, the couch, what a nice hostess. That is possibly the nicest thing anyone has ever done for me" Bingo. Sam said that with the biggest amount of sarcasm I have ever heard anyone use in my whole life(excluding Sam himself, he is indeed the sarcasm king).

"Okay, have fun walking home a couple miles in the dark at two o'clock in the morning." I said, as we finally came to the front of my house.

Sam, finally gaining a little more seriousness said "Nah, I'd rather not. It's just a couple of miles, no big deal. See you tomorrow though

Zoey, GOOD NIGHT!" Sam yelled the last two words, possibly the loudest he could. He KNOWS that the kids are sleeping, that carnival little demon. He is trying to wake them up!

"SHHHHHHHHH" I automatically said, as he laughed like it was the funniest joke ever. "Good bye" I said in a whisper, really praying that they all didn't wake up. Sam waved in goodbye, then began jogging away. I gave a huff in annoyance, it is like having the little brother that I never wanted. I grabbed the keys out of my bag, and began unlocking the door. Slowly I opened it, trying not to make a sound and destroy anything more than Sam already did. The light was on in Summer's and my room. Not in Tim and Scott's room. I began debating this one out. Whether or not I should go into the room and comfort Summer right then and there, or try and slip into the bathroom without getting noticed so that I can change into a clean set of clothes(for the pair that I am wearing has so much dirt and grind on it, and is torn at a couple places. Though, unusually enough, there was no blood on my clothing at all.). Plus there is the fact that I need to disinfect and check out the huge mark on my forehead, for I haven't had a chance to look at it and who KNOWS how ugly it is. For both Summer's well-being and my own, I quickly slipped into the bathroom, making exceptional timing and without being loud, good.

I quickly shut the door behind me and locked it, by now Summer would know that I am here and she probably figures that I am getting changed into my night clothes and that I will be there to comfort her afterwards. Though it is always safe to make sure. I quickly darted my hands towards the light switch and flicked it on. I took a shower. Then I grabbed my pajamas that I stored in the closest the other day and got changed. Then I looked right towards the mirror to asses my one and only injury. Where that tazer hit me, there was a pretty big quarter-sized bruise, along with some torn skin here and there where there was a little bit of blood seeping out(though not fast at all). The mark was right near the other scratch that I got a couple days before, so I'm pretty sure that I will be able to hide it with my hair, well, most of it at least. I opened the medicine cabinet that was over the sink and took out some disinfectant ointment. I squeezed a little bit out, and then I massaged it over the bruise, rubbing it in all of the way. Once it was rubbed in all of the way, I placed the ointment back into the cupboard and began washing my hands. I then took out my comb from the cabinet, and began combing my hair.

Thoughts began running through my mind. Okay, so the kid had a police tazer when he attacked me, so what are the possibilities of it all? One possibility that I can for sure rule out is the possibility of him being a police officer himself, I can rule it out for a number of reasons. Such as the fact that he is too young, duh, and why would a police officer risk his career by doing such a crime, such a thing is almost impossible, isn't it? Okay, next one. He stole it, good chance(and the most wanted one of the three in my view, that way it isn't the whole good guy actually being a bad guy type of thing, those things mess with my emotions way too often), pretty plausible. Then there is that other fact, that someone gave it to him to do the job for that person. This idea brings me chills through my mind. The thought of a police officer, wanting to kill me, being the MURDERER of my adoptive parents, just brutally sickens me. It really does. It has to be the worst scenario of my parent's death by far. I shake out the thoughts as I finally finish combing through my hair. I studied my clothes on the ground for a moment, the shirt was ripped on the side in a couple of places on the bottom of it. On the knees of my pants, there were multiple holes in them, not fit for running in any more. I really didn't care about the rest(like the socks) so I didn't even bother assessing how bad they are because either way by now they are going into the garbage. Above all, that whole set of clothes were just plain old. So I grabbed all of my clothes, walked over to the garbage and threw them out. They were pretty cheap clothes anyways, and I couldn't stitch up holes in articles of clothing if it were to save my life.

I yawned a big yawn, wow, this night so far really was tiring. I walked over to the room where Summer sat on her bed. Her mouth gaped open as wide as an apricot as she saw me. Crap, I forgot to cover the bruise up. "I fell and hit my head on a chair when I was hanging out with Sam, no big deal, don't worry" I said, already coming up with an excuse before she even asked. I am possibly the first sixteen year old girl who ever had to come up with an excuse to a seven year old. Wow, that's just sad.

"You okay!?" she asked, sounding very worried as she jumped off of her bed and came right towards me. One good thing about the younger kids are their gullibility. Unlike Scott, who I will have to tell him a way better story before I can even THINK about getting his understanding. I also have to remember he is actually on the list now, though that really doesn't prove anything, though it does prove that even Sam sees Scott as some type of threat.

"Yeah, yeah I'm fine. Now how about you Summer, did SAM wake you up?" I asked, emphasizing Sam's name just to draw out the point on who she should really blame if she would like to blame someone.

Summer nodded in understanding "So it was Sam!!!! I KNEW it.", I shushed her for a quick second as her volume increased a bit, I turned back to the door and shut it quietly so that the other, more harder two, didn't wake up. "This stinks, I have my third to last day of school tomorrow too! Now I'm going to be all groggy tomorrow" Summer said.

I laughed "don't worry, I'll punish Sam for waking you up tomorrow, we will get pay back. Now, get back into your bed so that I can turn off the light without having to worry about you tripping over something, okay?" I said, patting Summer's shoulder light with my hand in comfort.

Summer nodded, then she began walking over to her bed as she said "by the way, Tim ate all of those delicious pancakes you left. He told me to tell you, and I quote in which he MUST of gotten from the television or something, his "compliments to the chef"." Summer sat on her bed and laid down, she looked towards me and rolled her eyes as she said it. I laughed.

"Yeah Summer, he definitely did." I said, making SURE to set my alarm clock, then turning out the lights and going over to my bed to sleep.

CHAPTER 6

I woke up, thankfully to my alarm clock. I got up and turned it right off. Quickly I went over to the kitchen to eat something before I got ready quick. I grabbed the second-to-last hard boiled egg out(the other was in Summer's lunch pal), and began un-shelling it at the garbage. I then went over to the cabinet and grabbed the salt. I salted the egg over the sink, and the began eating it. Running over review thoughts in my head for the regents, I felt pretty darn sure that I was going to pass the regents with flying colors. I ate the rest of the egg, thinking about more important matters(though seeing the regents IS important because the grade I am going to get is going to affect me for the rest of my life because it determines the college I get to get into, and the type of career I'll be able to have, it's not AS important as a life and death type of scenario), I began thinking about the whole Banditing business thing. What ARE the police going to do if they do find me? Kill me on point, or interrogate me until I can't bare no more? Will they send me to life in prison or something, make me 'disappear'. I gulped at the thought. Lite in prison for what? Simply trying to HELP people!? Seriously, that is probably what they will do, because they can easily say that I 'intervene' with all their cases way too much. Which in a way, I do. I'll admit that, it probably isn't the BRIGHTEST idea to go outside at night into the streets of the city to save some victims when the fact is that I can become a victim myself, and then what will happen from there? They'd have to waste some extra time on a case that really DIDN'T have to happen, when they SHOULD be figuring out REAL cases.

But still, life in jail doesn't seem to fit the crime either… My best bets if this does happen, if they DO catch me, is the whole "innocent until proven guilty" scheme. That's ALWAYS the path to go. But why am I worrying about all of this NOW? I don't even KNOW if they are going to find me, let alone serve me that punishment, it's all just a hunch I am going on. So I should probably cool down. I took a glance towards where my hand was gripping the back of a chair, I slowly unclenched it from there. I realized that both of my hands seemed to have been trembling with the paranoia that was happening all inside of my head. I slowly stopped it, and took in a deep breath. What has began as a calm way of sorting my thoughts, turned into a huge thought-disaster. I probably SHOULDN'T let that happen again unless I want to end up being forever paranoid-stricken. I sighed. Got out some orange juice from the fridge, poured myself a glace, and began drinking it, trying to forget all the thoughts that just passed through my mind a few moments ago. Closing my eyes as I did so, I was slightly surprised to hear the quick opening and shutting(rather SLAMMING) of the front door, my eyes shot open to see who it was(though I kind of had a pretty good thought on who it was). I placed my cup on the table and looked towards Ms.Smith. She seemed really angry.

"He LEFT!" she yelled, anger bubbling up in her. So wake up the kids, that's nice... I thought in spite.

"WHO left!?" I asked, trying to keep my own voice down. Who was she talking about?!

"My BOYFRIEND you idiot!" she spat at me, her eyes shooting out such meanness and hate, that I had to look away just to stop myself from punching her in the face right then-and-there. "He LEFT because he said that I wear down on him" she said, snidely as she said the 'wear down on him' part. Join the group, I thought slyly(maybe a bit too slyly), rolling my eyes(and making sure she didn't see me rolling my eyes, another rule she has, don't roll your eyes at her unless you want to get kicked out of the house).

"That's too bad." was all that I could say as I saw the creeping of curious figures in the corner of my eyes.

She huffed a big huff, obviously not getting the reaction she wanted from me, and stomped out of the room like an annoyed child(with a little more balance than yesterday morning, which I'm surprised because you'd think she would have drunken away her sadness like most people do, but instead she seems a little more sober. Interesting). The other three casted worried glances towards each other, and then towards me. 'Ignore it' I mouthed, then I said "Cereal, anyone? There are three new boxes of cereal that I bought just a week ago that no one has touched yet" I began looking in the cupboard where we keep the cereal. "There is some fruity cereal, some wheat cereal and chocolate cereal" I added, taking them all out, and of course every one of them went towards the chocolate cereal. A kid's favorite breakfast.

"What happened to your forehead?" Scott said, noticing the bruise on my forehead, I cursed under my breath. He never asked that question before, but as I had imagined, this injury is too big to by-pass for him, and it is indeed going to be way harder trying to persuade Scott on how I managed to have it inflicted on me. Always fun trying to persuade a twelve year old, nosy and smart-mouthed as anything boy, real fun.

I looked right towards Scott, he still looks tired as anything. Why? The other two don't look like that, and he never looked this tired before, so why now? "Because, I was at the store with Sam, messing around with him, when I accidentally tripped over a buckled up piece of carpet and hit my head" I said, trying to coat my words with embarrassment as much as possible, though of course I am no Sam when it comes to the acting business and I failed epically. Scott narrowed his eyes to such an extent that there was only a sliver of his eye balls peaking through. "It's the truth" I said, as Summer slammed the door of the fridge as she got out some milk.

"Come on Scott, get your bowl of cereal ready that way the milk doesn't get warm!" Summer said, pouring the milk over her cereal, then giving it to Tim to pour over his(Tim is honestly the biggest eater I've seen, his bowl is filled all the way to the top now, and from what I can tell, most of it is the chocolate cereal). Scott stared me down for another five seconds, then he walked over to the cupboard and began getting his bowl out of it. What's his problem!? I walked out of the kitchen and into my room, got a pair of clothes, and walked into the bathroom to change. After I was done changing, I grabbed my necklace and put it on, it has always been a small comfort for me. I would almost DIE not having this necklace, if it was ever lost, tears are sure to come rolling down my face. I looked at myself in the mirror, not my favorite set of attire, but it will have to do seeing I don't have much time to linger on how I look at the moment unless I'd like to take a lovely(sarcasm!) taxi ride to the test again. I walked to the front door, waving good bye to them all, I walked out and began walking towards the school(which is approximately a two and a half mile trek along the side walks). It's not really busy on these sidewalks, so deciding that it were to be useless by trying do as Sam says and listen to people who AREN'T here, I just tuned out. Funny, I never really realized it, but I guess I do sort of zone out, still doesn't give Sam the right to say that I do, but at least it's a fact what he said...

Finally, as the school began to near, and the crowds began thickening, I decided to take a crack at it and start listening. Conversations ranged from: Dinner, sports, relationships(PDI?), and yes, surprisingly the 'mysterious Bandit'. Huh, Sam was right, not that I really doubted him, well, maybe a little, but still, it's not like I thought he was a liar or anything, right? But then again, I'd rather him be a liar at this point, not so much to prove me right, and DEFINITELY not the fact that I want to have a liar as a best friend, but it is the fact about how scary it is to think that this many people are paying attention to my 'Banditing' at all...

I grind my teeth, listening to all of that mumble-jumble, makes my stomach curl(mostly the relationships in which yes, you CAN hear people kissing each other. Just nasty, go do that somewhere else! I have no problem with the hugs, and even a quick peck on the cheek, actually I think it is quite cute, but there is that line that has been drawn, and that line has to be when people stop right in front of you as you are still walking and start kissing mouth-to-mouth for over five seconds. You'd think that they'd have SOME sort of common sense to move out of the way or something at the very LEAST.). I walked across the street and to the school. Time to take a test, I swooped some hair over the bruise and then I went inside the building.

*　　　　　*　　　　　*

The test, was quite simple, well, as simple as a huge two hour test can be that is. It felt like a breeze going through the multiple choice questions one by one, not thinking about all the crap I've been having to deal with lately. And it was pretty decent going through the short-response questions. I handed the test in to the advisor with a quick smile, and then I left the class. I started to walk back home when suddenly I felt a hand on my shoulder and then Sam's voice ringing in my ear. "Hey, I thought you were going to WAIT for me, young water-bringer?! Haven't you learned anything young water-bringer" Sam said, as I turned around, he flashed another one of his Cheshire cat grins.

I rolled my eyes "And young Bear, are you really stupid enough to jump into the water when you know you can't swim?" I said, knocking the stupid baseball cap off his head. It was the same one that Summer had, not cool at all.

"You like it?" Sam said, picking up the hat and dusting it off he added "I knew you'd love it" he placed the cap right on top of his head and grinned once again. "Kind of a real-men-wear-pink act don't you think? Only a little more classier if I do say so myself. I bought it purely out of a joke, but actually, It's been growing on me. I might wear it more often." Sam flashed another grin.

I snorted "Sam, you are a joke" I said, knocking the cap right off his head again only this time turning back around to walk away.

"Hey, wait up!" Sam said, laughing as he came right back next to me with that same hat on again, you'd think he'd learn by now… "I also bought another thing for you also, that's what took me so long and why I wasn't talking to you and gracing you with my lovely presence the second you walked out of the school." before I could say that I didn't want to have yet another one of his jokes for my joke-collection(I now have a total of fifty seven useless items including the stupid dog collar he gave me several days ago), he grabbed something out of his man-bag(which he continues to tell me that it is a 'satchel' to make it sound manlier, in which it makes him sound even LESS manlier just SAYING that), and pulled out a pair of really dark looking shades. "To hide your identity!" He said, grinning a now even(and what I thought was impossible) bigger grin than a Cheshire cat grin.

"Har-D-Har-Har, where did you get these sunglasses from? The same place where you bought that lovely hat, incase you haven't realized it from the moment you got it, but that is the same hat that Summer, a seven year old girl, has." I said grabbing the shades from his hands as we kept on walking and I began examining them. VERY well tinted if I do say so myself, though maybe a bit too much.

"No, I bought this hat in Mexico and then I dropped by to Italy to get those shades. YES I bought them from the same place, and yes I realize that it is the same hat that Summer has, but hey, they were two for five dollars, too good of a deal to pass up just because my best friend doesn't APPRECIATE what I do for her" Sam said, kicking a loose stone off of the side walk with his left foot, landing it right in the drainage gate.

"Hey, I appreciate you SAM!" I said, tempted to knock his hat off once again but decided against it, due to the fact that I have already pushed my luck in such a crowded sidewalk two times already, and I'm pretty sure this next time will be the time that the luck turns into unluckiness and it ends up clouting someone in the head, a very large someone with huge anger management problems and a gun right on hand(VERY descriptive dream I once had when I was like four years old, no one should ever ask...).

"Yeah, I know. It IS very hard to not appreciate such a wonderful person like myself. But you must prove it and put those nice shades on, I wasted two dollars and fifty cents on those shades and I'd rather not see them go to waste" Sam laughed, pointing his finger to the sunglasses, and then 'demonstrated' how to put them on by using himself as a practice dummy and a fake pair of glasses.

"If you say so" I laughed as I placed them on. The world around me felt ten times darker than usual.

"NICE!" Sam hooted, and took off his cap with his right hand, threw it in the air and caught it with his left hand.

"Impressive" I said, as we began to near my house, "but weren't you going to get into running clothes?" I added, they looked like running clothes to me, though why would he go take a test in running clothes? I guess guys don't really care what they look like in public, maybe....?

"Yes, I'm going to run in these, if that is what you were thinking, Zoey." Sam said, rolling his eyes and he sat down on the rail leading up to my house "Get ready, I will stay out here. Need to make a quick phone call to my dad anyways, just to tell him whether or not I thought I did well on the test. AND before you say anything, yes, my dad is indeed a little over-protective on certain things, no need to point it out." Sam took out his phone and began dialing the number, "Oh, and here!" he said, taking off the cap and throwing it to me(I gladly caught it with one hand), and then he unslung his bag and handed it to me "can you keep these inside when we are out running, I'd rather not have a ten pound weight strapped along my shoulder when I run". I nodded. Holding the bag up and down a couple of times, I began trying to resize the weight of the bag, definitely not ten pounds, at all!

I wagged a joking finger to him in 'shame', and then I took out my key and opened the front door. Dropping his stuff out on to a table, I quickly jogged over to my room and began taking out running things, and so that I don't forget to take off my necklace in the later time, I took it off right then and there. Even when I run for just pure enjoyment(?), I'd rather not have the chance of it breaking on me somehow and me not being able to find it. Then I changed into the proper attire in the nick of time. I then began walking to the front door(being as quiet as possible when I went past Ms.Smith's bedroom this time, rather NOT wake her up). Then realizing that I still had the stupid pair of sunglasses on(no clue how I forgot to take them off!) I walked back to my room and placed them on that little shelf along with all the other jokes Sam gave me. Then I walked back to the front door and opened it up, I shut the door behind me, and as I passed Sam who was still on the phone with his dad, I believe beginning to say good bye to him, I smacked Sam at the back of the head.

Sam mouthed the word 'Hey' and began rubbing the back of his head as if it hurt him(which I know it shouldn't because I MADE sure to lightly smack him, again leading back to the points of him being a weakling and him being yet an extremely good actor.). "That's for waking up Summer last night with your obnoxious voice" I said, beginning to stretch my arm(something that I usually just skip all together, but I kind of figure that I mine as well seeing that I'm waiting anyways). Sam rolled his eyes and then went back to talking to his dad on the phone. His Dad really is overprotective of Sam, so, I have to wonder what his Dad said when he got up at three o'clock in the morning(roughly). Yell at him, question him, say how worried he was, or maybe even a little bit of both. Obviously his Dad either didn't find out somehow, or his Dad wasn't that mad, because there is no way that a mad parent would allow history to keep replaying itself(Sam hanging out with me). I guess Sam could have

EASILY lied his way out of it too.

I heard his phone snap shut, so I turned back to Sam. “Ready?” I asked, looking back to the streets and trying to plan a nice route to go jogging on.

“Yes, and just in case you are curious as to how much more information I collected from my Dad since last night, I can tell you it is a lot. Lets go” Sam grinned while saying this and then began jogging. I grimaced, very funny. He only told me that he knew more information, he didn’t actually tell me that new information. He KNOWS what he is doing, he is driving himself for a smaller run because he believes that I am so curious that I’d want to know straight away. Fight fire with fire I suppose. I began running to catch up with him for he was already turning a corner by the time I collected my thoughts. So within a few moments, I’ve managed to catch up with him, dodging the few strays of people on the sidewalk(again, the road that I live on, isn’t that busy, at all. So we can easily run on the sidewalks here without totally ticking people off and having someone yell at us or something.).

“Nice one” I said under my breath, but loud enough for Sam to hear as we ran in a single-file line, Sam in front of me(of course, Sam likes to 'lead'. He is the captain of the school's track team and President of our class, so, one can pretty much get the point. In fact the time when Sam ended up getting runner-up to some kid in like seventh grade or something around that year as school president, he declined the offer as Vice president cause it annoyed him so much to be 'second in command' as he would say it. Not the best way one should live life, but I have to admit it was pretty amusing to see.). Sam ignored me, well, at least I BELIEVE that he did, I can't, like MOST people, really tell whether or not someone is grinning from the back. Curiosity was beginning to eat me up alive as we neared the third time of running around the block my house is on(Sam basically insisted on us running around in circles like dogs rather than run to an actual destination, I suppose I really don't care.). We had to have ran only about a mile and a half, and I'm really not planning on stopping at such a low amount of running. Trying to shove out that curiosity, I begin thinking about something else.

My regents, I had to do good on them right? There weren't any questions that really stumped me or anything, but some teachers do say that it's a bad thing when you think a test is TOO easy, because that means that you didn't take the test seriously. I stumbled for a brief second, regaining my footing, I decided that forcing myself to think about something that quite frankly I don't really care about, isn't the best thing to do when I am running along a pretty messed up and old side walk at a pretty fast speed(how much, I don't know, and in reality, I don't care nor' does it matter.), So, then how DO I stop that gnawing feeling of wanting to know right in the pit of my stomach? Counting HAS to be the answer doesn't exactly take much concentration and yet it is enough to take up all of my thoughts.

One, two, three, four, five, six, seven... I began counting in my head, reaching to ten and then dropping back to one again. Simple enough. I didn't end up stumbling or anything, but when I looked up, Sam was gone. "ahh crap" I said under my breath, looking around for him. We've been going around the block for so many times now, how is it that I lost him!? I had to have ran about seven miles so far, maybe I was running them by myself that whole time? No, that really doesn't make sense because I saw him just a few moments ago. So, how does two sixteen year olds loose each other by going on the same route a thousand times over!? Grinding my teeth, I know I should probably just go back home and wait for Sam to call me or something....

Two hands went right across my shoulders, I quickly turned around, my heart pounding, only to see Sam. "Payback" was all he said, with a wide grin.

"SAM!" I yelled, annoyed and embarrassed that I allowed him to do that stupid joke on me. I should have KNOWN that that was going to happen, how could I be so Brainless!? I let out an exaggerated sigh. "You scared the heck out of me Sam!" I said, not liking the fact that I am practically giving him what he wanted, a response, but really, why on Earth would he choose that joke, out of all the other jokes in the world, at a time like this?

"I know" he said with a grin, "It was a mean joke, but it HAD to be done. You should have SEEN yourself zoning out the way you were, it was as if you weren't there! I had to mess with you, it was way too easy. And I'm sorry that you gave me the chance to play such a FUNNY joke on you, considering the events that have been unfolding, but come on, you have to admit it was HILLARIOUS.". I allowed for my heart rate to slow down before I replied(My heart rate was fast both from running, and from that Idiotic joke!).

"Sam, you were this close to getting punched in the face from that joke" I said, holding out my hand and using my finger to show just how close(very close) he was. I exhaled a deep breath and then went on "PLEASE don't do that again?" I said, part ordering, part asking, and part begging.

"Yeah, yeah, don't worry" Sam said, inhaling a deep breath and added "Lets go to the coffee shop to get some coffee, jogging is quite frankly boring and I kind of want to have something to eat also", and without waiting for me to reply, he began heading to the coffee house. I rolled my eyes out of habit, obviously he was a bit too far away and not facing me to see the rolling of the eyes, and followed after him. Personally, I'm not a fan of going to the coffee house in my jogging clothes, because they make me look like a complete slob, but I guess it is pretty visible that I was jogging, but still. We talked and joked about nothing in particular on our way there(that nothing in particular NOT being about the whole Banditing ordeal, I think we kind of without really saying it decided that it was not to be talked about in public or anything of the sorts, only in the privacy of my place, or at our little 'hangout'. Not his place, his Dad is sort of nosy from what I can tell, though probably at my place we'd have to watch out too). It felt nice not talking about it all, but strange, as if something was truly missing. But all in all, it was truly pleasant(yes, in actuality it was MORE THAN nice.). We took the elevator up(not that crowded, surprisingly). We ordered two iced coffees and two chicken wraps to go. I made sure to grab some napkins and straws to put in the bag(for this place is notorious for not giving enough napkins, usually, you'd be happy if you got like one napkin, and that is if there were with like FIVE other people.). After picking up our order, we left, joking about how stupid it was of them to give us literally one napkin, and no straws. We took the elevator downstairs, it was pretty packed this time but Sam insisted on taking it or he'd just take it by himself.

We both went to the little old building, doing the usual to get in, and then we sat at the desk and began unwrapping our wraps. I grabbed my coffee and took a sip out of it, while Sam began to gorge himself to such an extent, that he was eating as fast as little Tim does. I laughed "You act like you haven't seen food in ages" I said, taking a bite out of myn.

"I forgot to eat breakfast" he said, taking quick bites in between words.

"I always wondered how you survived this long, forgetting to eat breakfast n' such" I said, taking a sip of my coffee, and glancing over to one of the corners of the room at which I heard a quick scuttling noise that could have very well have been a rat. Grotesque, really grotesque, an involuntary shudder went down my spine at the thought of a rat.

"Ha-HA, at least I haven't lived in New York City my whole life and yet I'm still afraid of rats" Sam said, he must of seen the shudder. Sam laughed, crinkling up his empty wrapper where the wrap was and throwing it to the corner of the room.

"You are going to have to pick that up" I said in a flat tone, then added "And what does that have to do with anything? Doesn't stop you from eating like a slob" I stuck my tongue out at him like a little kid.

"Nothing, I just think it's comical, and thought that I should point it out is all. Now that it seems like you have barely taken a bite out of one half of the wrap, can I have the other half?" Sam said, he then took the other half.

"Thanks for asking" I said dryly.

"No problem, what are friends for?" he said, making another huge Cheshire grin, then he took a bite of the wrap, making sure to add sound affects.

I rolled my eyes, I wasn't that hungry anyways, and I took a bite of the rest of the wrap I had left, and then placed it back on the wrapper. I swallowed and then said "So, you have managed to get more information, how about you share it with me before you end up swallowing your tongue down. Hmmm?".

Sam laughed, as he finished the last bite of the wrap. "Okay, so I guess they ARE placing up more patrols in this general area at night, they are also going to start putting up more and better security cameras along the streets at the end of July, in which you shouldn't be worrying about now, because we are in the middle of June. On the plus side, he said that all of the cops that are lining along your path are complete rookies, basically just got out of the Police Academy and barely have more than a year or two under their belt. This is of course, as most people were to think, because the more wiser and more experienced cops rather not have such a late-night shift, though I'm sure if you came out at the times that they choose for you to come out, they would have easily have said yes for the idea of becoming 'great'. And the money on the side that they were to earn...." Sam broke off with his words suddenly.

My jaw went rigid "Money?" I asked, pretty darn sure that I already know what he means, okay, one hundred percent sure, but I'd like him to specify a little bit better.

"Yeah, the government I guess put like a bounty on your head." Sam said, his eyes WERE looking right at myn, now they are wandering towards different areas of the room. "Five thousand dollars, and that is if anyone has any type of information on it all, if you are caught, and erm..... Alive, of course, ten thousand dollars. Now this is anybody, but of course a police officer has more of a chance of doing so...".

"Well, I'd probably hope it is alive, because they do realize that I were to be dead if I'm not alive, and that would be murder..." I said, trying to laugh it all off, of course it really, REALLY doesn't work...

"Yeah, that was mostly so that people don't go hunting in the night with a rifle and start shooting up a storm, killing other people, and killing you, which yes, it would be called murder and they were to be charged and fined with murder. But none or less, if they did end up killing ya', now lets hope that this NEVER happens, but anyways, if they did, they wouldn't be able to even tell if you are The Bandit or not, because they can't interrogate the dead, right?" Sam said, he is also trying to provide with some laughs, but again, it does not work. He sighed, "Well, I guess it really can't get worse, can it? If you do end up getting caught, you know what is ahead so there is really no surprises. The worst of the storm is already here, now lets just hope the clouds end up breaking somewhere else and not above us, hmmm?".

If there wasn't the facts that the kid who pushed me down was way younger than us, I know Sam's voice and that it wasn't Sam's voice, and the fact that I trust Sam way too much, I would think that Sam was the one that tackled me down, you know, with the metaphor he just used and all. "Sam, that metaphor honestly scared me, I'm not going to lie, and when it comes to that, you are indeed right. Now, something tells me that you are holding back on something and I'd like to know what it is, please.".

Sam laughed, nodding his head in realization at what he just did, "Whoops sorry about that, metaphors are great, aren't they?" I was going to say not really but something tells me he realized this and so he quickly cut me off before I could speak "Anyways, yes, but no. It was just an idea I had in my mind, that I crossed out the second it came up, due to how you are…".

"How I am, oh really now? Please do tell me this wonderful idea" I said.

Sam laughed "See, you haven't even gave it a CHANCE yet, you already denied it before even a sliver of it can come out of my mouth." Sam said, taking another sip of his coffee then going on "It is truly an idea that can go either way with a fifty-fifty chance of it helping the problem, or making it worse. My idea was that maybe I should go out there with you. You know, in case you need back up or something. You do realize that the only reason why that monkey-brain ended up getting the upper hand was because you were caught off guard, how your guard can be down at any point while you roam through possibly one of the worst parts of New York City by yourself at night is beyond me, but it is simply that. Now tell me, how can someone catch TWO people off guard, especially that feeble kid. I WILL be of some help now Zoey, remember, I might not be so called as 'tough' as you when it comes to getting my guts punched out, in fact I'm a complete stranger to that other than the times when I'm around you, but I can ensure you that SOME help is better than none. And I do have some strengths in which you do lack in..." Sam trailed off at that last part, he is now treading dangerous waters on that note.

"And these strengths are?" I said, quite curious as to what these lovely strengths are that he has in mind, I can name a few, but I suppose it will be just interesting to see what HE thinks they are.

Sam paused, he is hesitant. That's never a good sign, finally he drew in a large breath and began to speak "Well, I don't zone out quite as much as you do. I am on alert more while you just seem so at ease... Then there is the fact that you aren't the best at really examining a situation, I mean, I'm definitely not, but you are... Yeah, lets just leave it at that" Sam laughed uneasily, as if he didn't feel like upsetting me, quite amusing and ironic seeing that usually everyday we work on upsetting each other in a sort of comical way, and yet we never want to TRULY upset each other. Intriguing, quite intriguing.

I laughed "Fair enough, now do me a favor and tell me no more or

I'd be forced to tell you all the things you lack in that I seem to thrive in" I said with a quick smirk and then I went on "But no, I'd rather not put your life in danger anymore than I have, it is bad enough that I might be leading the Feds and criminals right towards your doorstep let alone push you up against a blade. I'd never forgive myself if somehow one night you get killed, and I'm still very well alive, that just doesn't seem right, let alone off the lines of WRONG. Besides, don't you need your sleep? You don't do too well without more than eight hours of sleep", I added the last part, raking my gaze(pointedly) along the tired-bags underneath his eyes due to the lack of sleep he had from last night, sleep was something that I managed to deprive him from last night..

"Yeah, yeah, I already know that flaw in the plan and in me. But come on Zoey, what is the harm in me tagging along?" Sam said, his fist pounded the table slightly as if to emphasize it all.

"I already told you, if you remembered or LISTENED to what I said" I said, teasingly slamming my hands in a fist against the desk, only doing it twice as hard. Both laughing, but I can still tell from the look in his eyes that he isn't ready to give up just yet. Not even after I tried deluding the conversation with some humor. Humor works for a lot of situations, just not right now, not today, not this situation.

"Yes, I always have to listen, you are so loud not even earplugs can save me from the wraith of your voice" Sam said, grinning and winking his left eye towards me, he definitely caught on to me trying to push the conversation away and decided to show it to me that he noticed by using his own joke and winking. I scowled inside my mind and whether or not it showed across my face is a different story now. "And Zoey, weren't you like eleven years old when you started this? You can't possibly think, me, a sixteen year old male, is at more danger than an eleven year old girl going out there, do you?".

He brings up a good and valid point, other than the fact that I was angry at the world at the time and very confused, though come to think of it, I'm not too far from the second one right now at this moment of my life. And the whole adding the gender thing into it, what does gender have to do with anything? So, putting those thoughts to words(well at least PART of the thoughts to words) I said "And what does gender have to do with anything now? You aren't going all 'boys are better than girls' on me now, because that Is so elementary school my friend and I believe we all know by now that it's totally false, right?", half-way serious, and half-way joking, both ways a hundred percent trying to get off of this horrid topic right now.

"Good try, you KNOW that's not what I mean, and I can also tell that you are trying to get off topic. Don't, we have to focus until I finally drive the point home and you give up. It's either that, or I'm just going to have to follow you tonight without you knowing, maybe even get robbed myself then you'd have a whole lot more to worry about than just yourself." Sam said, tapping his fingers on the desk impatiently as if he is just waiting for me to give in, not HOPING for me to give in, but yes, WAITING for me to give in, as if he already KNOWS that I'm going to give in somehow. Really, is that seriously how he wants to go?

I rolled my eyes still even though I know it's just pointless, he isn't even facing me, but more or less towards the wall "You do realize that you will NEVER ever do such a stupid thing. That is truly a stupid thing to do on so many levels, it's really NOT funny, at all actually. And if you really want to HELP me then you won't keep on begging to place your life in danger and telling me all these stupid plans you have in order to achieve another plan just so that you can 'Help' me. I appreciate it, but I believe it is unnecessary and dangerous. I don't like it one bit, not at

ALL." I took in a deep breath and then went on "Honestly Sam, you help me enough as it is, I will forever be in your debt, for I dug the hole and yet you continue to risk your own self trying to help me out of it. And yes, I'd appreciate it if you just ignore the metaphor, we all know that the metaphors in my head sound a lot better in my head than out loud so just yes, deal with it." I laughed lightly at the very last part, and then continued on once again "Thank you Sam, just thank you so much. It means a lot to me, It really does".

"Then ALLOW me to help you, even just this night, let me prove that I will be more than more weight when it comes to the night, I will actually help you, I WANT to help you. And if it doesn't work out, then fine, tell me if I need to be told that I just got in the way of things, but seriously, I definitely believe that I will be able to help you. So just one night, that is all that I ask of you" Sam said, moving his gaze around several times until he finally managed to lock gazes with me, he is VERY serious, I can just feel it.

I sighed, wow, Sam was RIGHT, he really did know that I was going to give in, not that I would necessarily call it peer-pressure, but I will definitely have to call it something pretty stubborn and bull headed enough to PUSH me to giving in. Yes, it's amazing how even your best friend can peer-pressure you. AMAZING. "Sam, don't make me regret this", praying to God that this is more of a right choice than the other choice I made last night that ended up as a complete and utter failure "But yes, I will allow you to come with me to do my little 'Banditing' tonight. As long as you promise one thing" I paused for a moment, and thinking better of it, I changed it "Actually TWO things, the first one, that you WILL follow and listen to every single thing I tell you to, don't flag down a police car because you THINK I'm ready to go, LISTEN. And second, if this doesn't work out, and not to be arrogant but it probably ISN'T going to work out, I don't want you complaining to me for the next two days that you are here and then once you get back from camping making me suffer for practically the rest of my Summer vacation. I will NOT be a happy camper if you do, and I'd probably end up giving you a pretty nasty scar on your forehead the shape of my fist if you do end up going insane on me. Now, please, PLEASE promise or that scar might come sooner than expected" I laughed. Sort of amusing how I can be so brutal with Sam and everything, most people would have most certainly have framed me for bullying or something like that by now if I have been doing that to them. But I know Sam all too well to know that he won't do that, his version of 'contentness' is a little thing called payback and the only person that believes and feels the sweetness has to be the 'pay backer'.

Sam grinned, he knows he won the battle. "Of course, I mean, it's not like I'm going to end up being useless to you, I am indeed going to prove myself 'worthy' of coming with you, you'll see" Sam said, adding a pinch of sarcasm to the proving himself worthy part. He already thinks that it is all in the basket. Seriously? He can't be more wrong than if he believed that pigs can fly with their own set of wings(Because technically speaking pigs can fly, they'd just have to be in a fully-operated airplane driven by people.).

"Yeah, okay." I said, rolling my eyes. Then I grabbed my phone out of my pocket(always buy a pair of running shorts with a pocket in them!) and flipped it open, checking the time. The time is now five-twelve, and the others are going to need dinner... "Okay, so lets both get back to our houses and get ready, I do recommend you wear something other than a pair of shorts to protect your knees if you end up falling or something. Now eat something, just make sure it isn't TOO heavy, because that will just weigh you down. We'll meet up OUTSIDE my house at nine fifty, don't knock or you will have to face something more than just the wraith of me. Try to make sure your lovely police father doesn't follow you, please. And make sure to have all necessary materials that you'd need after tonight, out and ready to use so that you won't have to make much noise when you get in. Got it?".

Sam laughed at the whole plan "My dad is gone for the weekend, something about a whole meeting just about you, they are telling every police officer one weekend at a time about you, well, um, reviewing what you have done basically. So far, my dad says all the other police officers that went there already are amazed and terrified all at the same time at how much you did. He says that most of them are fifty-fifty when it comes to believing about whether or not you are a hoax now. Dropped pretty quickly if I do say so myself, but hey, who knows WHAT goes on in that police department of theirs!? Anyhow, so I really don't have to worry about him, he went to a hotel closer to where it is at so that he wouldn't have to wake up so early for it. And in case you're wondering, that trip of ours is still going to go on", Sam said, adding humor to the whole mix. Slightly a joke and yet slightly serious, always interesting when Sam incorporates both.

"Okay, that's great. Well then, see you tonight I suppose. Now I don't HAVE to lie to the other three, I can simply say that I am going to go hang out with Sam, great, I guess that is one pro that I can have from all of this, compared to a zillion cons hmmm?" I said, emphasizing the zillion.

Sam rolled his eyes, "You switched that one, at first I thought you said one PRO and a zillion CONS, when in fact we all know it is the other way around, one CON and a zillion PROS, which is basically something you manage to get when hanging out with me in general" Sam said, getting up.

"Okay then, what ever YOU say" I said, getting up also, grabbing all of the garbage and placing it in the bag. We walked out of the building and to my place. Then Sam waved goodbye or rather see you later as he made sure to shout out, and began his trek to his place. I opened the front door and came in. The kids bouncing around the house like jelly beans. Shoot, I forgot that today is FrIday. Well, not necessarily FORGOT but I forgot to incorporate that when making the plan. The weekend is never good, the kids can stay up as long as they like because they have no school, and so, in actuality, how am I going to get the heck out of this place without them being way too curious? Sam is definitely going to have to come in, only way. I walked over to the kitchen and pulled out some pasta from the cupboard. Then I grabbed out a huge boiling-pan and got some water into it. I placed it on the stove top and turned it on high. I then began getting everything else out for dinner as usual.

My hands fumbled for just about everything I came in contact with, I guess I just don't like the fact of Sam going out. It does NOT sit in my stomach too well. I have been doing this for years, how would Sam know anything about this!? He is going to end up getting hurt! How does he even THINK that he is going to be able to help without getting totally injured in some way or another, if his dad finds out, he'll explode on Sam, EXPLODE. And we both know that they are looking for 'The Bandit' right now, and are waiting to tack it on the next person they see. Sam SHOULDN'T get in trouble for what I did. Would his dad turn him in, the answer is probably a yes. Though I would NEVER want to think bad about his dad, one has to have more of a realist thought in order to correctly think about this situation. Would his dad want something bad happen to Sam, NO, but that doesn't necessarily stop them from punishing Sam, Okay, maybe I am over-thinking this a bit too much. But still, it is all basically eating me alive. I honestly don't think I can take much more of it.

I sighed, looking out of the kitchen window, I took in a deep breath, telling myself to shake it all off, I washed my hands in the kitchen sink then dried them. Afterwards, I walked over to the now boiling water and cracked in the pasta into the boiling water. I then went over to another cupboard and pulled out a strainer and I placed it into the sink, ready to be used when the pasta is done. I then walked over to Scott's and Tim's room and knocked on the door. I heard the scuffling of feet and then the door drew open. "Yes?" Scott said, looking up towards me with his hard, and annoyed looking eyes.

"Dinner is almost ready, you BOTH need to wash up." I said, and not saying anymore, I walked away towards the living room to get Summer. She was on the couch watching some cartoon, while drawing, going back and forth between our room and the living room getting the supplies. Scratch it off about the whole 'ALL' of the kids were like jelly beans, I mean, only Summer was, while the other two were in their room. "Hey, mind if I interrupt the artist to tell her to wash up, dinner is almost ready." I said.

She laughed and nodded, then I added "Do me a favor and put all of this away before Ms.Smith comes out and gives us 'brats' another lecture about keeping HER house clean, hmm?" I laughed at the end part, for everyone, no matter what age, knows just how poisonous Ms.Smith's rules are and just how awful the ways are that she will enforce them with. Not that I believe the rule of having a clean house is bad, I just believe how she SAYS this rule is pretty annoying. She demeans us when she says this rule and does even worse when she enforces it.

Summer nodded, brushing her hair back away from her face all of the way, she sprung up from where she was coloring and began grabbing every loose crayon she could find and then she went back to our room to put it all away. I walked back to the kitchen and began pouring out the noodles into the strainer, the steam rising and hitting my face as I did so, it sort of felt nice on the lingering-throbbing effect of the bruise on my forehead. I then dumped all the pasta in a bowl, and placed it on the table. Scott was just coming in, followed by Tim and then by Summer. All of them getting their dishes ready, I sat down. I scooped some pasta for me and lightly salted it. We sat there eating in silence, and out of the corner of my eye, I kept on catching glances from Scott. He honestly is beginning to worry me, for his well-being and my own. How much information can he possibly know, or suspect? That kid just needs to chill. Trying to pretend that I'm NOT noticing the glances Scott keeps on placing on me, I concentrated on my food. After a couple of scoops of pasta, I managed to think of a better idea. "Summer, anything interesting happened on your third-to-last day of school today?" I said, trying to start a conversation to blur out Scott's insanely creepy suspicious looks he is giving me. My fists tightened up when Summer hesitated to reply, not good when Summer doesn't have anything to say. But then after she ate a couple more scoops of pasta, she took in a big breath, and opened her mouth.

"YES! We had a presentation from a bunch of cops today, they were telling us about The Bandit" Summer said, bouncing in her chair. My fork almost fell right out of my hand, and I tried not to twitch in reply. Scott was now staring directly at me now, as if seeing my reaction, maybe?

"Sounds.... Entertaining..." I said, not sure how to use a decent adjective to such a horrible thing. Also, trying NOT to show the surprise in my voice, though I had to shoot my head straight down(not too fast, a set of eyes are still REALLY watching me right now...) so that they COULDN'T see my face just in case it was clear as day written on it, practically screaming out to them.

Summer must of not have gotten the reaction she wanted, because she quickly blew over that topic and went on to what happened at lunch today for her, and how some kid almost started a full-out food fight in the cafeteria by throwing food at numeral tables, but was quickly stopped by a cafeteria monitor. She was really glad that he got detention because he pushed her over in the halls the other day and needed some major payback. After that, I began zoning out, deep in thought. Due to that shocking change of events, I didn't feel too eager to finish up the meager amount of pasta that was still on my plate. My stomach feels like it is being clenched, and my heart feels as if it dropped a hundred floors down into a canyon. That event that just happened, is just another reminder about what is happening to my LIFE. Even at home it has managed to infiltrate my thoughts(not that it really hasn't already, but definitely WORSE).

Catching yet another glance from Scott, I snapped. "Okay Scott, what are YOU looking at. You have been staring at me during the whole dinner time with those beady eyes and you won't let up" I said, frustrated out of my mind. What does he WANT from me!? For me to smack him silly, is that it???

Scott shot his eyes right towards mine, as if he thought I didn't see him the whole time. His jaw dropped open slightly, but he managed to close it back up within a snap. "Nothing, I can't look around now? That's okay, I'm done anyways. Lets go Tim" Scott said, getting up, throwing away the rest of the pasta on his plate and then waving Tim on. Tim looked at his half-empty plate with sorrow, as if he was loosing a dear friend, but easily obliged to Scott, and got up, and threw away his pasta, leaving.

I looked towards both of them as they left, Summer's jaw hanging open mid-speech. "Wow, you sure showed him" Summer said, with humor, but a bit nervously.

I scowled, "He WAS looking at me for the longest of time Summer, with almost a malicious glare, you realize that right?" I said, still trying to get over the whole fact. Summer nodded quickly.

"Of COURSE I saw all of that, how wouldn't I? Scott is just messed up in the head is all, ignore him like we usually do. I'm sure he hasn't had his daily douse of sane-medicine is all" Summer said, laughing at the last part. She flashed a quick grin, "So, did you get Sam back for waking me up today?" Summer said, as if she was actually TRYING to get off of the subject, smart little girl she is...

I grinned "You know it. Don't worry, he is going to have a pretty big bruise on the back of his head tomorrow. Revenge is indeed SWEET." I said, laughing at the dumb joke I made, it's a kid's joke n' all. One meant for a little kid like Summer. As I know all too well, I didn't ACTUALLY made a single mark on Sam, much less a BRUISE! Unless he bruises so easily that he can't even take such a light slap as it was! Which, on second thought, Sam just MIGHT bruise easily, but still point taken, right? Summer smiled.

"Knuckle touch?" I said, something that we do every now and then as sort of a joke. Because Summer and I always made fun of kids doing it and MISSING each other's knuckles in the park. So we got onto the fact of making fun of it by doing it ourselves, kind of a weird-twisted(in a weird way, not in a 'bad' way) joke, but it is OUR joke that we share together, and it makes Summer happy which I'd do anything for all of them. Summer brought up her knuckle, I brought up myn and we 'pounded' them together, then broke free.

"Yeah, we are SO cool." Summer said, laughing as she grabbed her plate and began scrapping off the rest of the pasta with her fork over the garbage. I got up also, shoveling in the last bits n' pieces of pasta into my mouth(not healthy, but I have to eat SOMETHING more!), and began putting away everything. I told Summer that she could go and watch T.V, as I began putting away the condiments. Then I went towards my room, and began grabbing out a fresh change of clothes for tonight. I then went over to the bathroom to take a shower and get ready.

*   *   *

I slipped right outside of the house, not really caring about the fact that it is a good ten minutes before Sam arrives. I just couldn't help but see the opportunity right in front of me, Scott was in his room with Tim, and Summer was watching T.V, so all I had to do was tell Summer that I was going to go hang out with Sam, and then leave. Hopefully none of them is going to look out of the window because that's all that I need, one of them noticing me still sitting on the porch. I began looking around at the increasingly darkening buildings surrounding me, not too long before the sun will be finally past the horizon. And yet even though the sun is almost out of sight, It is still comfortably warm outside, well, for now. Tonight probably is going to be unbearable, running in heat, but still, not as bad when the sun is up all the way I suppose. I yawned as I looked up towards the sky above me. So many clouds, huge big gray ones from what I can see in the low-light and in between the buildings(not that tall of buildings compared to the rest of New York City, but still tall enough to crop someone's view a bit. Not really on the side that my place is on, this side only has two-story buildings, but the other side has twenty story buildings for more building was added on to them some years ago so that more people can live around here). I gulped, I really don't feel like having to run in the rain tonight while having to worry about Sam, hopefully the clouds will hold off.

My hands tensed up as yet the same thought of something bad happening tomorrow crossed my mind. I STILL don't like the idea of Sam coming, but I already said yes and there is no way I can persuade Sam to turn back, not even for a million dollars. Probably not even if I told him that if he kept going it would mean certain death. Sam is way too determined to prove himself, and for what, I have no clue!? I huffed out a breath, getting agitated with how long I was waiting(my fault of course due to the fact that I came out earlier), I began stretching my arms. I swung my left arm over my head and across my shoulder and held it there for ten seconds then did the same for my other arm. Kind of lamely I reached down and touched my toes for a few seconds then stood back up, stretching is sort of boring. Not my cup of tea at all(though my 'cup of tea' wouldn't be an actual cup of tea, I'm not a tea fan, not that it REALLY matters or anything, those thoughts just cross my mind). I was turning the opposite direction to try out a different stretch when I saw Sam turning the corner and onto my street. He kept on making sideways glances over his shoulder, almost wearily. But definitely reluctant to show it, he quickly stopped looking over his shoulder once he caught my eye and 'slyly' held his head up high as if he ruled the world, not scared of anything the world threw at him. He is truly the best actor I've seen. I laughed as he finally got within reasonable ear-shot distance then I said "feeling almighty there aren't you now?". I teased him the lightest way I could, though I have to admit it is indeed sort of weird talking during the night. I've always went solo, so there is really no reason to talk at night, but now that Sam decided to tag along, I'm definitely going to have to communicate.

"Funny. So which direction are WE going today?" Sam asked, as if he did this for years, plus he said the word 'we' with a sort of ring to it, as if he is very proud of being a part of it all, this is most certainly going to be a long night. But I guess it is worth giving it a try.... Maybe....

"Um, well I went that way" I pointed to my right "the last few times, so I think we can go the other way this time. And seeing that the night is still pretty young and I'd rather not stay too close to this place, we are going to run several miles away before we even TRY to listen for um, news" I said using a whisper voice to it. Time to be serious, BOTH of our lives are now hanging on the line now, it's not just mine that I have to worry about, one mistake and I just ruined two people's lives.

"Great, I can go for another ten mile run tonight" Sam said dryly. He seems to be regretting it all, good, maybe it will detour him from tagging along with me tomorrow. I drew my gaze across Sam's whole outfit, he was wearing a dark green t-shirt with a small logo that I can't really make out due to the decrease in lighting(not the BEST color seeing we are running in the middle of the night in New York City, not in the forest, but not the worst either...), and then a pair of grey sweats. If I could and if we had time, I would send him back right now to get a pair of darker pants, but quite frankly we don't have the time and I don't have the patience, so it will have to deal and I guess I'll just have to hope that our target isn't too smart and won't notice a flash of grey out of the corner of his eyes. I grinded my teeth, rethinking it, I think it would be best getting away from the thicker population in this general area and going for a place where it is darker.

"Okay, actually, we will go straight, not left" I said, pointing across the street and towards a road that was going straight and was kitty-corner from us. "That way your, lovely pants won't show up too much." I added, pausing a second to come up with a word for the pair of pants he was wearing.

Sam looked down at his pants and then looked back at me grinning "Oh yeah, I thought you'd like these. It turns out that my dad threw away my only pair of black pants like a few months ago because he thought I'd never use them and didn't want them taking up closet space" Sam said, my jaw dropped "Wait, what did I say wrong" he added after a moment of silence from me, after another moment he said "Really Zoey, what did I say wrong there?" it's funny how easy Sam can be at the weirdest of times.

"Nothing, just surprised that your Dad still goes through your closet is all" I finally said, and then added "You walked into that one, just saying" and began running past him, making sure to land a light blow to his head again as I passed him, I looked back to make sure he was following, he was, and then we ran across the street. I dropped back a little bit, allowing Sam to 're-claim' the leading position so that I can keep watch towards the back, even though Sam says I zone out all the time, I know I won't when it's Sam's life in danger on top of it too, so I guess I'm just going to have to concentrate. Sam kept on the same straight-forward road, as we ran, the street lights around us were going from less-often to barely once every two blocks or so. We were heading into the worse area, a place in which I'm a little less familiar with, but we should be okay, though it was a pretty stupid idea taking Sam on a run down a street that I'm less acquainted with. After who knows how many miles(can't be much seeing I'm barely out-of-breath, my heart rate has to be just slightly more faster.), probably just one or two at the most, we stopped, well, rather Sam stopped and I fumbled a little bit trying NOT to run into him, giving him a quick questioning glance.

"Listen" Sam whispered, pointing his finger into an alley. We heard the shattering of glace, someone was robbing an apartment. I bit my lip, not liking the fact that Sam managed to hear it faster than I did, but gracious that he was here to hear it, because I might not have caught it and the robber would have gotten away(though some other crime would have been stopped too I have to remember that). "I say we wait until the guy is half-way out of the window, and then smack his head against the window pane until he is unconscious, easy win" Sam grinned.

I rolled my eyes "Sam, it is never that easy, and for a kid who has a father as a cop, I'm surprised you don't know anything more about criminals" I said, then I added "For instance, MOST have a second hand, they usually don't steal alone when they know someone is gone, and judging by the fact that there is no screaming, that apartment is vacant at the moment. Also, knowing the fact that they managed to target an empty house, I'm pretty sure they are not amateurs and definitely brought some backup." I began looking around for some car idling somewhere. "Usually in a car", I put in after that.

"Oh, well, there goes my plan and my idea of the fact that I know how to plan right, what is yours?" Sam whispered, keeping his eyes on the apartment window, probably expecting the thief to jump out of the window all of a sudden holding a gun and staring right at us, which isn't a too far-fetched scenario is you ask me. Shoot. He has me there, no plan what-so-ever. Thinking quickly about a usable plan, I began speaking it as

I thought, my words coming out in a rush as my brain tried keeping up with the plans.

"Okay, my idea is that we wait until the one inside gets out of the place with what ever he is stealing and wait until his little ride home comes to pick him up, you ambush the car, but be careful. Whoever is in it might have a gun, so your first move is to knock the guy out unconscious and to pull the key out of the car as fast as possible. I'll take on the little thief, and we'll go from there, 'kay?", I said.

"Sounds good to me" Sam said, pausing a brief moment, then going on "Now, two people seems to be the only way to have handled it, what do you do without someone else lending another hand?".

"I never really deal with thieves trying to steal from an empty apartment, and if I had to, I'd figure out a one-person plan that were to most certainly have left me with a few more extra scars, but would have been full-proof" I said, looking around trying to spot the car. Now, I am ninety percent sure that the thief is a 'pro' at this and definitely will have an escape-car. Though that ten percent of me is telling me, kind of yelling at me that it is just another straggler, just stealing for drugs or something, and that I should really be jumping inside of that window myself, wrestling the guy to the ground, but I held myself still, looking around for that darn car.

"Interesting, then if it's not STEALING then what on Earth do you deal with? Murders? Serial-killers even?" Sam said, sarcastically. Deciding it would be best to ignore the sarcasm for both of our well-beings, I answered him in a serious manner without any anger, or annoyance.

"Kind of, well, beatings that can amount to murders. Kidnappings that definitely would have became murders. I kind of never really have been to a murder. I wouldn't want to Sam, too much sorrow, not the best for my mind." I said, Sam's jaw dropped and he was quiet, though I definitely didn't used the BEST of words, or explained too much, but he most certainly got what I was saying. In the shadow of a building, I saw a car slowly pulling up, it's headlights not on, and the only way that I managed to spot it was the sound of slow-moving tires over pavement. I forced back a yawn(Not the best thing to be tired on the job?), and getting ready to run, I quickly shot back to Sam "You know the plan right?". He nodded, and not waiting for any type of signal or anything, he began running towards the car, obviously hiding in the deepest of shadows from the buildings as he ran. Seeing my only chance without having a warning from his buddy to sack the guy, I began running at top speed across the street and to the place. He wasn't out yet but my chance is quickly slimming down every second now, and pretty soon I would be beaten into a pulp if I don't act now! Getting to the apartment, I quickly tried(stumbled a bit...) dodging all the different electronics that the guy already had out to steal, until I got to the window. I gulped, just thinking about the chances of this guy having a gun. This case might just help my case, if he has a gun, it will help me give SOME sort of idea of if robberies happen with guns and that would turn out that my case was in fact an attempted-robbery more than an achieved double-homicide(though I'm pretty sure just because one guy using a gun, doesn't mean every robbery takes place with a gun. Plus there is also the fact that I'm pretty darn sure it was indeed a hate crime. But I have to have SOMETHING to gnaw over to stop myself from TOTALLY being hopeless). Watching myself, trying not to scratch my hands on the shattered glace from the window(for I know all to well how much a cut on the hand hurts, and it hurts a lot.), I heaved myself up and into the apartment as soon as possible.

I took in a breath, scoring the house with quick movements of my eyes, trying to find the robber before any type of warning might arise from Sam's little mission, and before the thief finds me. My heart pounded in my chest at the thought of getting caught. Enclosed apartment, no place to run or hide, only hope is that I turn out to be the predator, not prey. I jumped lightly down from the window sill, surprised at how quiet it was but having no time to 'congratulate' myself, I kept on looking back and forth around me. Not daring to leave the window, the escape route. I KNOW he is going to come TO me, there is no way someone with half a brain would think that they can get away with breaking two windows and not having finger prints on either of them. Or, at least that is what I theorize, and hope. I finally heard the slightest creak of a cupboard, so slight that if I wasn't listening for any signs like that, it would have gone unnoticed. I froze, trying to pinpoint exactly where it came from, my head shot right towards the faint outline of a door as I heard foot steps coming from that exact direction. This room right here, seemed to be some sort of office-type room, the study of the place probably, so it's probably best NOT to look upwards, in case there might be cameras(you'd never know...). So walking with my head slightly tilted down to an extent that my facial features wouldn't show on even the best of security cameras, but up enough so that I can see where I'm going and be able to punch someone on-target if I had to(which is VERY likely) I came right towards where the door would open up, and held my breath. He might hear my breathing. He just might. Oh please GOD, don't let him! I tightened my fist, and wound it up ready to punch him right in the face. The knob began turning, it felt like hours, maybe even days how slow it turned, but somehow I just know right now what feels like days, is probably even less than just a second. And as soon as it opened up enough to an extent, I swung my hand as fast as I could, instantly feeling the impact of skin-to-skin. I felt blood pouring down my hand as he fell to the floor. Fast, good. I began grinding my teeth, debating what I should do next. Not at all my usual setting, so I can't really drag him anywhere unless I'd want to ruin this guy's carpet anymore then it was. Bending down, I checked the guy's pockets, seeing if he really did have a gun.

Nothing. Pretty dumb robber if you ask me. Making sure not to touch anything else(like the jewelry the guy had in his hand), so that my finger prints won't be on anything, I got back up and slipped right through the window, landing both my feet onto the pavement, I rummaged through my back pack and got out my phone dialing 911 quickly. I allowed it to ring, then didn't reply. If Sam's little 'reports' were true, a cop should be here any moment now. I really HOPE that they will be here any moment, who knows when this guy is going to wake up? I then began jogging towards where the car was and noticed that it was braked in front of the place, and Sam was sitting right on top of the hood, looking around again, only this time with what seems like a hint of pride in what little I could see of his face. So Sam did manage to carry it out, very good. Speeding up my pace I got to where Sam was, the car keys in his hands. He was about to say something(best bets, he was going to gloat), but I quickly stopped him. "No time, cops should be here any second now, drop those keys and begin running to our place, I'll catch up with you after I make sure they get here" I said, pointing the direction the place would be.

"Nah, the cops are definitely coming, see" Sam said, pointing in the direction behind me, I looked around and saw headlights in the distance. Shoot, Sam is way too comforted by a cop car, isn't he?

"Then lets MOVE!" I said, my eyes widening, who knows how close this cop is to actually seeing us? Sam jumped off the car and began running. I followed after him, taking cautious glances behind me as we went along, making sure that we weren't being followed, we weren't, thankfully. As we began to near the place, a shot of disbelief ran through me, as I took my phone out again, it was still on. "Shoot" I huffed under my breath, turning it off. HOPEFULLY they weren't tracking us right now with some sort of GPS signal emitting from the phone, that was such a stupid mistake.

Realizing that I dropped a little behind, I sped my pace up so that I was once again right behind Sam, running. Taking a few more turns, we finally arrived at the building. We did the usual routine to get in. And once we got in, Sam was like a firework being lit up. "That was pretty awesome! I can't believe you do that almost every night! That was the easiest and most exciting thing I've ever done!" he said, grinning. I huffed in reply, he DID achieve the plan, and he seems to like going out like that at night. This isn't good, tonight was supposed to DETOUR him, not fire him up. Though I do have to admit it was easier having a second hand, and a lot more comforting if something were to go wrong on my end of the deal... But I DON'T want to be risking my best friend's life just so that myn is a lot easier. What kind of PERSON(not even a friend, just a human being in general) would I be to knowingly put his life in danger like that just because I have some type of issues with those guys. We walked over to the room and both sat down. Finally, I said something. "You aren't ACTUALLY thinking about coming again tonight, are you?" I said, knowing that it has to be already in the morning right now.

"Of course, why wouldn't I be? You deserve to have some type of help, don't you? Besides, I feel as if I was born for this type of stuff" Sam grinned, not a Cheshire cat grin in which he usually does when he is making some sort of joke, but a pure happiness type of grin in which it pains me in this situation.

"Then become a cop. Honestly Sam, I DON'T like the thought of you getting hurt, not on my watch that is." I said, looking towards him directly in the eyes, I already pushed my chances by letting him go this one time, and I DON'T think that I can push my chances anymore without him getting hurt, real bad.

"And do YOU think I like allowing you to go out at night all these years, having it hang on my conscious that if something happened to you, I was the only person who knew you were going out and that I SHOULD have stopped you, huh? Come on Zoey, this can benefit the both of us. This can benefit the people. Two people means you are doing the same amount of work in half of the time, right?" Sam said, I was going to say not really, because it really ISN'T true, but Sam quickly cut me off "That might mean more cases can be picked up every night instead of your usual.... One?".

I began grinding my teeth. "Sam, don't you have an overprotective father to attend to, I highly doubt he would be too proud if you do this behind his back and when we end up getting caught he has to be on trial against his own son. Not that we'd really get a FAIR trial, they'd probably end up having their minds made, it is obvious that we, well rather I was messing up a bunch of cases by finding the criminals and beating them as much as I have, so basically, they'd use propaganda, and propaganda isn't good when you are trying to defend yourself AGAINST it." I said, practically BEGGING him to listen.

"And I'm going to play a Zoey Aquarius D'Bandit on you and say that I have already made up my mind and there is nothing you can do to persuade me in any shape or form to back down. Now you can either go with the flow, or struggle against it but either way it will happen, it is just a matter of how much effort you waste going against it." Sam said, then he added "And by the way, he isn't over protective at all, it is simply the times you see when he is over protective that makes you conclude that statement.".

I laughed, "Last time I knew, we weren't analyzing your father Sam, and the next time you use my whole name like that, you'll get it" I said, rolling my eyes. Fifty percent joke, and fifty percent truth.

"Very funny. Now how about it? I'll see you tomorrow night, no?" Sam said, grinning a huge grin as if he just won. And in actuality he really did. I huffed as a reply, not giving him a REAL answer. Sam laughed, he just realized that I gave up. "GREAT, see you then... Unless you don't have to work tomorrow?".

"My hours are opening until four tomorrow. Then I think I'm going to go back home and clean up, probably go to the grocery store and restock the fridge, even do some laundry." I said, making it clear that I'd rather not have any 'visitors'(meaning SAM) over for the day, tomorrow will be my day to gather my thoughts and sort through them all. Not a day to see Sam for every second of it.

Sam nodded his head, he understood, good. "Fine, I might just have to sleep in the whole day tomorrow also... this is by far one of the longest nights I ever had, right next to the other night when you woke me up from my sleep just because you were a little scaredy-cat" Sam laughed at the end part, obviously joking, I laughed with him and rolled my eyes as he went on "How about Sunday, are we going to be able to say good bye Sunday, or shall I just say adios tonight and be done with it?".

I laughed and rolled my eyes, joking I said "Hmmm, I don't know. I'd have to check my schedule and clear a few things first... Of course I will, and lets not act like you are going away forever it is only a week and lets not forget the fact that you have to come back twice to take your regents, it's either that or you are going to skip your regents".

"Yeah, definitely going to skip it, right after I'm finished digging my grave with my dad. Of course he is going to drive me back, Tuesday we are just going to wake up a little bit earlier than six o'clock in the morning as planned, so that we can take the trip back to New York City in time for the test, plus no, I have no clue what my dad would be doing during that time and Thursday, my dad said he'll drop me off at the school when he gets more supplies to camp with. He says, and I quote, 'it will be like an added part of the trip, only I believe I'm going to be the one appreciating that time seeing you have to take a test'. Above all, my dad is a real taunter." Sam said the ending with a straight face.

"And you're not? The apple does not fall far from the tree you know. And is taunter even a word? I mean I can taunt someone, but can I really be a taunter, hmm?" I laughed saying this, and then a thrummed my fingers on the desk as if in deep thought to add to the words.

"Very, VERY funny, Bandit" Sam said, tipping his chair back as if he has this little 'word-battle'(as I like to call it) in the palm of his hands. I scowled at this.

"Mature" I said the word flatly as I got up and unbalanced his chair so that he struggled to maintained himself upright. I laughed "Pawned", I said, as he finally re-balanced himself and got up from the chair.

"And you are?" he said, inquiring the fact that I unbalanced his chair, which would have most certainly have meant a face-plant against the cold floor for most people, but USUALY not Sam. Sam snorted with a laugh "Oh I forgot, it is indeed mature to kick someone's chair to try and make them fall".

"Yes, almost as mature as tipping back on your chair like a middle school student would do" I said sarcastically, as we began walking out of the place. And pushing back the aching thought that I should try and persuade Sam more to not go out with me during the nights, I opened the window and hopped out with Sam right behind me. He closed the window, my jaw dropped as I thought of something. I haven't been caught because there weren't any cameras in my area, now what about here? I lead a direct route from the scene of the crime all the way here without adding any more turns to try and stop the cameras from tracing on my path, so does that mean we are being watched? I shot my gaze across the street, trying to scan for any signs of cameras in this area, but the lack of light making it hard to tell, Sam must of saw what I was thinking about. Because he patted my shoulder in reply, almost in comfort. He turned towards me.

Sam then said "Don't worry, I'm sure they won't check the cameras until it is too late, and about the fact that they might come to a conclusion that we come here more often then just this time, I highly DOUBT the fact that they would conclude to that. They'd probably believe that it is simply the fact of a one-time hit on this place on that we, or again, rather YOU always were going here and practically snuck past them, such a large detail not being caught until now, would make them VERY embarrassed.".

I laughed uneasily, trying to shake the thoughts off, "Right, definitely right" I said, trying to persuade myself with the words, and trying to knock out the thoughts, well at least I HOPE he is right.

Sam said no more, he knows that this is all a matter in which I'm the only person that can fix it, he can't say anymore words that would make me feel any better about it, that I would have to persuade myself out of it. He began walking, I walked right behind him, it felt sort of weird, walking with another person during this time. Most certainly not lonely as it was, that's for sure. But still, odd. All these years, it has always been the same thing, the one thing that I did alone, as a sort of remembrance. My little second-life, my secret. Even though Sam always knew about it, he never truly knew the details of it all. He didn't know what it felt like to be walking the streets of New York City completely alone(or almost alone for he would never be COMEPLETELY alone for as long as I'm here), to figure out a plan, knowing that every portion of it can mean the difference between mending someone's life, and completely destroying it. Sam didn't truly know the importance of it all, and he still might not. But every bit, every ounce of information Sam managed to collect from this event, means one more piece that isn't just my own. That secret-second life is now being uncovered by Sam, and there is no turning back.

*   *   *

I got home, took a shower and I fell asleep by four o'clock in the morning, waking up at eight o'clock to go to work at nine. My sleep was clouded by a nightmare, more or less the same nightmare I seem to have AT LEAST fifteen times a month, and the pain doesn't get any duller, any less painful as it did the first time, not that reliving an event ever does. So my eyes tired due to the lack of(or rather the disruption) of sleep, I made breakfast for myself(kids were still asleep and probably will stay asleep until ten o'clock in the morning due to it being a weekend), and then I got ready. Getting dressed in the usual pink t-shirt, a pair of jean shorts and flip-flops, along with the necklace, was easy. Being annoyed and slightly embarrassed came along with it when I was about to head out of the door, I realized that my shirt was inside out. Great, stupid me. So I walked back to the bathroom(quietly), and corrected my shirt with a huff. Getting out of the place I was about a minute late already from my scheduled timing of events. So basically I just briskly walked to my job, arriving there right on time.

Work was hectic, we had a huge sale going on and so for every one person I usually had in the store on a day like today with these circumstances, crossing out the sale of course, there was about six more people there. More people in general, is equivalent to more jerk-offs also. This wore down on me quickly as one might imagined som about a quarter way through the shift, I ended up exploding on like three people already because they were ordering me around too much(not exploding as one might think, more or less NOT doing what they were telling me to do in a way that it was clear that I did not want to be their punching bag every time they pleased. Like the fact that some guy yelled at me because I wasn't ringing his wife up quick enough, so basically I just slowed down my pace to make a point because I was DEFINITELY ringing her up faster then anyone else in the store would, because she had like fifty articles of clothing, and as fast as I possibly could. This angered him greatly, but I could care less at that point). By the end of the day, I managed to tick off about twenty seven people that I know of. Not exactly what most would call customer satisfaction, but honestly, I tried as much as I could to please them but they acted as if I was trying to go out of my way to anger them(which towards the end of every 'journey' with each person I was, in which they deserved it), so I didn't feel an ounce of shame for doing so. Surprisingly, I did not get fired at the end of my shift.

Swinging back home, I decided to see if any of the others would want to go to the grocery store with me, it was just a short sub-way ride away, it would be nice for them to go out and it can be helpful to have more than one hand that way I'd be able to buy more than usual. They all said yes, and Scott reminded me of the video game he wanted which I made sure to tell him that we were heading to a GROCERY store, not a video game store and that I will get it for him, just not at the moment. I told him probably next week when he is off and there is plenty of time for us to take a good thirty minutes of traveling time out of our day to get the video game(just an excuse, in reality I think it would best for Scott to stay away from the video games for at LEAST a week of his summer vacation.). Once we got home, Scott and Tim helped out and began putting everything away while Summer and I went to do laundry. After that, we had dinner, and time slipped past me when suddenly I realized it was nine o'clock, about time to go out and do some 'Banditing'(I always have to say it now, it is almost RIGHT to have a word for it. Even though the name is sort of ironic in the fact that it does align with my last name if you subtract the 'D' in it, and then the fact that the word Bandit, meaning to steal or something like that, is the OPPOSITE of what I do. Instead of harming society, I almost help it, to a certain extent of course). I called up Sam, told him to come to my house as soon as possible and began getting ready. As I walked to the front door, I checked off things from my mental list, necklace is off, t-shirt/shorts, and my bag with my cell phone(and other supplies), time to leave now.

CHAPTER 7

I opened the door to see Sam standing right in front of it, taken aback, I took a quick step back as Sam said with a laugh "Oh, whoops, sorry forgot to tell you that I was here before I came to the door." sarcasm rang in his voice, I ignored it. Glancing Sam up and down, I realized that his outfit got better from yesterday, a pure black t-shirt, with pure-black pants. Very good.

"I see you changed your apparel from yesterday" I said, walking around Sam as I shut the door from behind me. Thankful that Scott was too busy messing around with Tim to come and start interrogating me about what Sam and I are going to do. Though in actuality Scott might not even have a case now, seeing that he actually sees Sam with me so he can't REALLY say that I'm going out alone.

"Like it? I just bought them today." Sam said with a grin, then he added "The most boring day I have ever had. Thought about dropping by at your work, but decided that you obviously wanted space, so I went shopping for five hours or so and managed to get this t-shirt" he pointed to his t-shirt "and these pants" he pointed to his pants(Interesting way of 'showing' me, but I ignored the pointing). "Then, I went back home, and sat on my bed looking up at the ceiling for several THOUSAND hours which lead me to here.".

I laughed "You couldn't find anyone to hang out with, oh really now?" I said, walking down the steps, and sitting down I began to re-tie my shoe laces.

"Will went to Canada for the weekend" Sam began, talking about my counselor's son Will, in which case ironically he is one of Sam's best friends "And other than that, I have no other friends".

"Yeah, okAY" I said, getting up after I tied my shoe laces "Lets go this way" I said, walking in the direction that I went several days ago. I began to pick up my pace, half-running and half-jogging. My eyes scanning the area in front of me(and towards the sides of me), watching for danger(criminals), but mostly the cops. The thought hit me last night when I got ready for bed, that I DIDN'T check for patrolling cops, which was of course totally my mistake, and not smart on my part AT ALL. We ran for a good ten minutes or so, and then began slowing down, breathing heavy(slightly), I kept my eyes wide open and alert for anyone that might sneak up on us due to the breathing blocking my hearing sort of.

"So, what are we going after now?" Sam asked, his breath beginning to slow down, along with my breath also.

"Bigfoot, what do you think?!" I whispered, shoving Sam slightly with my right hand. I laughed lightly, making sure that it wasn't too loud, didn't want any unwanted visitors coming towards us.

"You know what I mean" Sam said in a quiet voice also, he returned the shove only this time with a little more force than what I used. Classic Sam.

"Yeah, I do know what you mean but you are forgetting the fact that I can't see into the future like most human beings, so I don't know who is out there" I whispered with sarcasm, while rolling my eyes. Behind Sam, I saw someone. Walking, no, running towards us. "Sam, watch out!" I said, my eyes widening as our aggressor finally got within a few yards near us, close enough to see the thin outline of sunglasses on him. I cursed under my breath as I came to realization as to just how much trouble we are in. Sam turned around in just enough time to have a blow right to his face. Quickly I ran straight towards the guy as Sam stumbled backwards, without thinking I flung a punch right towards the guy. Bad move. He grabbed my hand, and began throwing his own blows towards me, each one coming within a hair line of my face. Trying to get out of his grip, I threw my body towards him, pushing up against him to get him to fall to the ground. Right before I fell along with him, I saw another shadow looming, another aggressor. Right as I was about to tell Sam to look out as he was trying to get back onto his feet, the aggressor tackled him. As I hit the ground, the guy immediately tried gaining the upper hand, I turned over and my first reflex was to grab his sunglasses off, see who it was. But knowing I couldn't I try, I went for a punch at his face, barely scrapping the edge, my breath was knocked out as he wrestled me off of him and into the road. Praying that a car doesn't come by so that I won't get ran over(or caught, though getting caught might just be the safest thing for Sam and I at the moment...), I tried as much as I could to gain the upper hand. Slipping out from underneath him I quickly jumped back on top of him and push his face right towards the ground, "WHO ARE YOU!?" I yelled in anger. This wasn't the kid who attacked me last time, way stronger, and much older.

Just then, I felt the slam of another body up against me. ANOTHER person! I gulped as I was forced to the ground, feeling no blood drip down me was a nice sign, but I definitely got bruised. Struggling to get up, I felt the pounding feeling of a coming head ache. Trying the best I could, I tried getting out from his grip, and using as much force as I possibly could, I heaved my legs up and tried kicking him off. He flew through the air a couple of feet, his grip rubbing against my wrists so hard that it felt like they were going to fall off, but it loosened towards the end of it and he landed away from me. Quickly trying to stumble up, trying to ignore the pain, I darted straight towards the first guy, and running as fast as I could, I ducked as soon as I got within punching distance and full-out pushed him to the ground. Erratically punching in front of me, trying the best I can to land at least one good blow on this guy before the other guy regained himself. A couple times I felt the agonizing pain of pavement as we wrestled on the ground when I threw my fists, but a couple of times I felt the relief of hitting him. Scratching my knees against the pavement, and trying to ignore the pain welling up all over me, I threw the hardest punch I could in the best direction I could and hoped it would hit him, and not the pavement. I breathed a quick sigh of relief when I felt the hit, but before I could check and make sure he was unconscious(or aim another blow if he wasn't), the other guy must have been running towards me for I felt the pressure of a hit against me as I flung through the air, landing on the road hardly, I tried regaining myself but not before I managed to get my breath knocked out of my lungs yet again with another punch to the face.

In defense, I tried rolling away, just to get some sort of look at who I'm facing up against, and where he is. But punch after punch kept on blocking my view. So, instead of trying to roll away, I tried kicking my legs as much as possible to get him off of me. I felt the punching beginning to ease, and so, rolling over for a quick moment, I heard a yelp as his hand must of hit concrete, then I rolled back to the same spot and threw my body upwards, and wrapping my arm around his neck, and using all my weight, I forced him down to my left, his head hitting the floor with a hard crush. I staggered up as fast as I could, searching for Sam, praying that he was alright, on the sidewalk him and the last guy(at least I HOPE he's the last guy) were wrestling on the ground. Running over, I noticed that Sam was on the bottom of the scramble, clearly loosing, but not by much, I grabbed the man's shoulders with both of my arms, and pulled him off of Sam, and not taking a moment to think, I flung him up against the concrete with enough force to knock him out. Sam groaned. My eyes darted right towards Sam, he had a huge gash along his forehead as if his face was knocked to the ground, and he had numeral cuts along his arms that were bleeding out. My heart pounding, I quickly said "Come on Sam, lets go before more come" without another word, he began staggering up, and while I helped him, we made our way to the closest place to us, which was our meeting place.

I glanced around us wearily, the sound of my pulse pounding in my ears, ready to pick up even the slightest disruption in the street around me that would tell me that another person was drawing near, thankfully there was nothing more than the usual honking of horns and rumbling engines of airplanes in the distance. We walked there in silence, neither of us saying a single word on the way, the night felt even more eerie than it would have even alone. Finally we got to the place, and I opened the window, letting Sam in first for the thought of more people following us made me paranoid and I didn't like the thought of letting Sam get the first punch when it was more than obvious me who started it all. I am the one who ticked them off, not Sam. We walked to the usual room and Sam staggered down with a groan. Hesitantly, I turned on the light, not really liking the thought of seeing the wounds in full-blown light. Squinting my eyes slightly to adjust to the increase of light, I began shifting through my bag to find the materials I wanted BEFORE I looked at Sam's injuries. Sam was the first to speak as I did this "Good thing I was out there with you because three against one would not have been good..." Sam started it off with a semi-real joke. He laughed a pretty hoarse laugh, and definitely a forced one due to how much pain he must be in right now... He really seemed to have taken a huge beating with that guy, he was caught off-guard, twice.

"In this case, with YOU being the second one, two against three didn't do me any better" I said, adding another joke to brighten things up a bit. Finally grabbing out the needed anti-bacterial ointment, some medical spray, some band aids, and a cloth, I went over to Sam to get a glance of the damage. He looked worse in the light, as I thought. Two deep looking gashes along his head as if his head was smashed into the edge of the sidewalk(and probably was), several scratches along both of his arms and even more bruises. Then the knees of his pants were torn to show a pair of very scratched up knees. My jaw went rigid when I thought about how awful all of those must feel, and even how he was going to explain all of the nasty, huge injuries to his dad. No way he can say he just fell, and probably won't even pass if he 'fell' down the stairs.

Breaking my thoughts Sam said "Prepared, I see. Why keep so much supplies in your bag when we all know you are in a safe huge city, with nice criminals, and you don't go out past five o'clock in the morning". Sam meet sarcasm, sarcasm, meet Sam, oh I forgot, both met each other already plenty of times before, how could I be so foolish? Sarcasm always meets Zoey when Sam manages to find Sarcasm.

"You have no idea how sarcastic my thoughts are right now" I said, grabbing the cloth and throwing it to Sam "Here, wipe off all the blood so that I'll be able to disinfect it properly".

"Thank you, you are such a lovely nurse Miss. D'Bandit" Sam said, I ignored the sarcasm only because of how many injuries he managed to gain that I definitely should have been the one to gain them. All I got were a few bruises and MAYBE a scratch somewhere, though I don't feel any blood dripping down from anywhere on my face, or my arms, and my legs were unharmed... I think it is safe to say that Sam had pretty darn bad luck tonight. Once Sam whipped off all of the blood, I began spraying down his arms with the medical spray, making sure to use as much as possible(without going overboard, OF COURSE). "Sho-o-o-ooootttttt" Sam said, pulling his arms back slightly, "that stuff really does hurt".

"It is disinfectant spray, haven't you ever used it before? You ARE in a sport, aren't you? Oh whoops, I forgot, track boys don't get hurt" I said, laughing slightly, making to pause like two seconds in between 'you' and 'oh' to add to the effect.

"Very funny" Sam said, moving his arms back, slowly. He really did get warn out, as much as I'd like to delude myself that it is no big deal, just pain that Sam would have to deal with when it comes to these injuries, but nope, definitely not just pain, more like tiredness, which isn't good when he has to walk a good three(or four, give or take a few miles..) back to his place. I'll probably make him stay the night so that he wouldn't have to stay up longer than he needed to and so that he didn't walk home alone(who knows if we are being watched at this very moment?), though of course he'd have to wake up early so that I(we!) don't have to hear it from Scott, I can just picture it now, and it WOULD NOT be good. Surprisingly, he didn't add anything more, which almost worries me more. But I am almost positive that those injuries aren't fatal(at least at the point I have them right now), but it still echoes in my mind like one of those annoying songs or melodies in your head that just won't go away.

After his arms were sprayed down, I walked back over to my bag and pulled out a spare wash cloth, and threw it to Sam(who barely caught it) "Here, take off all of the access disinfectant spray with that, try not to open up any more cuts even more then they already are, so rub gently", I said, remembering to add in that last part for I forgot to tell him that before.

"Ai, ai captain Bandit" Sam said, taking off all the access medical spray, he added "what about my face or my knees, you can't possibly think that it would be all right to spray that junk across my face, do you?".

"Yes because I gain strength in watching you squirm in pain like a little kid getting his first shot" I said, rolling my eyes "Of course I won't, I'll just use the ointment on it, and your knees I am not TOO worried about, you have a fully functional immune system that can fight off SOME type of bacteria or else you wouldn't have been able to survive in New York City your whole life let alone the first day you were born." I gave him the tube of ointment, which he seemed to gladly take and he quickly began rubbing it on all of his cuts.

"Very well then" Sam said, still cutting the jokes off short. He must be REALLY out of energy right now, not good. "Okay, I'm ready for the band aids" Sam added, holding out his hand.

"Here, I recommend only putting them on the deeper cuts, like the ones on your forehead, and that one right there on your hand, because I don't think your Dad would appreciate it too much when he comes home to see you all wrap up in band aids. Now, what ARE you going to tell your Dad to get him off your back about this? You fell down the stairs is the BEST option that I can think of, but that is most certainly very unbelievable." I said, walking over to my chair and sitting down, a worried look was most definitely crossing my face right now, Sam usually does have a plan though...

"I have no clue, Zoey." Sam said, unwrapping a band aid and placing it across one of the cuts on his forehead. I huffed, even SAM has no idea on what he should do, this is not good at all.

"Not a single clue at all?" I asked, not liking the idea of that, I ran through some more ideas in my head. Maybe a fighting dog attacked him, leaving him unable to defend himself, he landed face-first up against the concrete. He fell down the stairs yet again, only this plan would mean he'd have to tell his dad that somehow he managed to hit his head on the very bottom stair, very unrealistic(In a way…). He could also have just simply tripped and fell on the sidewalk, I mean, Sam MIGHT be an easy bruiser for all his Dad knows. Okay, lets face facts, it is probably not the best idea to tell him those last two plans unless I'd like to be made fun-of by how stupid they are, even if Sam was half-asleep, I still wouldn't hear the end of it, so instead I decided it will be best to tell him the first one. Inhaling a deep breath of air, I began to speak "Okay, how about a dog attacked you when you were walking, um… somewhere?" I laughed slightly for I didn't really think of where he'd be walking to that would get a dog to attack him, though in the general area where we live, we sort of aren't in the BEST place… Going on I said "He managed to attack you to the ground, where you landed face-first against the concrete where you were able smack the dog on the head hard enough to make it jump off of you". I stifled back a yawn, if one starts yawning, they WILL get tired.

"Nice one" Sam said, yawning freely, he added "Just where exactly would I be heading to which would allow the type of scenery at which a dog could be running lose in?", he placed another band aid on his arm, covering up one of the bigger scratches. I thought for a moment before I spoke.

"You were jogging around here to help keep up endurance for track" I said, decent idea...

"Yeah, okay, sounds good to me." Sam said, brushing the rest of the band aids he didn't use across the desk. I grabbed them and then placed them right inside my bag. Grabbing the rest of the materials, I placed them also in the bag, then I took out my phone. Flipped it open, and it was four thirty five in the morning.

"We should probably be heading back, you need some sleep for your little trip, more or less you need some sleep in general!" I said, pausing. Realizing that there is just one other question I should place on the table I added "So, are you going to stay at my place, or go back to your place, because I'd have to walk with you because you aren't in the best condition and I won't feel good letting you walk by yourself for that long of a way when you are so injured. Which means we'd have to speed up the pace a bit that way I could at least get a hour of sleep.". Sam looked at me blankly, his tiredness obviously clouding his thoughts to an extent that he didn't catch a word that I was saying(that, and I might of said it all in a confusing manner and at a pretty fast speed). So I decided for him. "Okay, looks like you are going to have to crash at my place for the night then, I don't think you'd be able to make it back to your place in one piece...".

"Yeah, yeah, what ever" Sam said, obviously struggling to keep his eyes open, worry struck me again. Fighting back the thought, I got up out of my seat, and Sam got up also, slowly, but he managed. We walked through the building to the window. When a bright light from some car began pouring in, "Duck" Sam quickly said, bending down, I bent down also, but kept my eyes slightly above the window ledge to see what it was. To my utter dismay, it was one of the patrolling cop cars, slowly making its way across the road. You'd think they'd be smart enough to station cop cars inside some shadows so their presence wasn't so pronounced, but Sam did say that they were mostly rookies, so it really does make sense now. Now tell me this, where were they when we were in that struggle with three buffed up guys(their muscles were sincerely the largest I have ever seen in my life, which confuses me at which how I'd ever knew them before and yet they were wearing shades, but it might have been just to keep their identity safe from me if we were to meet outside of that little fight, at which case I'd have to yell at the top of my lungs just how messed up that truly this.)!? It was a good thing they weren't there for a number of reasons, but still, are they serious?. "Is it gone yet?" Sam asked, as he slowly began getting up, trying to get his eyes over the ledge. Only until the car went around the corner, did I reply back.

"Yes, it's gone" I said, getting up, then holding my hand out so that Sam could get up also, Sam stopped from trying to peer up out of the window, then he greatfully took it and got up. He huffed.

"Let's go then" he said, opening the window up, he hoisted himself up into the window and jumped down. I jumped through after him, making sure to hang onto my bag. Looking around, I casted worried glances up and down the street, just expecting for another sheriff to drive by. "Shoot" Sam said looking back into the window "We forgot to turn off the light in there". I squinted my eyes looking through the window, and there it was, the faint glow of light emitting from around the corner.

"I'll get it" I said, not saying another word, I hopped through the window, and ran right towards the room. I quickly turned off the light, at which I was greeted with eerie darkness surrounding me. Memorizing the path out, I walked quickly right towards the window, regretting the fact that I let Sam out there alone by himself, but really can't change that mistake and I think he might have been capable of defending himself long enough for me to come if something DID happen. Jumping right through the window, Sam was leaning up against the building's wall, I turned around and closed the window. "Ready?" I asked, as Sam stood right up again. He began walking in the direction of my house, and without another word, I followed. My hands were bunched up in fists, ready for anything now. I DEFINITELY have to get back to the usual tomorrow(slash today due to the fact that it is in the morning right now), actual saving other people other than myself, or their items the more I think about it. Those guys HAVE to rest, they are honestly beginning to annoy the heck out of me, they keep on stopping me from doing what I came out to do, and it's not even like they are achieving what they set out to do, they haven't killed me or anything like that and they haven't even gotten me to stop! I'm beginning to think that this situation is a lot more complicated than I thought before...

Finally, we got back to my apartment. I gave Sam a warning glare not to yell or anything like he did the other time. He nodded in reply, hopefully he would heed my warning or he is getting kicked out of this house before he could even say that he is just joking. Unlocking the door, I silently and slowly opened the door, and coming inside, I walked silently through the house, hearing Sam lightly shut the door telling me that he wasn't going to mess around. Grabbing a pillow and blanket from the closet for Sam, I walked over to the couch where Sam was already sitting on it and threw him the pillow and blanket "Thanks" he whispered, exaggerating the whisper a little too much which shows just how little restraint Sam had when it came to being serious and not joking around. I rolled my eyes, even though Sam probably couldn't see them roll due to the darkness that surrounded us. Walking over to the bathroom, I lightly shut the door behind me and turned on the light. Looking in the mirror the only scratches I had on my face were the ones from the other nights that were healing up nicely. I had a bruise on the very corner of my forehead which was pretty self-explanatory how I got it because of the whole getting slammed to the ground and all. Looking down at my arms, I had a few bruises here and there and one scratch. Not bad at all, and I am very surprised too, seeing how much I got punched and wrestled to the ground by my attackers. Quickly, I placed my bag away and I took a shower, and got changed into my pajamas. Turning off the light before I opened the door of the bathroom, I walked out and went to my bedroom as quietly as possible. Laying on my bed, I was welcomed with sleep.

*   *   *

"Have fun on your little trip with your father for a whole week now Sam" I said, making sure to place as much smugness as I could in the words to try and annoy Sam(All as a joke of course).

"I will, Water-Bringer" Sam shot back at me, real smugness filling his voice as he said that awful nickname towards me. I rolled my eyes, letting him have the satisfaction of winning, he then went on, more serious now. "Now obviously you do realize you are now being watched to an extent that is so incomprehensible that I can't really give you any type of advise except for this, watch your back. Don't drop your guard down no matter what, whether it is at the store or at your house, and ESPECIALLY when you are out there, because that is definitely the time when they choose to get you at. What is happening now is more like a game of tricks and strategies more than anything, these guys, have something up their sleeves and we both know that we don't like it, nor' should we like it. This is dangerous stuff we are messing with here, no joke, Zoey.". I gulped, Sam always seems to point out the obvious, something that I know deep within me, but every time he says it, it almost seems like a huge brick just hit me in the head, as if I truly didn't know such information, it might be just the way that Sam says it, or even just the fact that he points it out that really hits me.

"Trust me, this is just another obstacle in my way, I'm sure I'll be fine" I said, trying to comfort(and convince) Sam's tired-worried and greatly scratched up face. Though I sort of feel as if I'm trying to convince and comfort myself more so than Sam in actuality. "Have fun on your lovely trip" I said, as we began to walk out of my place, and we stood on the steps. It was eight o'clock in the morning and we both had about three hours or so of sleep last night, so we were definitely tired, but Sam had to go back to his place, explain what happened to him once his dad comes home (which according to Sam earlier today at like seven thirty five, he said that his dad would be home at eight forty fiveish, interesting enough time though..), and be able to leave at their scheduled time of ten o'clock in the morning. So I had to get Sam out as fast as possible to give him enough time to prepare himself, so basically this would have to be good bye instead of our planned me meeting him at his place right before he left thanks to those guys last night mixing everything up right down to the bone. Not even Will(Sam's other best friend which again, I've only met twice now, and that wasn't even with Sam more so with my counselor) would be there to say good bye now because of his own weekend trip too. I guess this would have to suffice for Sam, though I'm sure a couple of his not-so-close friends would come to say good bye, still, not as fun.

Sam snorted. "Nice adjective" he said, rolling his eyes, he went down the steps, I didn't follow.

"Bye now Mr. Sarcasm" I said, waving good bye, he waved good bye, and then began walking towards his house, he was limping slightly due to the fact that one of his knees were greatly scratched up, but other than that he seemed back to his old energized self(tired from lack of sleep, but NOT tired from injuries, very good). Turning around, I opened the door in front of me, and went back inside. Cleaning up, I grabbed the blanket and began folding it. Hearing foot steps coming from one of the rooms, I quickly grabbed the blanket and pillow and went straight towards the closet where I quite sloppily shoved them in there, hoping to ride on the fact that Sam didn't sleep over to the others. Turning around

I saw Scott right in the kitchen, grabbing a box of cereal out of the cupboard and pouring himself a bowl of it. Grateful that he hadn't noticed me, I walked in the direction of my room, and then quickly turned around, walking towards Scott as if I just came from the room, his back towards me I said "So how was your guy's night, had fun?". I walked over to the fridge and got the milk out and placed it on the table for Scott, he turned around and looked at me, his eyes clouded with more tiredness than Sam and myn combined! What has he been doing!? If this goes on any longer I will have to confront him on that...

"Long, Tim and I played cards for quite sometime until Summer some how managed to hoax us to watch one of her little girly movies" Scott said, walking over to the table and sitting down, he poured the milk, and grimaced at the last part of what he said. "Then at ten o'clock the other two went to bed and I stayed up watching boxing for a good couple of hours. Now, how was YOUR night OUT?". How he said that, sincerely gave me the chills. Honestly, you'd think he knows every single little thing about it...

Blandly I said "It was decent, hung out with Sam the whole night, it was his last night here before getting stuck on a week long camping trip with his dad.", I tried moving onto a different topic by throwing in the whole Sam going on vacation thing, but Scott didn't budge in anyway what-so-ever.

"What did you do?" Scott said, looking up at me from his cereal, eyes sharp as nails or rather tacks. Is it simply just curiosity, or something more now? I want to say curiosity, for so many reasons I wish it is just curiosity, but quite frankly, I do not know, not good at all.

"HUNG OUT, now Scott, don't be so nosy, it's not polite. I hope you don't give the others just as much as a hard time because you'd be in a whole of a lot of trouble if we all had to pick sides between you and someone else in an argument" I said, trying to get him off of my back like that.

The door opened up and Ms.Smith marched passed us, grumbling about something, I paid no attention to her as Scott did because he added with agitation "I am not being nosy, I just want to know!". He looked down at his cereal and began eating it. I ignored him, not giving in to him being mad at me, I felt for my necklace, but felt nothing but my own skin on my neck. I must of forgotten to put it on when I got dressed earlier. So I walked to the spot where I kept my necklace(thankfully away from Scott), and grabbed it out of it's container, I clipped it along my neck and felt the sense of guidance wrap around me. I had a whole day open to do anything, and yet there seems to be nothing to do. I can't possibly sit around here with Scott breathing over my shoulder! And Sam is probably home right now, getting ready to deal with his dad, and getting ready to go on his vacation. We don't need any groceries seeing that I picked up some yesterday. I don't work today, seeing that I traded in Sunday to have off that way I can work the rest of the week(and gain some money!) except for Friday, at which I saved so that I can bring the kids to the park that day. Walking silently to my bedroom, I grabbed my laptop, deciding that it can be time to look over some of the evidence. I grabbed my other bag, that carries my average daily things such as my wallet and my main-phone, and I placed the laptop into the bag. Slinging it around my shoulder, I walked out of the room, still careful as to not disturb the sleeping Summer.

Walking passed Scott who was just finishing up on his cereal I said "Going to the café to work on a summer assignment for school, be back whenever. Watch the other two for me when I am gone". And now, more than ever, I made sure to cut him off short before he was able to even speak another word, and walked out of the house, shutting the door behind me.

*　　　　　　　　*　　　　　　　　*

I stared at the picture longer than I have ever stared before, with such intensity, that one would figure there is no possible way that I can miss a single detail, not even a single SLIVER of a detail. But somehow, in some way, I keep on missing it. I bought a regular coffee, making sure that it was black so that I could get as much caffeine in me as possible, sleep is not an option for any point of the day seeing that Scott is home, probably waiting for me to get there like a vulture, just waiting for me to show signs of anything he could question, in which sleep would definitely be one of them. So now, I am sitting at the same table that I sat at the other time with a view that was right near the window, and I am looking at that one picture on my computer that there seems to be something that I am missing, but I really can't figure out what it is. There is something there! Or even not there! I just KNOW it! But what on Earth could it possibly be!? And why can't I seem to pick it up, as to what it is? It just doesn't make sense. I KNOW it's not all just in my mind, this picture is definitely showing me something of the crime scene that I didn't catch, that the police department didn't catch, I just don't know what it is. Forcing my eyes off of the screen, I grabbed my coffee, and held it up to drink some of it. I began Closing my eyes to think straight as I started drinking the bitter-hot beverage. Bringing it down back onto the table, I still came up with nothing. Nothing is what seems to be echoing in my head as the answer to all of my questions at the moment. Nothing, is how much information I have on who is trying to silence me, or kill me as most would see it. Nothing is the answer I get when I wonder how I should go about saving myself from complete and foremost destruction.

So this picture, this one picture, almost seems to be holding the key to unlocking it all, the answer to my question, the start of a chain of events. But how is it going to help, if I can't seem to find that small detail, that small clue. Hopelessness seemed to bubble up inside me at the thought of it all, and then disappeared just as fast as I forced myself not to feel hopeless, the fact that being hopeless, means becoming weak, and becoming weak, means letting them win, and letting them win, means that justice has never been found for them. They must get justice, no matter what it takes. I breathed in a heavy breath, thinking what I should do next before I have a complete mental-breakdown. Taking another sip of my coffee, I closed the webpage and began to shut down my computer. Once the screen went blank, I closed it, and placed it in my bag. Walking over to the tip jar, I left a tip of four dollars, deciding that the new girl here was actually one of the more helpful of the employees(she actually asked if I wanted a napkin or anything, I told her no of course cause I mean, it's COFFEE, why would I need a napkin, and of course all I said was no thank you, I didn't add the last part. But she did deserve a tip of some sorts.). Walking out of the coffee shop, I went to the elevator that was just beginning to open, along with the three other people who were standing there waiting for one. One person pressed the first floor and no one touched a thing, everyone was going to the first floor. I stood there, watching the numbers tick by. Out of the corner of my eye, I saw someone reading a newspaper, focusing my eye slightly towards the newspaper, I was grateful not to see the headlines being anything about 'the Bandit'. Once we got to the first floor, I allowed everyone else to clear out, and then I went out afterwards. Walking out into the sidewalk, I made sure not to run into anyone as I checked my phone to see what time it was. It read twelve thirty five. As I dodged people on my way to my house, I thought about the next thing I should do. Jogging seemed good, but where? I definitely wasn't going to be jogging the same route Sam and I took last time, that is just weird, jogging in circles n' all.

Right now, I am tempted to go my usual route that I usually took. What more can happen? I highly doubt they made any sort of connection between me jogging there and the Bandit, because wouldn't that be a pretty far-off idea? Then again, SOMEONE made a connection between me and the Bandit, I'm just not sure HOW they did it. Going up against my better judgment, I think I just might jog my average, regular route. As I neared my house, I grabbed my keys out of my bag, not sure if Scott left the door unlocked or not. He'd probably wouldn't want to unlock it for me if he did lock it anyways. Walking up the steps, I unlocked the door. Coming in, the television was on with Tim and Summer sitting on the couch watching it, Scott was no where to be found. "Where is Scott?" I asked, seeing the fact that Tim and Scott are almost NEVER seen apart here, they do everything together.

"In his room, sleeping" Summer said, turning herself towards me, then turning back to the television as a commercial went back to the actual show.

"Okay then" I said, adding "I'm going to get into a change of clothes, and then go for a jog, if you need me, call me on my phone, you know the number right?",

"180-2956" Summer recited the number. I grinned, glad she remembered it, I walked to my room, grabbed the different set of clothes, went to the bathroom and changed. Taking off my necklace and placing it in it's usual spot, I walk to the front door, opened it, and left, saying goodbye to the others. Jogging to the little Government area, felt nerve wrecking. The thick huge clouds in the sky were a sure warning that a storm was going to break any second now, they definitely got bigger from a couple days ago that's for sure... My stomach felt like it was tied in a knot, now I KNOW I shouldn't be running in the direction I am running, to that piece of land, but part of me, the more curious and stupid side of me, is urging me on to keep going.

My hands sweating and sweat dripping down my forehead by the time I got within sight of the area. I felt almost numb with fear. Chickening out, I started to turn back, when suddenly I heard the whimpering of something, a dog most likely. Didn't really made sense as to why a dog would be anywhere near here, and it just yelled danger, but curiosity yanked at me like a chain, curiosity, and worry for the dog. Slowly, I began approaching the area at which it came from, some trees here and there still blocking my view, I advanced with caution, not sure exactly just HOW this was going to turn out. Walking right behind a bush,

I crouched down, and peered out from behind it, trying to find the cause of the noise. Looking around, I noticed that I was right across from the area at which I saw those three boys that one day, ironic in a sense that bigger things happen here, in this exact little spot than at any other place I've been to on this piece of land. Looking around, I spotted the movement of two figures in the slight distance right under a tree, and at the same time, I heard the same whimper. My guess, it came from the figure crouching down against the ground, then the one standing up 'higher' to it. Must be a dog and an owner, animal abuse, ug. I began grinding my teeth. How exactly should I take this on?

Getting up from where I was crouched, I quickly walked over to the side walk, and began jogging towards them on it, trying to make it seem as much as possible as if I was just simply jogging on it as a normal route, not trying to confront them. As I neared them, I made sure to make a worried look on my face as if I just noticed what is happening. "What is going on!?" I said, hoping that it wasn't so obvious that I KNEW what was going on and I intended to stop it. It probably was, seeing as I am not nearly as good as an actor as Sam, so in other words, I am not nearly as good as a LIER as Sam, as I'd like to say to sort of boost my self-esteem(only in a sort of funny way of course). The guy turned to me, the dog whimpering down a bit. It was a pit-bull looking type dog, my guess less then a year old, and probably was in a fight or something. The better thing versus animal abuse(not really), having two dogs attack each other until one of them(or both of them in some cases) are almost dead, the loser, gets a beating(and probably death) while the winner dog, gets another day to live. All of that, just to make a few bucks, and so that the owner can get some type of twisted entertainment, I do not look on highly at those who abuse animals as most would think. Now as I quickly look up at the guy(who took an aggressive step towards me, and I in return stopped jogging, his mouth open as if he was about to speak), I realize that I met him before(for this is where the whole eye-thing really, truly comes in handy, but only for my own curiosity), looking straight at his dark brown eyes, that shown almost confusion and hate(not to be mistaken by anger) emitting from them(not the emotion he shows now, but more like his personality).

Those eyes, I have seen three years ago, when I was thirteen years old, this was the guy that was beating on some kid for no apparent reason, it is pretty messed up that he moved to dogs, and that he is not in prison, but I suppose I am not the judge of that. One of the most pronoun things about this guy was firstly, the fact that he had to be one of the average guys that I get into a fight with. Not hard at all, and only takes about a minute to completely knock him out unconscious. Now the other thing, is the fact that he was pretty darn STUPID in the fact that he told me that if I didn't stop, he was going to call the police on me. Now keep in mind, I was beating him up, but that was simply because he was beating the child up. So, in other words, the guy who was beating a child up, was planning on calling the police on me, who was trying to protect the child, not the sharpest knife in the drawer if I do say so myself. Which makes sense why it is this guy again, seeing the fact that he was beating up a dog, which seemed pretty well-associated with dog-fighting, right in front of a governmentally owned piece of land, where there are cameras lining this whole area. He hasn't gained a bit of intelligence, has he? Thankfully, it really didn't seem like he recognized me.

"Mind your own business" he said, taking yet another aggressive step towards me. I wanted to say something along the lines of 'ooooohhh, scary' but I refrained from such levels of sarcasm for I believe it would only provoke his anger even more. So holding out my hands in a way to try and calm down this guy, I replied back to him(in a way that won't totally get me pounded to the ground by anger).

"Don't worry. I just want you to walk away from that dog, and let him be. I won't call the cops on you in anyway, I, promise" I said, choking down the last part. I don't want to let such scum walk away a free guy, without any repercussions other than being told off by a sixteen year old girl, I WANT to get this crook locked away behind bars. Though I know it would be worth more to let the dog live, then bring this guy through the justice system. AND, I am pretty darn sure he isn't going to stop, which is where that promise I made would go up in smoke, and he'd actually probably end up trying to attack me like an enraged bull when it sees red. So, the dog just might be safe after all. It MIGHT be.

"Oh really now, a sixteen year old girl thinks she can beat up on me, now I am so scared" he said, taking another aggressive step forward. No, I don't THINK I can beat up on this guy, I KNOW I can beat up on this guy. Because I did it when I was thirteen years old, and I am sure it would be just that much easier now that I have another three years under my belt. He took another aggressive step, so that now he is a little less than two yards away from me. I took an automatic step back, not liking how close he is getting(just close enough to run up and lunge for me with his fists). Bad move, he must of saw this as a sort of a sign of weakness(which I admit, only happens in movies, right?), he took another step forward, only this time, he began running towards me with his fist out. Right when he got a foot away from me, I quickly tucked down, and dodged to my left, and spinning back around to face my now stumbling aggressor. He turned around, annoyance striking through his eyes.

"I am telling you, leave now, that is all that I ask" I said, as his eyes got a hold of myn, he still didn't recognize me, which is really good. I really wanted to add in the words 'while you still have an ounce of dignity', but I also refrained from that comment too(taking every bit of strength that I had to do so). But without another word, he ran right towards me, throwing punches here and there wildly, obviously not aiming them in anyway, so this time, I just ducked when he was less then a foot away(dodging a few blows on my way down), and allowed him to fall right over me. Hearing a big thud on the ground behind me, I quickly ran over to the spot where he was last time, to give us some distance apart. "Come on, I am warning you" I said, looking up at the cameras that pointed our way, wondering if it was worth risking the chance of getting caught on film fighting him, just to teach this guy a lesson, I decided against it.

"Oh, don't worry about those cameras, I took out the wires just some minutes ago if you think you'd be caught fighting someone. So come on, try and actually FIGHT me, don't duck away like the little child you are" he said, wheezing slightly because of the fact he must of wasted some type of energy running back and forth like that and not getting anything in return to help increase his morale. So he DOES have an ounce of intelligence in him, at least enough to deactivate those cameras. I'm impressed. But still, very suspicious, he might just be lying just to get me to try and fight him at which case I think he believes that he would win the fight(and unless he got any stronger from last time, he definitely won't. And that is NOT arrogance coming into play, but more or less calculations due to past experiences). So I am better off just wearing him out a little longer, and allow him to chose whether or not we actually fight by how long he keeps on going.

Taking on a slightly different(yet similar) approach, I began running towards him, in which case, he thought I was ready to fight, so he charged right for me. Right before we clashed fists together, I swung a hooked fist up towards his face, and he, as I sort of figured, ducked to dodge it, seeing my chance, I jumped up, and onto his back, kicking him to the ground and landing on the opposite side of him(behind him), turning around, I walked backwards, waiting for him to turn around again, and really hoping that that move didn't show TOO much skill. A grin managed to escape as he turned around, his face cut up from the side walk and all dirty from the loose dirt. Quickly realizing that I grinned, I shot back to a straight face, hoping that he didn't see the grin.

"Oh, you think this is funny" he said, his face burning with rage. "That is it!" he added, and right when I thought he was going to give up, he charged right at me. Okay then, a fight it is. Running right towards him, I swung my left hand out, and got a blow right at his face(gaining myself a blow right at the stomach, wasn't TOO bad.), and right as he tilted slightly to the right, I back-handed him with my right hand, and as fast as possible, I placed all of my weight on my left leg, and swung my right leg right at his ankles, bringing him down with a hard crash. Backing away, I waited for him to get up. It wouldn't be smart to write anything 'Bandit-related' near this guy during the day. So I am going to have to let him run free with only bruises and scratches as a punishment, for now. I WILL see him later in the future, and he will be given some type of jail time for his idiotic crimes. I narrowed my eyes as I watched him stumble to his feet.

"Leave now, unless you would like to be knocked-out unconscious. I do indeed know karate, and as you can see, I am not afraid to use it. So LEAVE." I said, lying my pants off right now. I don't know karate, not an ounce of it, but hopefully he doesn't know what karate actually looks like. He looked at me. And without another word, he walked away, grumbling to himself. One could wish better for him, but honestly, I bet that I am going to see him again, no questions asked. I watched him until he was out of sight, then I turned back to the dog. It was on its backside, huffing and puffing as if it's already on death road, not good at all. I slowly, and cautiously walked towards it, preparing myself to sprint as fast as I could in case the dog didn't appreciate me scarring it's very abusive owner away like that. As I neared the dog, I realize that my thoughts were right, and it was indeed a pit-bull, probably a mix due to how thick it's fur looks, mixed with German Shepherd maybe? Under all the blood, and past the scratches, I could see the basic pattern of a German Shepherd(tan and black), along with the rounder head-shape of a pit-bull, though it's muzzle was a little bit longer than the average pit-bull's muzzle. His(Yes, a male) tale was long, and slightly shaggy. No scars along any part of his body told me that it was his first fight, though I really can't tell for certain if he truly has no scars under all the blood. As I took one more step forward so that I was a little more than a yard away from him, a growl broke from his throat. I stopped in my tracks, trying not to scare the dog.

"Don't worry" I said, trying out the best soothing voice I could "You are alright, I am not going to harm you", the growl stopped, he tipped his head to the side a little bit, in a sort of questioning manner, I held back a laugh at how funny the little(not so little in actuality) dog looked, in fear of it agitating the dog some more. I took another step closer to him, this time, the dog remained silent. Taking yet another step closer, I was now about a foot away from the dog, in reaching distance of it. I bent down, and reached out to pet the dog, making sure to go nice and easy on the speed, not too fast because of that little saying of 'no sudden movements'(which I am not even sure if it is true, or even if it would relate to this situation, but mine as well...), cautious, I leaned in so that I could pet his head, and he stayed still. Holding my breath, I finally got to rub up against his ragged, blood-ridden fur. I brushed his head for a couple seconds without him growling, and then all of a sudden he looked up at me with a whimper. His eyes a dark blue shade, which must of came from the pit-bull side of him because every German Shepherd dog I have ever seen had dark brown eyes. I rubbed the top of his head, "Don't worry little guy, I'll get you better" I said, feeling honestly disgusted at how someone could do such a thing to a poor helpless animal.

Giving him one last gentle pat on the head, I got back up and began thinking what I should do with him. Can't leave him here, that's for sure. Dropping him off at a pound is out of the options list also, that would be equivalent to me putting him down myself, for sure. DEFINITELY can't bring him home, Ms.Smith would indeed have a fit(not that she is home that often but it is her place, and she is just a cranky woman to begin with). So, only place I could think of is Sam's and my little place. I huffed, I am going to gain myself a lot of glares for bringing an almost beaten to death dog down the streets of New York City, especially seeing as I don't have a leash or a collar. Thinking about the closest mini-market type store, made me think that I might be able to leave the dog here for a couple minutes to buy a leash and a collar, seeing as it is only about a block away, but the real problem is the fact that I have no money on me(seeing the fact that I have my jogging attire on). I huffed. There is that cash store Sam and I placed at our place just in case of an emergency(Well, something that I placed in there that is, but for both of our uses). I believe it was a hundred dollars, stuffed in the drawer of the desk we usually sit at(which if that place were to be somehow sold at this very moment, then I'd probably never see that hundred dollars again). Which still leads me to the fact that I'd still have to bring the dog down the streets with no leash and collar because of the fact that it would take way too long going back and forth between places just so that I don't have to walk around getting a couple glares. Kicking a rock out of my way, I turned back around to the dog. Pretty big dog, though based on how 'childish'(should I say?) it looks, it indeed can't be any more than a year old.

This dog, is going to need some food, water, and lots of it. After a couple seconds of looking at the dog, the dog got up and walked over to me, then sat down right at my side. I patted his head again, deciding that now was the time that I should get this dog to the place, that way I can buy the needed supplies for him(including medical supplies, he really NEEDS it), as soon as possible. His cuts really do need to be treated. I looked around, one helpless time, wondering if by some chance, this guy had a leash and collar laying around here somewhere. Narrowing my eyes, I saw a flash of blue as my eyes went past the fence. I breathed a sigh of relief as I noticed that it was a leash and collar, that is truly GOOD luck. Walking over to it, I grabbed both of them, and walked back over to the dog. The leash and collar both had skulls on them, which also proved to me that he wanted his dog to look tough, which is equal to dog-fighting. Now why he'd choose a fabric leash and collar with skulls on it is beyond me, seeing as the fact that most dog-fighting guys get their dogs spiked-collars and chained leashes to make them look tough. Gently, I clipped the collar around the dog's neck, trying not to hurt any of his wounds. Then I hooked the leash to the collar, the dog stood there patiently as I did so.

Glancing back over this dog, made me realize that it definitely will help that I have a leash and collar for him, because I am going to get enough glares just for the fact at how beaten up he is. "Come on" I said, walking a little ways but not tugging on the dog so as not to hurt him(with his injuries n' all). The dog looked up at me, his round blue eyes staring at me as if I was doing something wrong. "Come on little dog" I said, not sure exactly how to 'talk' to a dog, seeing as the fact that I've never even owned a dog in my entire life! He didn't budge. I tugged the rope slightly, he still didn't budge. I looked right down towards him, disbelief clouding my thoughts. Great, I managed to save the one dog that has the stubbornness of a mule! I gave an exaggerated deep breath in annoyance. Gritting my teeth, I gave one quick tug of the leash, the dog barked a huge walloping bark, but got up, and began following me. Walking, I briefly prayed that this all wasn't going to come back and bite me in the butt later on today. It felt odd walking with the dog. I KNEW he wasn't my dog first of all, so I couldn't help but get the feeling that somehow I am going to be arrested for 'stealing' someone else's property. Second, the fact that I got lots of glares obviously from how wounded he was didn't help either. Too many glares to count. But as the amount of people began to wear down as I walked through the less populated areas(and less commercial) the glares wavered to a point that for every ten people I saw(which I saw a total of ten people every five minutes by now), I'd get like one glare(estimation).

Once I finally got to the place(or rather WE got to the place), I popped open the window, and thought about how I was going to get such a huge dog inside the window. He definitely won't be able to jump in himself, that's for sure, he is way too wounded for that. Now, I guess lifting him up is indeed the only way. I inhaled a huge breath in annoyance. Looking at him, I thought to myself that I hope he wants to live because I am going to MAKE him live due to how many more problems he is giving me to solve other than the lot-some amount of problems I already have. Bending down, I patted his head to try and calm him a bit. Looping my right arm around his shoulders, I looped my left arm around his ribs cage and connected them together from there. Taking in another deep breath(this time to get ready for the load I am about to carry), I lifted him up. Immediately I felt the dog's neck muscles tense, as if it was about to lunge at me. "Please don't" I said, startled a bit as he began struggling, I most certainly DID NOT think this through all the way. Taking a quick step closer to the window, I tried placing his paws on the window sill, in which I managed to get a quick scratch right next to my huge scar along my arm for that move. Finally, his paws managed to get a hold of the window sill, and the dog pushed himself in(kicking me with his hind legs as he struggled to get in, probably landing a bruise right along my stomach area). "Stupid dog" I muttered to myself as I wiped off a little drip of blood coming from that scratch along my arm, thankful that it was just one of his nails that managed to rake across my arm. Making sure that the dog wasn't right underneath the window sill, I slid in after him, and closed the window even though I knew I'd be back in a minute.

The dog was walking away as I hurried towards him and grabbed his leash(afraid that somehow he'd find another way out and get lose in the city.). Taking him to the room, I tied his leash up onto one of the legs of the desk, hoping that somehow the average-sized desk would be able to hold down such a huge dog(though seeing the fact that most of his strength HAS to have ran out due to all of the injuries he has, I doubt he'd break loose). But just for good-measure I said "Stay", not that this dog ever heard a single obedient command in his life or anything. Opening up the drawer, the folded hundred dollar bill was right where I left it(proudly came from my first paycheck!). I grabbed it out of the drawer, wishing that it was five twenty dollar bills, that way I could at least leave a twenty dollar bill or so here so that we have SOMETHING in safe keepings. But reminding myself to replenish the store some time soon, I closed the drawer with a loud clank. Looking up, I folded the hundred dollar bill up and placed it in my shoe(no pockets this time). I heard a heavy huff and the clattering of nails against the floor, the dog was laying down. Glancing over to him, I saw him close his eyes. He was really tired, signaling to me that I should leave and get him the things he needs, and fast. I jogged out of the room, noticing that it was the first time in a long time that I didn't need to turn on the light in here to see due to the fact that Sam and I have been coming here VERY late lately so the lantern was greatly needed. Felt kind of, ODD, I suppose.

Opening up the window, I went right through it, and then shut it. Looking up at the dark cloud-filled sky, I had to wonder what time it is. Had to be at the very least past one, right? Keeping at a speed-walk pace, I made my way to a store, approximately fifteen minutes, it was not exactly a 'joy' walk either, horrible thoughts of death(of many sorts...)

clouding my mind, I practically managed to beat myself up(mentally, of course) by the time I arrived at the store. Walking in, I went to first get some of the medical type spray. I grabbed one can of it, and then went over to get a towel(to wipe away all the access blood on the dog). Getting a couple of glares from people who saw me holding them in my hands, I went to the cashier and asked her if I can leave those there, she said yes of course. Getting the dog food was more interesting than a challenge, seeing as the fact that they had a whole isle worth of different kinds of dog food to choose from, and each one of them saying that they were the best for your dog(which one would learn that EVERY type of product believes that they are the best, so never buy something simply because the container says it is the best, learned that when I was like eleven and bought the best type of soda ever, and when I took a sip out of it, it tasted purely of carbonated sugar and nothing else.). Deciding that there was no way that I was going to pick the right bag of dog food just by glancing over them, I did a quick price check and grabbed the bag that stood in the middle of high priced dog food, and low priced dog food per pound. I slung it over my shoulder to help lift some of the weight, and then grabbed two dog bowls in my left hand, holding the dog food with my right. Walking over to the water-bottle area, I grabbed a jug of water and went over to the cashier who just finished ringing someone else up.

She shot me an uneasy grin when I placed the dog-food on the counter. I can just guess that she actually thinks that I am the one who actually dog-fights, part of me wants to explain the whole story so that she doesn't get the wrong idea and thinks bad of me or anything like that, but that other part that just keeps my mouth shut, is telling me that I have nothing to prove. She began ringing everything up, grinding my teeth, I decided that it was safe to say that I won't be attending dinner tonight, so I walked over to the small little produce section that they have and grabbed a bag of apples, walking back to the cashier, I had her ring it up. "Anything else?" she asked, almost hesitantly.

I looked over to one of the mini-fridges that they had right at the cashier's desk and grabbed out a water and placed it right on the thing "This" I said. Once she rang it up, she told me that it totaled to seventy seven dollars. Taking out the hundred dollar bill(which I embarrassedly forgot to take out of my shoe before I came into the store), I handed her it. She took it, and began tallying up the change. She gave the change to me and then I said "Have a nice day", I grabbed the bag with everything in it(amazingly it all fit, except for the dog food), then I slung the dog food bag over my shoulder. It was still daylight out so I shouldn't really get into a troublesome situation in which I'd be robbed, but, if I were to be robbed, I think if everyone knew exactly what I do, their best bets would be on me, and not the robber(unless he had a gun that was pointed right at me, in which case, I wouldn't necessarily LET him have everything I just bought, and the money, but I'd probably mine as well because I'd end up coming right at him with my fists and getting shot if he has at least half as a good aim as an amateur. Guns, not my best competitor... at all). If I had a ten dollar bill, for every glare I got so far today, I'd probably have at the very least five hundred dollars. Once I got to the place, I opened the window, after placing the bag of dog food on the ground, and dropped everything inside. Grabbing the dog food bag, I dropped it into the window also, almost being dragged in with it after letting go possibly a second too late. Regaining myself, I went into the place through the window, and closed the window right behind me. Grabbing the things, I walked over to the room that the dog was at.

Turning around the corner into the room, I saw the dog still attached to the desk, sleeping(I hope!). Dropping everything in front of me, hoping that it would wake the dog up, that way I'd know that he is alive! He looked up at me, his eyes bleary with sleep, every bit of blood on him now dried to his fur. Moving the bag of stuff with my foot as I went towards him, I bent down and grabbed out the towel and gallon of water. Pouring a little bit of the water onto the tip of the towel, I began wiping the dog's face down gently, trying to get as much blood off of his face as possible(his head moved a little bit, but nothing that stopped me from cleaning his face). Moving over to his back, I poured a little more water on the tip of the towel and began taking the blood off of his back. So many cuts and abrasions. Teeth marks for sure. Once I got done with his back, and all of his limbs, I went over to the neck at which I realized was the worst for sure. Taking off the collar to get a better look, there were two huge gashes along his neck, obviously from where the other dog must of bit down at. The blood over it was dried up, but as I wiped it away, disturbingly I noticed that the gashes went down into his neck a good inch and was sure to be infected by this point. Grabbing out the medical spray, I opened it up and thought about the best possible way to spray it on the dog. It was the same type of stuff that really stung Sam(and myself), so how was I going to hold such a huge dog down as I basically, in his view, hurt him? I huffed, and hoping for the best, I grabbed a hold of his head, and began rubbing it gently, getting a good hold on him, but still trying to comfort him.

I aimed the container towards the two cuts, and began spraying. Immediately, I felt his body lurching as I tried the best I could to hold him down. Whimpering broke through his throat followed by a growl. Sliding my hand right towards his muzzle, I clamped it hoping that it would be enough to stop him from biting a huge chunk out of me. As I stopped spraying him with the medical spray, I placed it onto the floor, and keeping my other hand across his muzzle in fear of him still trying to bit me, I placed my other hand on his head, rubbing it. After a few moments he started to rub his head into my hand which signaled that I gained his trust again. Getting up and then repositioning myself right next to his back, I sat back down and reached over to the spray. Grabbing it, I placed it in my right and began shaking it up. I placed my left hand draped along his shoulder blades to keep him calm, and still sitting there. "It shouldn't hurt as much" I said, trying to soothe the dog. I started to spray along the back of his neck, it definitely made him uncomfortable for he tried shifting away from me, but that was all. Lifting my hand off of his shoulder blades cautiously, I began spraying along his back, and then finally at his tail just in case there were some cuts that I didn't notice on it. The dog, still calm(whimpering slightly, but still pretty calm), I leaned over and began spraying down his legs which were buckled down on the side of him. After that, I moved over back in front of the dog's face, and turned the towel to the part I didn't use and sprayed it down. Then grabbing the dog's head gently, I began rubbing it along the different bite marks on his face, careful not to get the stuff into his eyes. When I was just about done, he pulled back, he definitely had enough.

Grabbing the two bowls out, I set them down, just out of reach of the dog(I kind of DON'T want to have a dog hurtling at me as I try to pour him some food and water). Walking over to the huge bag of dog food, I grabbed a hold of the top part that said 'tear here' and ripped it off. Dragging it over, I poured some dog food into the bowl, which seemed to get the tired and dreary dog's attention, he got up and pulled on the desk a little bit, whimpering as he realized he couldn't get at the food. Quickly, I grabbed the gallon of water out, and poured it into the second bowl, pushing the two bowls closer to the dog, the dog hastily plunged his face right into the dog food, moving my hands quickly away just in time. As he began eating, his tail wagged in delight. Grabbing the bag full of my water and apples, I went over to my chair and sat down. Opening the bag up, I took out an apple, opened my water up and poured it onto the apple to clean it a bit. Then I bit into the apple and leaned into the chair, closing my eyes for a brief second to think about what exactly I should do with this dog. I can't possibly keep him, can I? That would be like animal abuse in itself, seeing as the fact that I'd have to keep him in here, with practically no chance of him having any type of company during the night, and where he will use the um, bathroom is still a huge mystery.

With a huff, I decided to push those thoughts back a bit, I have to keep him for at least a couple of days so that he could regain his strength, I will think about it when the time comes and hopefully I can train this dog to go down stairs into the basement when he needs to go for now(because basically all Sam and I use is this room, meaning that the rest of this building is as the public views it, vacant, and the basement isn't even thought of.). Now I guess the only question to ask is, what should I name him(because there is no way I am going to take care of this dog for at least a couple of days without giving him a name.)? What do people name their dogs anyways? I have heard of the names 'Bear', 'Moose', 'Max', and even 'Tony'(I know the last one isn't really a dog's name pursae, but hey, I have indeed heard someone call their dog Tony before), but believe it or not, none of them seem to stick to the dog. I mean, 'Moose' and 'Bear' represents big dogs, which this dog is most certainly big, but I just don't see it(there is also the fact that 'Bear' is the last name of Sam, so yeah...). Then the name 'Max' for some strange reason always ends up being the name for a dumb dog, or a dumb kid, and this dog doesn't seem dumb at all. Now the last name, Tony, was probably wiped off of my list even before I thought about that, the name is so bad for a dog, I don't even want to know why that name came into my mind!

Taking another bite of the apple I thought of some more names. I can name him 'Sam' just for a sort of joke, but again, that is the same reason why I crossed out the name 'Bear', it would be just, odd. Gunner, Oak, Tank, Bailey, Skylar, and Wolf, all were crossed out the second I thought of them. Naming something is usually quite fun, you gather around with friends or family and joke around as to what you should name it, as seen on movies and shows. But the problem is probably the fact that I am not with anyone else at the moment, no one else to laugh with or joke around with, it is just me, my thoughts, and the naming subject(which is indeed a DOG).Taking another couple bites of my apple, I heard the crackling of thunder and then the sudden pouring of rain. Great, so now I am trapped here, for who knows how long, thinking of a name, until the rain lets up. I definitely knew that it was going to start raining some time today, I just didn't know when(or this soon!), finishing the last bite of my apple, I placed the core on top of the desk, and then got up, stretching. Who knows what time it is, seeing the fact that I didn't bring my phone with me(I don't usually bring my phone while I'm jogging, only sometimes. But if I knew how it was going to end up, I'd have definitely brought my phone with me!). Looking over towards the dog, he was sitting down, staring at me. This is not seriously happening, it literally looks like he is GLARING at me. Can a dog really GLARE at someone, or is it just in my head? Focusing my eyes back onto him, he was still doing it.

Really? Okay, I am guessing that this is not all in my head then. "What!?" I said, expecting no true reply but I needed some way to channel the agitation and questioning out of me. The dog continued to stare at me, with his huge blue eyes, a big contrast to his dark red scratches. I walked closer to him, and then turned a little bit out of his view, seeing if he was actually glaring AT me, or just glaring for no reason. Turning around to see him, his head was still angled towards me, still glaring. I can already tell right now that this dog isn't going to make me an animal person, but push me farther away. The thunder rang out again, only this time the dog barked at me, a loud bark. This dog better not think that I AM causing the noise! The thunder sounded again, and yet again the dog barked at me. This dog honestly has the biggest attitude I have ever seen on a dog! I mean seriously! I walked over to him and bent down. "Little no-name, can you stop barking, please." I said, patting his head lightly, and rubbing the bottom of his head where the neck area was soothingly, making sure not to disturb any of his injuries. I debated whether or not I should just give him a random name and get it over with, at least then I'd be able to run in the rain all the way home without having to worry about giving him a name, instead of waiting for the rain to stop as I try giving him a name(how one affects the other, I have no clue, but that would be my plan still!). The thunder roared again, and yet again the dog barked. My nerves are definitely on their very end because of this.

"THUNDER! How's that? Seeing as you like thunder so much?!" I said, replaying the name back and forth in my head afterwards, seeing how it fit. Thunder really isn't much of a dog's name, but it kind of stuck to him. When one thinks of thunder, they think of big, loud, and powerful, which is exactly what this dog is. Plus, it works in the fact that he seems to bark at thunder which almost represents an event that is part of him. "Thunder" I said the name out loud one more time, deciding that it would be good enough for the dog. Leaning up against the desk, I sat down right next to, Thunder. He came closer and sat down on me, barking every time thunder sounded(which is definitely going to get old after awhile, I am sure of it. But it is kind of entertaining in the mean time...). Rubbing his head, I slowly managed to get him to sleep.

Brushing my hands through his fur, I allowed my mind to drift a little bit, guessing that it will be some time until the rain is over and until Thunder is off of my lap(not the most comfortable thing to have a ninety pound dog laying on your lap while sitting on an uncarpeted floor by the way.). I have to wonder how Sam's little camping trip is going. Hopefully it isn't raining where he is, though it would be very amusing to learn that Sam was soaked during his whole trip or ended up stuck in a small little camper with his dad(n' such) the whole trip. But I definitely don't wish it upon him seeing Sam is indeed my friend and he wouldn't want that to happen to me(I hope!). Though me getting caught fishing, is very impossible seeing the fact that first, I don't want to kill a fish. Second, fish are scaly(plus slimy!) and gross, so I'd rather not touch one to get it off the hook, so it is just impractical. I also have to wonder as to how the whole injured-Sam thing turned out with his Dad. I REALLY hope that he believed Sam, and that everything turned out just fine(which it is a pretty big coincidence that a fighting dog was Sam's excuse, and that I found a fighting dog just today, interesting how things play out like that, VERY interesting).

Thinking of Sam, tonight will be the first of seven nights(or so) without having to worry about Sam when I go out now. That makes me feel SO much better, because honestly, it is nice to have someone around, someone to rely on in case something goes horribly wrong on my part, but other then that, it just completely messes with my mind having Sam come out with me. I feel like I am almost doing something wrong. I mean, yeah, Sam CHOOSE'S to go out at night with me, it is not like I am forcing him to or that he is not old enough to decide for himself or something like that, it is just that I feel kind of like it is my fault that he has that type of thought in his head, I mean, it is as if he doesn't realize just how DANGEROUS it actually is! The only reason why I started doing that in the first place is because in actuality, I really didn't have anything to lose, but Sam does! He has his father to think of for crying out loud, his family. Now I know that I have Summer and the other two to think of, but honestly, that was just a responsibility that I placed on myself and I don't even think they realized that, so what exactly would they lose, yes it probably would be sad for them if they found out that I was dead, but it wouldn't be like losing a family member. Sam has to think about his dad and his family. Besides, truthfully, I can do just as much by myself, I can help just as many people, cancelling out Sam's theory which definitely won't in reality work to save time, it would only work to save injuries. So in actuality, there is no need for Sam to risk his life anyways, he really has no kind of obligation to nor' any sort of reason to because it isn't making matters that much better. I guess out of all the things I've managed to understand Sam on, this is one of the things I really CAN'T.

Just add that to the list of things that I don't understand in life I suppose. Stopping right in my thoughts, I realized that I was grinding my teeth together, a nasty habit that I should really stop unless I'd like to be twenty five years old and toothless. Stress and frustration is the obvious supporter of the habit, to such an extent as if I needed to create an ad for it, the end would have something like 'Grinding your teeth together to such an extent that it is bad for you is brought to you by stress and frustration, yes, STRESS and Frustration'. Someone would probably say, 'then get rid of all that built up stress and do something to stop it'. Then I would say 'like what?', which would be followed by the person saying 'exercise, work out all of that built-up frustration, it can make you feel better' and me saying 'I run miles on end every week, possibly amounting to more than fifty miles a week, trust me, I think I have enough exercise', which would be followed by a sharp 'oh' and then 'well then, can I recommend you a nice brand of dentures?'. That guy would need a pair of dentures after I am done with him or her(does Ms.Thomas come to mind, anyone?). Which leaves me at a dead end of ideas because there truly is no way to relinquish stress and frustration(which could be considered over-worked and enraged), at least there truly is no way FOR ME that is. Concentrating on NOT grinding my teeth, I tried going for a more happier topic as the sound of thunder still rolled in the background(surprisingly Thunder is sleeping like a baby, not to be twisted into the fact that babies rarely fall into a heavy sleep, but more so the fact that Thunder is sleeping peacefully),

I have work every day this week, but Friday. Which yes, most people were to complain about it, but I really can't because I ASKED for it. I mean, more work means more money, right? That is definitely the way that I look at it, and if I really wanted to I bet I can just quite the job right now and go get a new one(though maybe asking for another day off would be a better idea, hmm?). Plus there is the fact that it would make spending time with the kids(mostly Scott of course... Scratch that off, ALL the way Scott of course, Summer and Tim are pretty good in my books, it is just Scott is so.... Scott...) seem that much more pleasant of a day. I stretched up, and fumbled for the switch of the lantern, flicking the switch on, the room brightened. I just began to realize how dark it was getting in here because of the rain clouds n' such(though it might be getting later in the day too...). Listening, the rain was going down to a drizzle and the thunder was gone too. I should be out of here in no time, good. Thunder raised his head and looked up towards me, the big lump of fur got up, and began stretching. Walking a little of a ways until the leash was stretched out to its maximum length, then he turned and walked back, lying down beside me with a thump as if he decided that it would be better use of his time to go back to sleep. Getting up before he had the chance to jump on me again, I walked over to the dog food bowl and poured in some more dog food for Thunder so that he had some more to hold him over until the next time I get here to feed him again. I poured some more water also, making sure not to spill any and also not to make a noise in fear that Thunder fell asleep and I didn't want to wake up the poor little dog just because I was too loud, especially if he JUST got back to sleep. I walked back towards his leash, and untangled it from the table, enough that incase he wanted to leave, he could(and hopefully use the bathroom somewhere else, I would show him the basement but, I'd rather not wake him up and I am definitely not going to wait until he wakes up again because who knows how long THAT would be!? He is a VERY sleepy dog.). I grabbed the bag of apples, and the water-bottle, debating whether or not I should bring them back home(carrying a bag of apples through drizzling rain isn't the most fun thing to do, and these might come in handy the next time I come here). Deciding that the others might want some apples, I opened the bag up again and took out an apple, one with a couple bruises and holes in it that made it unappetizing, then I dropped it on the ground, maybe Thunder might find some sort of entertainment playing with an apple. Then I place my water bottle in the apple bag, and grabbed my apple core with my free hand. I then walked out of the room.

Walking over to the window, I looked outside to see just how much it was raining, now it was only a very, very light drizzle, no problem for a short walk. I opened the window up, and went through it. Shutting it, I looked up at the sky to see if I could see the sun through the clouds by any chance and where exactly it was in the sky. Squinting my eyes, trying to shield away the rain, I saw just a bit of sun peaking through the clouds just slightly above the horizon told me that it had to be seven o'clock, maybe even eight. Walking in the direction of my place, I began speeding up my pace, the rain was surprisingly falling down much faster than it appeared and was beginning to really soak me, and walking in wet clothes is not fun. I yawned, remembering that I didn't take that much needed nap I wanted to today due to my little 'rescue mission', I MIGHT be able to cram one in between getting ready for tonight and leaving for the night, but that is highly doubtful seeing as the fact that it takes me so LONG to fall asleep during the day(or early night, which ever way someone would put it), then there is the whole fact of making sure to wake up!

Once I finally got to the house, I tried to see if the door was unlocked because I managed to forget my keys. As I turned the knob, the door opened. Thank God it was, because quite frankly, I don't think I would have wanted to be out in the rain much longer, the rain and I, aren't best friends, at all. Opening the door slowly, and quietly just in case it was later than I thought, I came in and then shut the door behind me. The television was roaring and I quickly glanced at the clock, it read seven forty five, they are so lucky that it isn't past eight o'clock or they would have it. Walking into the living room, all three of them were sitting on the couch, my squeaky shoes made my presence known because before I even got within a couple of feet they were all turned towards me. "Got caught in the storm" I said, laughing both because it is sort of amusing, and true. Tim turned back to the television without replying, the show was back on.

Summer was the first to speak, both her and Scott didn't turn their attention back to the television, in fact, they both seemed to find just as much amusement out of it as I did(for a different reason, of course) "Wow, you are WET, you must of REALLY got caught in the storm for how wet you are. Where did you go jogging to, China town and back five times?!". Scott grinned, obviously liking the thought of me getting caught in the storm with how our last conversation left off, needless to say, I ignored that grin.

Making up a quick story in my head I said "Well I was jogging for the whole time and I THOUGHT it was all going to blow over, but it didn't. So I ended up taking shelter in a store, still pretty soaked. I got bored pretty fast, so basically I just decided to tough out the storm and come back even when it was still raining", I really don't have to explain it to a seven year old, but honestly, I wanted to make it sound as believable as possible because not only was Summer listening, but Scott was too, and I'd rather not get questioned by him, and then blurt out about Thunder, and me beating up some guy who is like twice my size(in weight, maybe not muscle...), which would practically give him an arrow pointing from me, straight to 'the Bandit' for him. HOPEFULLY he isn't that close yet though.

Scott finally spoke up after listening to us both, "you truly are a Water-Bringer" he said, laughing like crazy, I felt my face flash red. He has been listening to Sam way too much and took on one of his wise-guy-jokes. I don't know whether I should treat it the same way that I treat it with Sam, another comeback, or to be infuriated with Scott right now. He doesn't LOOK like he is trying to get on my nerves, maybe he is just trying to joke around... Just maybe though... This middle name will probably be the first thing I change the second I turn eighteen, it is becoming too much. But giving Scott the benefit of the doubt, I decided to laugh it off and not totally explode on him, he is lucky this wasn't one of my school days in which I would have been called that about twenty times and it was way too worn out on me, because then that would have been a problem, and like a ticking time bomb, I would have exploded on him. That would not have been good, for BOTH of us. "You bought apples?" Scott questioned, glancing the bag of apples I had in my hand up and down. I held out the apple pit, almost in relation to what I was about to say just then.

"I got hungry when I was waiting in the store, so I figured why not?" I said, walking over to the kitchen, throwing out the pit into the garbage, and grabbing out a bowl to wash the apples in. Turning on the water, I poured the apples into the bowl, making sure to grab my water bottle before it fell into the bowl and had the same fate as the apples. Once the bowl filled up, I turned off the water and poured the water back in the sink, leaving the apples that I placed onto the table. "I'm going to go take a shower, okay?" I said, taking off my shoes and placing them in the hall way so that they could dry.

"Okay then" Summer said, as she turned to face the screen. Out of the corner of my eyes, I noticed that Scott was looking directly at me for a split second, his eyes narrowed. As soon as I turned around(or by the time that I turned around), he was already facing the television screen. What does he WANT from me!? I mean seriously! Since day one, Scott and I have butt heads together, and you'd think as the days go by it would begin to cinder down a bit, but it doesn't. In fact, if anything, the flames almost get fed more, especially with Scott's increased suspicion, which in this scenario seems to be the oxygen for the flames, it seems to be feeding the flames even more. How could someone think such a thing? Well how can Scott turn on a dime like that?! He went from joking, to suspicious, maybe he had that in his head to begin with and didn't want to show it around Summer, but still, I have enough problems to deal without having to deal with the most foul little twelve year old boy I have ever met! Walking upstairs to my room, I grabbed my night-clothes(not to be mistake with my pajamas, but yes, my BANDITING clothes.), and went right into the bathroom and got ready for tonight(Showering, getting dressed...).

*   *   *

After I got ready, I heard the sharp scream of Summer. My eyes widened as I went straight towards the living room at which I heard it coming from. As I raced to the room(which seemed like forever, though it probably took approximately five seconds or so), thoughts began to surface inside my mind. Was someone breaking in!? Was that someone because of me? Did I just put their lives in danger because I go out at night and possibly catch the eyes of some unwanted people as I do so? Is it that guy, coming to succeed in his promise to kill me because I didn't back off? As I turned around the wall to the living room, I held my right hand out in a bundled up fist at shoulder-height ready to lunge at the first guy I see. But there was no one there. Bewildered, I crept my way towards the couch, trying to see if there was someone hiding right behind it in my blind-view(couch covering up the spot). My breath came in shallow breaths as I walked over to see what was behind the couch.

My heart almost felt as if it just stopped as I caught sight of the scene. There, on the ground was Summer and Scott, wrestling each other.

"ARE YOU guys SERIOUS!?" I said, in an extremely annoyed voice. They were seriously WRESTLING each other. WHY on Earth did Summer scream like that!? That sound sounded equivalent to a MURDER for heaven's sake! They both stopped still right where they were(Summer on top of Scott), and looked up to face me. They know that they just did something wrong, slowly, Summer got up off of Scott and hung her head, almost in shame, or the fact that she didn't want to look me straight in the eyes at fear of what would be next. As Scott got up, I began again "By all means, what," I took a deep breath "WHAT on Earth could be so bad and serious, that you had to SCREAM like that!?". I am now not angry at the fact that they were wrestling each other, because it only affected them, but to scream like that? They KNOW just how badly that sort of stuff messes with my mind, don't get me wrong, I am VERY happy that there really isn't something horrible going on here, but I mean, seriously!?

"Scott stole the remote from me" Summer said, obviously trying to make her voice sound apologetic, and shameful, but I knew all too well that she felt that she had a good reason to and sincerely believed she did nothing wrong but was trying to make her being wronged by Scott, right.

I exhaled a very aggravated breath out, trying not to completely blow my head off. I guess I really DON'T want to know her reasoning, at all. I took a swift glance towards Scott, who wasn't looking at me, or at the floor, rather in a different direction, in annoyance. As if I was doing something wrong. "Anything else?" I said, turning towards Scott to show that I was asking HIM anything else, to see his little 'side' of the story. He didn't reply back, just stared out into space. Trying to keep my cool I said "You know what, why don't you guys all go to bed, now", I looked towards Tim who was peering out from behind the couch's back, eyes wide in curiosity, and sort of frightened, maybe. Both Summer and Scott nodded, Scott a little less than Summer, but all three of them walked in the direction of their rooms. A nice way to start the night, I thought with bitter sarcasm as I made my way towards the door for the night ahead.

CHAPTER 8

Walking out into the dark summer night, somehow managed to calm me down a bit, shake off all the worries that I have been having lately. Sam wasn't here, removing the constant reminder that everything is now changing, that I am now in danger(and probably always was, just never really brought to my attention, and the fact that I am in even MORE danger) with various threats to try and watch my back with. I huffed, as I debated where I should go exactly. Deciding that it would probably be best(and possibly more interesting), to go out farther than usually, stretch my range n' such. That way, there is less of a possibility of being found, right? Listening carefully for any signs of a patrolling police car, I began heading the same direction I headed last time, only this time, my view on an area much more farther. I kept at a pretty even pace the whole time, probably right in between a jog, and a full out run. Once I finally got to the 'out-skirts' of the area at which I usually am at(surprisingly not hearing anything 'bad' happening along the way, being almost a huge coincidence and something that is basically screaming at me to push forward, because I definitely would have stopped if I heard anything going on), I began to slow down a bit. Making sure to keep track of every turn I made so that way I won't get lost when I come back.

A gentle breeze stirred a strand of my hair that wasn't in the pony tail, making it blow into my face a bit, as I went to go move it from my face, I saw possibly two figures moving up ahead, and turning around the corner. Picking up the speed, I ran towards them, trying to keep as quiet as possible(and realizing that it is IMPOSSIBLE for me when I am going at such a speed, I hoped that the two guys were too busy with each other, to listen for anything else. As I turned around the bend, I saw nothing but street in front of me. Looking around, I tried listening for any type of sign that would lead me to where they went. A couple minutes passed and I heard nothing, then up ahead, I heard the slamming of something to the ground, making a loud and echoing crunching sound. It must be a garbage can, running once again, I tried pinpointing exactly where the sound came from, listening again, I heard the scuffling of feet on the ground towards my left, turning in the direction the sound came from, I began sprinting towards the alley that I saw. Two figures were crashing up against each other in the alley, one throwing a fist at the other, the other ducking and so on. As I got within a yard or two away from the situation, the bigger one took one last punch, and punched the more smaller one(female, if I can determine the shadow figures correctly, one dim street light as far as I could see both ways around me). Right when he began turning around, I came up, and punched the guy right in the face, landing a blow at which he fell right to the ground. Unconscious.

Definitely one of the easiest jobs I had to do. My first reaction was to check and make sure both of them were still alive, unslinging my bag from around me, I set it on the ground next to what appears to be the garbage can that was knocked over. Looking down, I checked the first figure. It was a female as I suspected, her long hair covering up her face, the faint whisper of a breath coming from her mouth. Numeral abrasions along her arms as if she was being handled. Very well under, but still alive. My guess, boyfriend and girlfriend date gone wrong(or a robbery gone wrong also). Looking towards the guy, he was definitely still breathing, and the only mark on him was a gash along the side of his face at which he landed on, definitely the event to thank for him getting knocked out unconscious. Leaning over to grab my bag, I placed it in front of me, and grabbed out the rope. Doing my usual routine of wrapping his arms and legs up together so that there is no possible way of him getting out and untangled from it, I tied a triple knot, then I decided to cut the rope away with a nearby sharper rock(which took me a good minute or so to fully cut through it). Throwing the rock to the side(and out of reach of the... captive?), throwing the rest of the rope back inside my bag, I grabbed out a piece of paper(and a pen) and wrote 'The guy who is wrapped up in rope, seems to be the aggressor. Punched the female victim(?) out unconscious as I neared the scene of the situation. Do as you must to seek real justice. -B . -P.S, thanks for the nickname'. I laughed a short laugh at the semi-witty remark, it should probably get them pretty good. Picking up the piece of paper from the ground, I placed it neatly on top of the guy, in clear sight, slightly under his hand so it won't blow away.

With a quick sharp exhale, I got up from where I was bending over, shot the pen right back into the bag, and grabbed out the phone from the bag. Dialing nine one-one, I waited a moment for it to be picked up. When the usual '9-11, what is your emergency' began, I cut it off short and quickly as possible I said(careful to put not a single ounce of a feminine sound to my voice), "Two people unconscious, one victim and one aggressor." I went on by saying the street name, and then at the end just to almost urk them I said 'from your's truly' and hung up. Quickly shutting off the phone, I threw it back into my bag, and slung the bag back around my shoulder. Taking one last glance at the little scene of what happened, making sure that I didn't miss anything, I walked towards the exit of the alley, glancing back and forth, making sure the coast is clear and that there weren't any patrolling police cars or something around here also. Then I turned all the way around, and began running as fast as I could, 'fleeing the scene of the crime', just knowing that they would be here soon enough. Going the opposite direction at which my place was, I decided that since I am already going to be out here longer than I thought I would, I could do one more.

Listening, I turned around a building and did a 'loop-around', angling myself back in the direction towards my house, but on a different path(street). Slowing my pace back down to a jog, I kept on listening, wondering if there really was so much crime around here that I'd actually be able to find another. Looking longingly at my bag, where I know my phone laid shut off to stop myself from being tracked, I decided that it was times like these that I really did wish I had a watch. I mean, I would really like to know what time it is, I could only guess and quite frankly my guessing skills aren't exactly the best. Suddenly, a huge blur darted right past me, my eyes whipping straight to where the blur came from, and then where it is, I huffed a loud huff. Am I serious? I was spending so much time thinking about what time it was, I couldn't even see a crime that was going on not one building away from me?! There, in the shadow of a building, laid a figure on the ground moaning, and in front of me(and getting farther by the second), was someone running away, with what seems to be a bat in his hand. My first thought was to run after him, running full-speed, I ran after the guy, ignoring the other thought that seemed to cloud into my head to go check on the victim, in my head, I told myself that he or she would be okay, I mean, if they are moaning that HAS to mean that they are semi-okay, right?

As I got closer to the guy who was fleeing, he turned around the corner, after a few seconds, I turned the bend, only to witness to my lesser-satisfaction, the picking up of the guy into what seems to be(and MUST be) the escape car. "SHOOT" I said, using the word as a substitution for multiple swearwords I had in mind, kicking the brick wall of the building closest to me with the bottom of my foot in outrage. Clenching my hands into fists, almost in a last type of act to control my anger, I made my way to the victim, who, as I finally got there, moaned one big moan, signifying to me that he was still conscious, and still very well alive. I guess all of this wasn't totally for nothing. Walking over towards a shadow coming from the building, I grabbed out my pen and paper, and scribbled down "Victim(the one on the ground), apparently beaten to an extent that he cannot get up. The doer, ran away and into an escape car,-" I broke off writing for a second, trying to recall something about the vehicle. It was low light, so very hard to tell what color it was, could have been dark blue, but then again, it could have been any other color off of the color spectrum as well, so that type of description would be useless, and a complete waste of time to write down. It was a pretty big figure that I saw, so I suppose that it would be safe to say that it is a van, right? Deciding that it would I went on "pretty big, possibly a van or a pickup truck. -B". Shoving the pen back into my bag, I walked over to the victim and placed it right onto the ground next to him, making sure it was close to him so that it wouldn't blow away. Groaning as I noticed that the paper got wet. Grinding my teeth, I made the decision that the writing was still legible, and placed that thought aside.

Taking out my phone, I turned it on, and dialed nine-one-one, stating the things that I usually do, I clipped the phone shut, and turned it off. Throwing it back into my back pack, I looked both ways across the street, and then turned in the direction of my apartment, deciding that it was probably time to go home and rest. Work in the morning tomorrow, followed by checking on the dog Thunder and seeing if he made it through the night(hoping he DID make it through the night.), is indeed going to take a beating out of me, so rest is definitely necessary. Starting off with a brisk jog, I began full-out sprinting by the time I was at my block, getting possibly a bit too arrogant that there weren't any cops(probably too busy with the two crime scenes I left them, snooping around for me...). All in all, I didn't get caught, and that was indeed the most important part. Once I got to my door steps, I took out my keys and unlocked the door, silently I opened it up, and went inside, shutting the door behind me, I looked up towards the wall clock, it read three fifty five, surprisingly. It actually felt more later into the night than that, but hey, that is such a welcomed time in my opinion. Walking more into the house, I got what I needed and went into the bathroom, performing everything as usual. I made sure to run the shower nice and hot, it felt like heaven.

After I got myself ready, I headed to my room(being as silent as ever), I went straight towards my bed, flopping down on it, I was surprised when sleep didn't come towards me within a minute. In fact, my mind felt like it was buzzing with the thoughts of that guy getting away today. I huffed. My eyes wide open, staring up at the ceiling, they began to sting as I blinked them shut. How could I let that happen!? See this, THIS isn't good, at all. It just, agitates me. I mean, it probably shouldn't have. He was going to get away anyways, I mean, the only thing different is the fact that someone(someone being ME) witnessed it. But still, that sort of stuff only has happened to me on several occasions over the years, and I hate it, more like DESPISE it every time. This is just one of those added things that is keeping me up, I suppose... Finally though, after what seemed like decades, I was able to gradually fall asleep, one of the small things that feel so good, and yet are so simple, sleep.

* * *

I was woken up by Summer, yet again, NOT by my alarm clock. Now why I keep on making that mistake is a mystery, I mean, it is not that hard to set the stupid thing, is it? So yet again, I rushed to get ready, possibly a bit too pleased with the fact that it were to be only work that I am missing if I end up being late, not the regents, which brings up the fact that I should probably quit the job sooner or later, because

OBVIOUSLY I don't like it, but knocking the thought right out of my head, I took an apple to go, and walked right out, saying good bye to everyone as I did so. I fast-walked to the store, at which I arrived five minutes late, luckily no one noticed me sneaking in and I was able to open up another cash register without some angry customers screaming at my 'higher' about there only being one cash register. Pretty average shift for the most part, nothing close to a paradise, but not necessarily a huge nightmare either. So in other words, completely uneventful and a waste of my time. Getting out at twelve thirty, I went straight to the coffee shop and got myself an Iced coffee to go, I walked back to the store and picked up one more jug of water and another huge bag of dog food, not sure as to how much a dog needs. Hesitantly, I made my way to the building, opened the window, and came right in, shutting the window behind me, slightly un-eased as to what I was going to walk in on when I came in, not liking the thoughts that flooded my head.

As I turned around the corner, my breath was almost knocked out of me as I saw Thunder sprawled out across the floor. Right before I had enough time to fully react, the dog brought his head up and looked at me with tired eyes. I huffed in annoyance, I should have known that he wasn't going to die so easy. Dropping the food into the corner I came up to Thunder and rubbed his head, checking in on him, I noticed that he looked a lot better. The cuts don't look as infected, I mean, they are most certainly still there, some even seem to have opened up even more, probably due to Thunder biting at them, but they were all definitely more clean looking. A couple of them has even scabbed over. His dark blue eyes looked straight at me, they almost seemed much more lighter and less haunted now. "Good boy" I said, rubbing his head even more, he must of liked it because his tail began wagging back and forth at such a rate that I was afraid that he was going to open up more cuts. Walking over to his bowls I realized that he ate every last morsel of food in the bowl, and had maybe a couple sips left of water in his water bowl. Going over to the opened carton of water, I unscrewed the cap, and poured more water into the bowl. Grabbing the opened bag of food, I did the same with the food bowl. Looking around made me realize that the floor around me is spotless, and figuring that he must of went somewhere else, I drew my attention back to him and whether or not I should spray his wounds with more of the anti infection stuff. His neck definitely needed it, seeing as to how fragile the neck really is, but the rest of his wounds might not need it, because animals have an immune system for a reason, he should be able to fight off SOME sort of infection, I mean, if he ends up looking worse tomorrow, then I would spray him down more, but I already have limited supplies of the stuff, and there is no sense in using it on something that DOESN'T need it. Especially when it was my FIRST thought, too. When in doubt, always go with the first thought.

Taking out the anti-infection stuff from my bag, I went over to Thunder and grabbed a hold of his head. This time, I made sure to be a little more looser than last time to try and gain some sort of his trust. I then began spraying down his neck, he pulled back a little bit and whimpered a bit, showing that he had some sort of pain and there were definitely a good amount of bacteria in his cuts, but still, less than last time showing that he is indeed getting better. After a couple seconds of spraying his neck down, I heard a sort of hissing noise, which told me that I was all out of the stuff, so even if I WANTED to spray down the rest of his body for infection, I wouldn't be able to seeing the fact that I spent the rest of my money on the dog food and water, and I am not even sure if I have any left at home(possibly a fifty-fifty type of chance). Throwing the can to the side, and making a mental note to pick it up later, I grabbed the leash and tied it back onto Thunder's collar, debating whether or not I should take him for a walk when he is in such a condition like this. It could either be good for him, or catastrophic, depending on what type of day I am having when it comes to luck. I decided to make a list in my head of the pros that could happen, and the cons that could happen, and then I'd weigh them all out. So the pros has to be the fact that it is fresh air for him(good for health, right?), exercise for him, and of course just plain nice for him(dogs HAVE to enjoy going outside, I think...). Now the cons just keep on ringing in my head, like the fact that out of all of the dogs, Thunder has to be the one who hates outside. Or the fact that he might get too tired and can't go on the walk any longer, making us both stranded, waiting for him to regain his strength. Plus, I believe that I might get 'pulled over' by animal police as to why I have a dog that is so badly beaten as Thunder is. Which could get me into trouble, and Thunder straight into the pound and on his way to death. Honestly, I would NEVER forgive myself for that, all just to take him on a WALK!? With a huff, I unclenched the leash from his collar and placed it back onto the table. Looking back to him, I said(though most definitely didn't need to explain to a dog!) "Maybe tomorrow, for right now you should rest". He probably didn't even understand exactly what was going on, because he got up from where he was laying, and sat down, looking up at me, his tail wagged back and forth, as he tipped his head slightly giving me that sort of questioning-cute type of look. I held back that aching feeling to laugh at him, trying to stop myself from looking weird in front of... well myself. Laughing when there is only a dog around to hear, isn't exactly the most SANE thing to do.

Reaching over, I rubbed Thunder's head again, wondering if keeping him here really was the best thing to do, for all of us. So, when I was thinking about that, I had to wonder what Sam would think about all of this. I mean, keeping a large dog in an abandoned building by himself for most of the day isn't exactly the safest thing to do, and there is the fact that who knows how much of a bill I am going to rack up on feeding such a LARGE dog? On second thought, it isn't whether or not Sam would approve of it, that sure doesn't matter cause in actuality it is indeed none of his business, but more or less the fact on whether or not Sam would LAUGH at it all, and I am pretty darn sure I KNOW the answer to that: he would laugh, HARD. Plus, that little Cheshire cat type grin, he'd definitely throw in a couple of those along the way, and probably say something about how desperate I am to get myself into tight situations. Ah, Sam, one of the many things that depending on what mood I am in, I either miss, or glad that he is gone on vacation because of it. Now, I have to wonder exactly what he is doing right now, is there still a chance that he is still getting interrogated by his dad from the injuries? I really hope not because I am the MAIN reason why he got those in the first place.

Honestly, it is just mistake after mistake that I make, I mean, SERIOUSLY!? I clenched my left hand(and only free hand) into a fist, realizing just how fast I was to get back onto the topic of Sam, I sincerely need a life of my own, but then again, what other things have I really been thinking about? There is the whole crime thing, now Thunder(maybe it is a pro to have a dog that I need to heal up), and yes, Sam. I huffed, amazing how my thoughts could practically be grouped into three different labels.

Unclenching my hand, I turned back to Thunder, I mean, I shouldn't be over-analyzing it all like this, I don't think it is healthy, or practical, and maybe even the analysis isn't realistic, maybe it is WRONG? Just maybe though. A huge loud bark that managed to make my ears pop sounded. "Are you serious!?" I said, annoyed and not able to hold back the temptation to say that aloud to a dog. Good thing has to be the fact that I am the only one around to see my weirdness surface, bad thing is, I'd rather not consider myself weird. Making a promise in my head to both myself and Thunder, that I will teach him obedience training some time soon, if not tomorrow. Definitely a must, because a dog barking in public is like a baby crying in public, right? Uncalled for, and will definitely get you an array of glares. ESPECIALLY with how loud Thunder barks, Thunder barked several more times before stopping all together. Thunder then began whimpering, and he looked into one of the corners behind me, his paws scratching along the floor. I looked behind me, to see a rat in the corner. An involuntary shudder ran down my back(not that a shudder could really be voluntary or anything) as it's red beady eyes gleamed at me. I looked back to Thunder who was still whimpering to an extent that it began to sound like nails on a chalkboard after a couple seconds.

"What!?" I said, looking back and forth between Thunder, and the nasty rodent in the corner(which by now its focus was on nibbling something it found in the corner, judging by the ripping sound, the paper we had. Also drawing in the question of 'rats eat PAPER?'). Thunder continued to do it, this time, looking straight at me. I stomped my foot, as I dropped my right hand that was petting him back to my side, because it was just out in front of me, staying there stupidly for I stopped petting him. I mean, I can see the dog's point in not liking rats, I too hate those useless lumps of skin, bones and what little fur they have, but, he's a dog! Dogs are supposed to CHASE all things that could run and are disgusting, not whimper at them for Pete's-sake! "KILL it if you don't like it! Go get it!" I said, yelling at him with frustration. Thunder stopped whimpering immediately(thankfully), tipped his head in questioning again, and before I knew it, charged straight towards the rat. I heard the shuffling of paws as I turned around to see what was happening, all I saw was Thunder hunched over something(the rat, most likely), and a squeal as he bent done to possibly bite it. It was definitely dead as he picked it up and held it almost proudly and walked over to me, dropping it right at my feet. I stared in disbelief, trying to sort through all the thoughts that were bubbling up inside my mind at the moment.

Thunder, who was whimpering just twenty seconds or so ago for what seemed to have been in freight, seemed to have listened to my commands to go kill the stupid rat. Now, that means that he was indeed trained, and most obviously that command was used for, um, battle(against other dogs...). And he is very injured, yet he had the reflexes of a cat in getting that rat(dogs aren't really supposed to get a rat like that I don't think, and definitely not when they are as injured as Thunder). Another thought seemed to have swarm in my mind, and took almost all of my strength to stop myself from full-out puking at the thought. The rat, more likely than less, is diseased(more than the average rat that is), and what ever was wrong with that rat, is now inside Thunder's mouth, just waiting to infect him also. My heart dropped as I came into realization as to what I should do, discard the rat away from Thunder so he doesn't get sick.

Looking down at the rat, and then back to the more than ecstatic Thunder, I debated as to how I was supposed to pick up the filthy little thing. Not with my bare hands, that is for sure. I glanced around the room, looking for something to pick it up with. Looking towards the paper, I decided that it was my best option. With a sigh, I walked over and grabbed like ten pieces of paper and walked back over, bending down, I gagged a little as I looked at the rat, realizing now that I have definitely lost my appetite for my coffee and its fate is for sure in the garbage now. Holding the paper on the palm of my hand, I drew it down, and picked up the rat, feeling my stomach churn due to the fat that the paper might mask the actual rat-to-hand contact, but it most certainly didn't destroy the feel of loose limbs in my hand. Holding the rat as far from me as possible, I began walking out of the room, with Thunder following. Looking back and forth, I tried finding a room as far away from there as possible, and one that had a door that I could shut. The clicking of Thunder's nails against the floor told me that he was still following as I neared a room at the very far side of the building, I reached out my other hand, and turned the handle of the door, and without looking, as quick as possible I threw the rat into the room, and slammed the door as fast as possible, relieved that nothing more happened, cause quite honestly I DON'T think I could stomach it.

Turning, I looked back to Thunder who was staring right at me with huge-round dark blue eyes. I wasn't exactly sure as to what to think of it. Ignoring the expression he gave me all together, I walked around him and back to the room, glad to have that all done. His paw steps trailing behind me, I walked back to the room, and sat down in my chair, he sat right in front of me, and placed his head right on top of my lap, he looked up at me. I stroked his forehead for a couple minutes, enjoying the moments of silence that I usually don't get when I am home, or anywhere I am usually at for that matter(having to think back to the nights when there are still the sound of cars honking in the distance, and fighting someone definitely isn't the most QUIET thing to be doing). I allowed my mind to drift a little bit, thinking about nothing really in particular. School, work, average stuff, the kind of stuff that really doesn't matter necessarily. Suddenly, my phone rang, and I jumped slightly, making Thunder jump a little bit too, his eyes stretched out to the size of sugar plums, I laughed and patted his head in comfort. Getting up, I walked over to my bag that I must of placed on the far side of the table at one point and grabbed my phone out, opening up, I said "Hello?". I got no answer. Looking back at my phone screen to see if my caller hung up, I realized that it wasn't a call after all and just a text message, from Sam, of course.

I laughed to myself, thinking about when Sam changed my text message settings to a ring, how he got my phone is indeed a mystery that I am going to have to ask him when he gets back, seeing as he probably doesn't have much time to text because of how busy he is going to be, and there is no sense on wasting the time on a stupid text message that is probably going to go nowhere seeing the fact that Sam isn't really into explaining things by texting(curiosity is definitely going to eat me alive for the next week, but oh-well). Opening up the message, the words 'missing me?' appeared on my screen. I had to roll my eyes at that one, and began typing in 'very' hoping he'd 'hear' the sarcasm that rang in that word. Then I went on 'what have you been up to today, have you gotten attacked by a Grizzly-BEAR yet? Ironic would definitely have to be the first words that came into mind as that happened', sending the message, I walked back over to my chair and sat down, looking down towards Thunder who was laying on the ground a few feet away from me, his eyes closed and his nosed tucked into his front paws, he looked like a big baby, it is really one of the cutest things I have seen in awhile. Tapping my fingers against the desk, boredly waiting for a reply text message from Sam(Sam is a pretty slow texter, not that I'm not, but still, then you have to add on the fact that he might still be some-what busy).

After a few minutes or so, I got a reply back, the sound ringing in my ears, I quickly flipped open the phone so that it wouldn't wake up Thunder(if he is even sleeping that is, how can something go to sleep that fast, I have no clue!?). I opened the message up and it read 'ha-ha, very funny. We actually SAW a bear though, not that u would really care, I am sure you r just DIEING 2 tell me about all the exciting things u have been doing for the past couple of days without me. I am sure u went for a nice sweaty jog, followed by some billion loads of laundry, and the occasional ten hour working shifts only to gain minimum wage. Am I right, or REALLY right?'. It MUST be raining there or something, that long of a text message is very uncommon with Sam, and to top it all off he SHOULD be busy doing 'out-doorsy' type stuff, makes me believe even more that he is stuck inside waiting out a storm. Which sort of pops in that question of, shouldn't there be bad reception in a highly wooded area? Or is that just on television? I shook my head, deciding to hold that question to myself, seeing the fact that it was obviously answered by the fact that he is texting me at all!

The sarcasm of his words finally soaked into me, and without thinking another second, I replied back to him with the next words as they flowed through my mind 'very interesting words for someone who probably still has his dad do his laundry, am I right, or am I REALLY right?', the last part, was more or less a mockery of Sam's mockery. Then I thought for a few more moments before sending it, deciding that I should text him something about Thunder, I added 'Anyhow, I found a dog yesterday, named him Thunder, and is rehabilitating him at the very moment, now, when you get back I sha'll get into more specific information, sounds like fun, right?'. I clicked the send button, and then flipped the phone shut and placed it onto the little table.

Closing my eyes, I leaned back into my chair and hummed a little melody to myself out of boredom. Struggling to keep myself awake with my eyes still close has to be a pretty big challenge, especially when I am as exhausted as I am. Giving up, I opened my eyes again, that way there was no chance of me sleeping seeing the fact that my eyes are wide open, though boredom never ceases to leave me either. My mind, some how finding the moment of emptiness as a chance, flipped into thinking about that picture, the picture. I went through each piece of it in my head, having already memorized it inside my mind after the past tens years of looking at it, I had no problem bringing the picture up inside my mind as if it was right there, right in my hands, as clear as daylight. Looking at it inside my head for a couple minutes or so full-filled my boredom for a bit(though whether it replaced it with sorrow is a quite arguable question), but only then did I become conscious of the fact that my attempts at finally seeing what I was missing in the picture, were for nothing because how I memorized it is without actually seeing the part that I want to see, so of course I am not going to suddenly dig up that thing that I am missing from the picture just out of my memory. Stupid, stupid me. The ringing of my phone, drew my attention right back out of my mind and to the physical plain of reality. Grabbing the phone, I flipped it open, still hoping that it didn't wake poor little Thunder up. I opened up the message to see what it read.

'Wow... what did you do, steal him or something?☺' rolling my eyes at the little smiley face, I went on 'it is great... I mean, if U want him is all. where are you keeping him? Wait, don't tell me, I want it 2 b a surprise when I get back from camping. Anyhow, I have gotta go, ttyl!', I yawned, sort of glad that the texting was over so that maybe I can head home and get some sleep. Texting back 'kk, bye', and without another thought I sent it. Clicking my phone shut, and placing it back on the desk, I looked back towards Thunder, who was still, and now most definitely, sleeping away. His snoring finally processing into my conscious mind, it practically echoing off every wall in this room, and probably on the walls in the next rooms. I laughed, hearing it is just too funny because this is the exact type of snore I'd expect from such a BIG dog. Now why anyone would want to have THAT in their house as they try to go to sleep is a HUGE mystery. No matter how much I love an animal, I would not let it keep me up at night all because it has a SNORING problem.

Getting up, I walked a few steps to the side of Thunder that wasn't exactly facing me(his right side to be exact), and bent down and began stroking his head. Even though he was most certainly 'out for the count', his ears still twitched as I rubbed his head. Sitting down next to him, I brought my other hand down towards Thunder and rubbed him also. I yawned, suddenly the cold hard surface below me, right next to a huge, snoring dog seemed to call my name. My eyes felt tired and dreary, and my limbs felt as if they were about to practically fall off. Finally, giving into to the quite.... ODD temptation of it all, I lowered myself closer to the ground and wrapped my arm around Thunder(careful to make sure not to hurt Thunder's cuts, and even not to get whatever bit of dried blood that was still on him on me, I'd have to admit). His snoring felt as is it got louder, but quite frankly, I couldn't have cared less.

Laying my head on top of my other arm for support(and comfort!), I closed my eyes slowly, trying not to think about how very dangerous this is for me to be sleeping in an unlocked abandoned building alone(well, basically alone), on a pretty bad street, and how the only thing that could possibly make this situation worse is if it was at night, and wait, one other thing would be is if I wasn't used to beating up criminal scum at night anyhow. Listening to Thunder snore, made me feel(amazingly enough), safe, in a sort of weird kind of way. Shifting through a whole different list of thoughts, my thoughts kept on feeling more and more blurred as I went along, the effects of the most sure sign of a coming sleep wearing down on me. At one point, I really did feel like I was sincerely on some sort of drug or something at how dull my senses have gotten, but little by little, my thoughts began to flood out, tiredness beckoning me to give in. Finally, I shut out all of my thoughts like someone closing the top of a pot full of steaming water.

CHAPTER 9

Two gun shots rang through my head, misery sweeping inside of me. I screamed, terror washing over me like waves on a beach. This can't be happening, this shouldn't be happening! With a jolt, I opened my eyes yet again to the walls of my room, and Summer sleeping soundly in her bed. It wasn't happening, it already happened. Trying to revert myself back into reality, into the present, I realized that it has been nearly three days since I fell asleep next to Thunder that one day. Today is a Thursday, and so far, Thunder has definitely healed up to an extent that every wound, even the deep neck-wound is scabbed over, some are even beginning to fade away as the skin cells make their way into the area, replacing the scabs. Over all, Thunder is pretty darn healthy, and as for the training, he knows how to sit, stay and follow, so it is indeed good enough for me. Now as for taking him on the walk, I have decided to hold it off until today, thinking about this, made me also realize that today is the day that I promised the others(or was it I promised MYSELF?) to take them to the park today. Maybe they could meet Thunder? Just, maybe though, I don't like the thought of someone snitching on me or anything to Ms.Smith, what they'd gain, I have no clue, Scott might just gain vengeance the more that I think about it though.

Now as for my little 'nights out', I have indeed been going farther and farther, to a point that two nights ago I got lost half way through the night and ended up racking up two other people as I was lost. Other than that, my nights were pretty ordinary, I didn't cross paths with any cops, and thankfully I didn't cross paths with the idiots who seem to have a wolf's head over me(Idiots is just one word of many worse words that I could call them...). Swinging my legs over the edge of the bed, I wiped a bead of sweat off of my forehead with my index finger. Looking over to my alarm clock, the time six sixteen shown on it, a bit too early for a day that I don't have to work or go to school, though seeing the fact that I'd rather not go back into that awful nightmare again I guess it is a reasonable time to wake up.

Walking as quietly as I could, I made my way to the bedroom door, slipped out of the room, and closed the door behind me. Going to the kitchen, I grabbed two eggs and cracked them onto a frying pan to fry up. Grabbing the toaster out, I plugged it in and popped in two pieces of toast. Taking out a plate, I set it down and grabbed a spatula out, flipping the eggs. After a minute or two, I sat down with two pieces of toast, eggs and a glass of orange juice for myself. Grabbing the newspaper that I bought yesterday(and was too lazy to read) off of the countertop behind me, I flipped it open and bit into a piece of toast. The headlines consisted of World-news, that quite frankly, at the moment I didn't care about(not that I ever really did, but besides the point!). Scrolling through the entire newspaper, I was relieved that it had nothing to do with 'The Bandit', then I choked a bit on my own spit in horror, and annoyance once I noticed that the back of the newspaper was filled with it. The title read 'The Bandit: Who is he?', I laughed a forced, slightly devilish laugh at how foolish they are still. Seriously, who is he? Gosh, they are still way farther off of finding the 'truth' than one would think! I mean, obviously Sam and I must be right when we say that there are no cameras, or really crappy cameras, seriously! Plus, you'd think that they would question the criminals too or something, cause there is no way that every single person didn't get a good look at me(I know that for a fact for some MOUTHY ones, Criminal: 'look, it is only a little girl', Me: 'Yeah, a 'little' girl that just got done kickin' your butt to a pulp!'.). Shoveling the last scrap of egg off of my plate and into my mouth, I read on.

Blah, blah, blah, 'Not someone you want to mess with, that's for sure.', blah, blah, blah, 'planning on capturing him sometime to make him talk as to why he is doing it, no one is certain as to what his plan exactly is. All we know for certain is that he is indeed alone at the moment so it can't be too hard of a trial to rope him in', blah, blah, blah, BLAH. Above all, the title didn't exactly match the information in the article, not that journalism ever really does. They are very ill-informed is all I managed to REALLY get from the article, though I guess I do suppose that they must be keeping SOME information that they have away from the public for some very obvious reasons. Rolling my eyes in annoyance towards the stupid article, I crumbled up the newspaper, got up, tossed it into the trash can, and placed my dishes into the dish washer. Going to my room, I opened my door slowly so as not to disturb Summer, grabbed my clothes for the day, and went to the bathroom to get ready. Once I was done with everything, I slipped on my necklace and walked to the living room, at which I heard the faint sound of the Television crackling on. Looking towards the couch, Scott was sitting there, flipping through the channels. Deciding to start the conversation up a bit, I said with as much effort as possible in a cheerful voice "Hey Scott, ready to go to the park today?".

Scott looked up at me, and for sure I saw his eyes roll, but I ignored it. "Yeah, I will get ready as soon as you get the other two up. So, what's your plan for GETTING us there, I know you hate riding in taxis, so do you have any other good ideas for transportation?" he said, very hard to read the emotion in his voice as to whether he is excited and just trying to help, or completely unexcited and is just a huge pain in the butt by coming up with problems in his head just to make it more difficult.

Picking my words wisely, I replied back by saying "We all have two legs that work perfectly fine, I believe we could WALK there. Now, do me a favor, and wake up the other two, I am going to run to the store and pick up a football or something to play with, OKAY?".

"Fine" Scott said with an agitated huff, he got up, and went towards the other two rooms to wake them up. I went over to my purse and grabbed out a couple twenty dollar bills, and shoved them into my jean pocket. Slipping on a pair of flip flops, I headed out. Walking over to the closest convenience store, with the sun beating down on me felt nice. By the time that I got to the store, I could already tell that today was going to be a good day, with how nice the weather is, and having no work so that I could just relax and maybe even have some fun with the others. I walked straight towards the pet supply section, picking out a nice light blue leash and collar for Thunder(deciding that introducing him to the others wouldn't exactly start off too well if the supposedly 'nice dog' I'm introducing them to has skulls on his leash and collar, that just screams violence, not good at all.). Then walked to the sports-type area and grabbed a football, Frisbee, and a kickball(we might have one of these back at the house, and we might even have EVERY one of them, but I'd rather not take any chances). Walking over to the cashier, he rung them up, and placed them all in the bag. I told him to have a nice day, and got the same back in return, then left the store.

Slinging the bag around my right arm, I started with a brisk walk towards the hangout place to retrieve Thunder, ignoring the thought that somehow one of the other three were going to snitch on me. Honestly, I really do hope that they are all BETTER than that, but hoping isn't the same as reality. Once I finally got there, I opened up the window, and jumped right in, deciding to take the chance of getting caught and leaving the window up, I went straight towards Thunder's little area at which I was immediately greeted with a huge bark, followed by the staggering force of impact as he jumped up onto his hind legs and pressed his front legs against me, licking my face. I closed my eyes, and walked back a step to get him off of me. Gross, just really grotesque. Whipping the saliva off of my cheek, I bent down and rubbed his head adding a little "Goood-Boooy" for good measure. Then, I unclipped his old collar and threw it towards the desk, aiming to have it go right on top of the leash, but it missed and slid right passed it, landing with a light thunk on the floor. I rolled my eyes at how bad of an aim I had as I opened up the bag and took out the new leash and collar for Thunder. Opening the collar, I strapped it nicely around Thunder's neck, making sure that it was tight enough, but not too tight that it would hurt him. Clipping the leash up onto the collar I got up, and lightly pulling the leash, Thunder followed without any hesitation, his tail wagging madly with happiness.

As I got to the window, I grabbed Thunder's front paws and placed them through the window, and then I lifted up his back legs, pushing him as hard as I could to get him out. Without any type of movements in protest, Thunder slipped right through and stumbled onto the sidewalk. Quickly, I jumped right through, landing on both feet, and making sure not to land on Thunder. Shutting the window behind me, I lifted my bag up higher onto my shoulder, and grabbed Thunder's leash, then I lead him all the way to my house. As we walked, I noticed how much healthier Thunder is beginning to look, not just the physical healthiness, but just the way his eyes shine, unlike that haunted, abused type look that I saw when I first found him, kind of hard to believe that it has only been less than a week and yet he changed so much!

As I finally neared the door, I heard a scream of excitement coming out from the apartment, and then suddenly the slamming of the front door as it swung open, which had both Thunder and myself taking a quick step back with uneasiness. Summer's eyes were brimming with excitement, as she came running down the steps, stopping when she reached us, me wondering as to how she saw us so fast, just to make sure, I looked quickly at the closest window feeling stunned, not exactly sure how she ran that fast. Laughing I said to Summer as she began rubbing Thunder's head with her hand "You like him, I..." I paused for a brief second, trying to come up with how exactly I was supposed to word it, definitely not something I thought about, thankfully, I don't think she noticed. "FOUND him the other day, he was pretty beaten up too. His name is Thunder, Summer.", I emphasized the 'found' part to get it in her head.

Summer laughed "That is NOT a name for a dog! It is original, I give you that, but definitely not a name for a dog. Name him Bear, or Riley, or even Albern!" she said, I stopped her chattering right there, feeling a bit defensive over the name, I felt the need to explain myself.

"Well.. I named him Thunder, Summer! There is actually a reason for such a name. It was because every time Thunder rumbled on, he barked. So yeah" I said, realizing that my explanation has to be the most crumbiest explanation in the history of explanations! Summer continued stroking Thunder.

"You don't like that awful name, do you buddy?" Summer said, looking down at Thunder and talking in a sort of baby-talk. I rolled my eyes, she was obviously trying to mess with me.

"And who are you, the dog expert?" I said, laughing as Summer began walking back to the house, casting quick glances back towards us every second, we followed. "Anyways" I started, as we finally entered the house, I shut the door behind me with the hand that wasn't clasped around Thunder's leash, the sound of feet pounding against the floors told me that both Scott and Tim were getting ready in their room, "where did that name Albern even come from!? It is most certainly not the first name that comes to mind when naming a dog. ESPECIALLY with someone your age!" I laughed for a quick second, before getting cut off short by Summer's reply(she coughed with dignity as if to tell me to 'shut up'!).

"Actually, during school about a month ago, we had a 'fun' assignment to search up five different names for five different types of animals and their meanings, to show differences between every name. Albern means 'strong warrior' and was the name I looked up for a horse. But I believe it could easily work for a dog, especially this dog, Zoey." Summer looked at me straight in the eyes as if we were complete equals, and in second thought, I suppose we actually are, but still, she has some nerve...

"Oh yeah, I forgot, they are teaching kids about names in English class at the end of the year, my BAD." I laughed, patting Thunder on the head lightly before adding "You almost ready to go to the park, I am going to bring Thunder along too, if you don't mind.". Summer nodded her head excitedly, wiping off that, that mood(???), instantly. Possibly the most interesting change of moods I have ever seen.

"Don't worry, I am all ready, now as for the boys..." Summer broke off, casting her gaze into the direction of their room, I had to laugh a bit as she went on "Could easily be a different story...".

"I'll go check on them, you watch Thunder for me and make sure he doesn't... go anywhere..." I said, not really waiting for a reply, because I know that Summer would be more than happy to hang out with Thunder for a few moments, she is truly an animal lover, as I left, I was practically praying that he doesn't 'relieve' himself anywhere in this house, Ms.Smith would definitely flip if she found out(and seeing that there is definitely a not too hard to persuade available snitch in this house, she

WOULD find out). Once I got to their bedroom door, I was about to knock when the door swung open(thankfully doors point inwards towards the room they come from), and I was almost tackled by Tim. "Woah, watch it there Tim", I said, feeling my eyes grow nearly twice their size as they widened, so many years and yet that sort of stuff still never ceases to surprise me. Isn't THAT amazing, I guess there are some things one never gets used to...

"Sorry! I wanta' go to the park now though!" Tim said, grinning slightly, and once I caught his eyes for a brief second, they quickly shot downwards, poor shy little Tim.

I laughed, to try to ease his flash of shyness that he tends to get every now and then, "So that means you are ready, right?" I said, throwing my glance back to Scott who was sitting on his bed, dressed in day clothes as he promised, throwing a ball against the wall, catching it, and then doing it again.

"Yeah" Tim said, in the background, the loud echo of Thunder's bark could be heard, just one large bark. "What's that!?" Tim asked, trying to look past me as if he'd be able to see the thing the sound came from right there behind me. Not a shot seeing as how weak the sound was, but he is just a kid I suppose.

"Go find out, Summer is with him near the front door." I said, letting Tim through and then looking back towards Scott, as he continued to throw the ball as if time continued unchanged throughout the whole couple of minutes(or so). "Now Scott, you are ready, right?" I said, taking another step through the doorway. A couple seconds went by without a reply, I rolled my eyes and said "If you don't want to go, you don't have to go, remember this is for YOU guys, not really me, I am just happy buying a coffee at the coffee shop and sitting down with my computer. And if you are just fine here, then there is no reason for me to drag you all the way out to practically 'torture' you.". He stopped throwing the ball.

"Sorry, I was just thinking.." Scott said without another word of explanation, he got up and walked out. So STRANGE! With a huff, I followed right out, walking back to where Summer was petting Thunder with Tim looking on curiously from a couple of feet away. Scott was bouncing the kickball that I just bought up and down against the floor, with no hint of even the slightest bit of interest in his eyes.

“Okay” I said, slightly glad that Scott didn’t have anything to say about having a dog around here, I grabbed my purse and made sure that there was enough money in it to buy some food with. Then walking over to the kitchen, I grabbed some bottles of water, some for drinking, the other one for Thunder to drink when he gets thirsty also(he’ll just have to lap it up as I pour it…), walking back I went on “everything is set?”, I grabbed the foot ball and Frisbee, giving one to Tim to hold(the football), and then giving little Thunder the Frisbee(he bit into it happily, his tail began whipping back and forth like a fish out of water, a bit amusing if I do say so myself). They all nodded, I opened the door, and we all exited the place.

As we walked, Summer gave me the leash because she said how she fears that she’d somehow let go of the leash and Thunder would run away, though I had no doubt that he wouldn’t, I grabbed the leash anyways because it looked as if it made Summer tense up a bit and I didn’t want her stressed out just because of walking a dog(quite absurd, actually).

By the time we got to the park(which I have to admit, it felt like ages, and Scott’s notion was probably more right than my own..), our mouths were pretty dry, and only then did I remember that I packed some bottles of water, making sure that my face expression was apologetic, I took out the water bottles from my purse and threw one to each person, then I grabbed one out for myself, guzzling down about half of it in a little more than three seconds. Capping it, I placed it back into my purse and grabbed out another for Thunder, pouring some right out in front of his mouth, he was able to catch on quickly and lapped it up with his tongue. Turning to the others, I got out some money and handed it to Scott, "You and Tim can go to the stands right there" I pointed to where they were, straight in sight so that I could still WATCH them "and get yourselves something to eat, get something for Summer also, please.".

Scott rolled his eyes(possibly at how I was sort of 'ordering' him to do that) but didn't say another word, instead he just nodded, and went towards the stands, with Tim hard on his heels. Sitting down right on a huge root of a tree(possibly an Oak tree), I watched as Summer began rubbing Thunder's head, and then trying to grab the Frisbee out of his mouth(without succeeding), then went back to Scott and Tim, who were just now getting in line at a hotdog stand, with about five other people in front of them, but they still surprisingly didn't seem to mind. Just then did I actually began to realize the huge glares I was getting from numeral people who were hanging out too. Looking up at the tree, I felt as if maybe there was like yellow caution tape around it, as if something happened here, but there was none. Looking back to the people around me, I still felt those glares coming straight at me like heat waves radiating off the fire place in the winter. Finally, the bitterness of it all hit me, these people have some honest issues because it must be the fact of all of our different races(Scott and Tim are both of Cuban dissent, while Summer is African American, and I Caucasian), I scowled in annoyance at this, when people see three different age groups hanging out together of different races, they begin to create conclusions, very false conclusions to be exact. People honestly have to get a life, and stop nosing in on other people's business, I mean serious! Catching the eyes of one of the people who were glaring at me, I made sure to smile back, to make him feel like a complete fool. And as I figured, his gaze dropped, and though it was at a slight-distance, I am pretty sure his face flushed with embarrassment, good.

When someone glares at me, I make sure to make them feel uncomfortable by smiling back, because in all honesty, it either makes them feel foolish for being so cruel, or fires up their anger even more, which are both pretty darn good vengeance in my book. Now about the whole glares n' all, all I could think about is the fact that this world is sincerely messed up, in more dimensions than one. Glancing back to Tim and Scott(who are now second in line), I made sure that they were completely unphased from the glares that we were all receiving, they definitely seemed it. Taking a swift look back to Summer, I knew for certain that she didn't notice yet because she was too busy trying to get the Frisbee out of Thunder's mouth(still wouldn't budge.), so she might not end up noticing it all, very good thing indeed. Getting up, I walked right towards Summer and said "Here let me try". She glanced up at me and laughed. "What!?" I said, almost defensively. Now, why on Earth would she be laughing!? There doesn't seem to be anything funny going on right about now, but if she is laughing at me, she is lost and won't get that Frisbee, I can guarantee it.

"You can try." Summer said, amusement twinkling in her eyes. I had to roll my eyes at that, whether she was complementing(?) Thunder's strength, or degrading my own, I am definitely not too certain, but that most certainly sounded like a challenge, even if it was from a little girl that hasn't even hit double-digits when it comes to her age, it is still a challenge, and a challenge is something I'd rather not back down from(dork, I know, but still, I really can't, something drives me to complete it, oddly enough...).

"Trying in my book is equivalent to succeeding, watch young Summer" I said with a bemused laugh, taking one quick glance at Scott and Tim(who are now getting their 'order' in), I bent down onto my knees and got face to face with Thunder. Grabbing a good grip on the Frisbee, I started to pull. A low growl came out from Thunder throat, but hoping that that growl is mostly a playful growl and not an aggressive growl, I kept going. His jaw was locked around the Frisbee, obviously using his old 'pit-bull locked-jaw' to his advantage, so instead of wasting all my energy on an already foiled plan, I did the next idea that popped into my mind that would still count as getting the Frisbee out of his mouth, and tickled his nose a bit with my left hand, Thunder sneezed and I pulled the Frisbee right out(of course all good plans come with even better back-fires, for I flung back plowing my head right into the ground), I huffed, getting up and dusting my pants off from all the dirt that was on them. "Here ya' go" I said to Summer pretty smugly as I handed her the Frisbee. Summer's eyes narrowed into playful skepticism.

"You are such a cheat Zoey!" she said, as she grabbed the

Frisbee and wiped it off(probably from all the saliva that was ONCE in Thunder's mouth.). I laughed for a second, then decided to reply back.

"Not really, you specifically told me that I could 'try' to get the Frisbee out of Thunder's mouth, you didn't really necessarily included HOW I'd go about doing it, so yes, I have indeed succeeded." I laughed, sticking my tongue out at her afterwards for good measure. Summer rolled her eyes, clearly trying to hold back a laugh. Thunder barked several times then waged his tail, turning around I saw Scott and Tim heading back over here, with two paper-trays full of food(I debated whether or not they knew not to blow all of the money just because I gave it to them). Once they got over, Scott and Tim set them down on a picnic table near us. Scott came over to me and held out some dollar bills.

"Here, we spent about half off the amount of money you gave us" Scott said, dropping it in my hand. "We bought four hotdogs, two large fries and an apple incase you don't want to eat a hot dog.".

I laughed "Yeah, I am not that hungry at the moment, you got me there. I bet you or one of the other two can finish off that extra hotdog with no problem" I said, as we walked over to a table and sat down, Tim opened his mouth as if he was about to speak, but Scott beat him to the punch.

"Sounds good to me, I guess I could fit in a second hotdog" Scott said, as he shoved Tim with his elbow, signifying that he realized what Tim was about to say. Deciding that it would be best not to interfere with the two siblings, and that they could debate it out with each other, I took the apple that they got me and bit into it, the usual tartness filling my mouth. After wrapping Thunder's leash up around a tree, Summer made her way towards us and sat down, her eyes still on Thunder as if someone was going to steal him or something. A mutt?! No way would anyone actually want to steal Thunder, even if his German shepherd origins is pretty visible, that doesn't take away the effect of him being half pit-bull also. Catching Summer's eyes, I shook my head, signaling that she really didn't have to worry about anyone stealing Thunder, now as for someone getting mad at how she tied him up to a tree like that, I have no clue. Summer seemed a bit hesitant, but before long began eating her hotdog. Taking a couple more bites of my apple, I looked around, taking a good look at my surroundings, all of the people jogging through the park, playing catch or just plain hanging out. Come to think of it, people watching is possibly the most 'interesting' thing anyone could do in a New York City park. Biting into the apple again, I scanned the whole crowd in front of me(still, every now and then gaining myself a glare), finally my eyes rested on one person in particular, which seemed to have sent chills going right through my back.

The guy had shades on, a fire seemed to have set off inside my head and I might be a bit paranoid at the moment seeing the fact that it is in the middle of the day, with the sun high up above us, it's indeed pretty common for someone to wear sunglasses on a day like today. But it seems like he is looking at me! His head was slightly crooked in a way that if you drew a line from his eyes, to me, it would be a direct angle. Keeping calm, I kept on watching him, seeing if maybe I was clearly paranoid, maybe I'm truly not being watched, I mean, being paranoid does those sort of things to you. Maybe he is looking for someone, and I happen to be in his path. Just then, my heart seemed to have dropped a hundred stories down as I saw him smirk, a very wicked smirk. It might of simply been because of the whole moment, but within a second, I saw him nod. A single, small, quick nod, that might of or might not of happened. Then he just walked away, I found my eyes tracing his every move until he was lost in the crowd. My mouth felt dry, and my eyes were stinging for how long they were opened for. Forcing my eyes closed, a thousand horrific thoughts flooded my mind, during that one second of closing my eyes. I gulped and shot my eyes open to try and block out the thoughts, I felt like my heart was pounding a thousand beats per second(obviously not).

"Zoey?!" Summer said, knocking me back into reality(well, at least out of my thoughts). "Are you even listening?", her voice seemed to be surprised as if she thought I was listening to what ever she was talking about, with a thick coat of annoyed, and a pinch of worriedness. Trying to flush out what ever horrific expression was on my face at the moment, before I turned back to them, I forced a quick smile, making sure to try and make it look as if I was 'caught' not listening.

"Whoops, sorry, what were you saying?" I said, biting the last bit of my apple and then wrapping the core up in a napkin.

"She was wondering about what we were going to do next" Scott said, roughness in his tone of voice as he butt into the conversation, he MUST know that something is up. Summer nodded in gratitude at Scott, obviously believing that Scott was on her 'side', which is mostly untrue, seeing the fact that Scott really isn't on a 'side', he is just always against me. Scott turned slightly, but I was still able to catch a quick roll of the eyes. I huffed in annoyance, the thought of it all burning inside me, yelling at me to get the heck out of here because I am probably putting the others in danger, but I have to stay calm. Common logic says that whoever is watching me isn't planning on going ballistic on me in public, because he/she/THEY are probably not on the government's good side, seeing if they really wanted to rat me out, they would have already, no, if someone has a secret/criminal record, they don't get the government's attention drawn onto them. Too bad common logic isn't able to swallow up complete and utter fear. I took in a deep breath.

"We can throw the football or Frisbee around, or we can even kick the kickball around" I said, not even bothering to try and make it sound appealing, because in all honestly, I feel sick to my stomach and I just want to go home and lay down forever until my troubles magically disappear(the awful thing about WANTING or HOPING for something is possibly the fact that it is sometimes just a constant reminder of the predicaments one is in). Tim coughed, his eyes drawing over right towards the football.

"Football" he said almost in a rushed tone, my guess to 'beat' Scott to the decision. My thoughts still very well crowded and blurred out, I decided to save myself the agonizing pain and I just nodded in reply.

*   *   *

After a whole day of strictly hanging out and throwing either the football, Frisbee or even kicking the kickball around, I was more than glad when we started back to the apartment at eight o'clock(approximately), and even gladder once we got back to home-sweet-home, for more than one reason that is. Yes, I was indeed exhausted and quite frankly pretty darn bored with the limited amount of events I had planned, but that aching feeling that we were being watched freaked me out and made me feel like a complete stranger on the streets I have grown used to(I made sure to stay behind of everyone, dreadful thoughts kept on turning through my head about one of them lagging behind). Plus, there was that chilling moment when I went to grab my keys to unlock the door and I felt the glaring eyes of someone watching me, and as soon as I turned around, there wasn't a single person on the streets in front of me(within a reasonable distance, of course there were people on the street, just not within ten yards of where I stood, not much, but enough!). So now, at the very moment, I wait with Thunder on my lap for Summer to say goodnight to him so that I could bring him back to the place(and take part in my usual night schedule, whether I really want to actually do it tonight, definitely a different story, at which I'd probably have to include the fact that I am not going to be lingering around in the same area for any huge amount of time.). Which, note to self, I should lock the door tonight, and bring my key with me, just to make sure....

"Do you have to take him back, can't he just stay here for tonight at least!?" Summer said, making me jump slightly at how close she was able to get towards me, to a point at which she was sitting cross-legged in her pajamas on the couch next to me, without me even noticing. Summer's face expression looked perplexed "You okay? I mean, if you want I can come with you if you are really that afraid of the dark.".

I felt the impulse to quickly blurt out 'NO!', but thankfully I was able to catch myself. "No Summer, I will be fine, thanks for asking though..." I paused for a quick second, but just to make sure I added "And um, promise me you won't come out looking for me, stay in bed, okay?".

"OF COURSE she will, she is used to it by now." Scott's voice crackled through the room as he stood in front of us, his arms crossed as if some sort of injustice has been brought down on him. He narrowed his eyes, as if ordering me to give in and tell him what exactly I do every night, or to admit that he is most definitely right. If he wasn't a kid, I'd probably have gotten in a couple fist-fights with him by now (and leg-fights, and what ever else I could use to harm him), of course this is all just my worst side speaking(though one could definitely not get any more worse I'd have to say...). Summer looked up to Scott, almost with uncertainty, but finally she looked back to me and nodded.

"M'kay then, say goodbye to Thunder, you'll probably see him tomorrow." I said getting up(plus moving the huge dog off of my lap also) and walking over to the kitchen which we left the leash on one of the counter tops. Grabbing it, I walked back over to Summer hugging Thunder on the couch. The dog's tongue was lolling out, and his mouth was positioned in a way that it was as if he was smiling. I stifled back a laugh at the picture I was seeing, and maneuvered my hand with the clip of the leash in it around Summer's arms so that I could hook it on

Thunder's collar.

"Had fun today Zoey" Scott broke in, surprisingly, I looked up and nodded in appreciation at how he lightened up. One last thing I'd have to worry about tonight I suppose. "Summer, stop hugging the mutt so that Zoey can take him back to the, um, place" Scott added, his voice half-joking and half-serious. Summer stopped hugging Thunder and got up off of the couch.

"Remember when I told you guys how I wanted a pure-bread dog when I turned 18" Summer said, we both nodded in reply, pretty sure where this was going "Well, now I know the breed I want, a hybrid just like Thunder". Ah, yes, Summer's vocabulary skills exceeds the normal criteria for a little girl her age, mostly when it comes to anything about animals, because I don't believe that the word 'hybrid' is a term usually used by seven year olds. I laughed a short laugh.

"German-shepherd, pit-bull mix, that is a very interesting bread to desire, but of course, anything for a day that special, hmm?" I said, tugging on the leash slightly to get Thunder up and off of the couch(and really wishing that he didn't shed too much on the couch).

Thunder got up and jumped off of the couch, and walked right up next to me and looked up at me as if this was his basic routine. “Have a nice night you guys and don’t stay up too late, I am not positive as of when I am going to come back, it’s a long walk” I said, walking toward the door with Thunder’s leash in one hand, and picking up my keys on the way from the kitchen with my other hand. I could have sworn I heard the agitated exhale of Scott in the background, but one really can’t be so sure. I opened the door as I walked through it, and making sure Thunder was still right by my side, I closed the door behind me. Natural light is just beginning to disappear from the streets around me, signifying to me that I was basically right on my usual time frame.

Scanning the area around me, I still kept on feeling those creepy-chills that someone gets when they believe someone is watching them. But there was still nothing, and actually no one anywhere(the streets on my block get abandoned earlier in the night than the commercial streets in New York City.). Making my way down the stairs, I held my breath, the thought of being attacked still rang through my mind. But nothing happened. Clenching my left hand(the hand that was free of the leash) into a fist(puncturing it a bit due to the key in my hand, but I ignored it), in case I did need to punch someone all of a sudden, I began a medium-pace jog, with Thunder keeping up just fine. The thoughts of police cars patrolling the streets managed to run through my mind, but at the moment, that is the last thing that is on my mind(though, not TOO far behind). After a little bit, I finally got to the place, realizing my speed increased dramatically as I went on, then making Thunder's speed increase also, I had to do a turn-around that way when I stopped I wasn't yanked off my feet by the running Thunder. Cracking the window open, I swiftly grabbed Thunder's front paws and draped them through the window, then his back paws up off of the ground, and he went right into the window. Deciding that it wouldn't hurt if I spent a few more minutes with Thunder(and to check his food and water bowls), I jumped in after him. Thunder made sure to get out of the way, but looked out of the window longingly. I stroked his head lightly in comfort.

Pulling his leash for him to follow, I made my way to the room, and flipped on the light as soon as possible(don't want to be followed is all...). Unclipping the leash from his collar, I set it down onto the table, then I went towards his bowls, and filled them both up with some food and water. Thunder hurried his way to the food bowl and began devouring it, seeing my time to leave guilt-free, I patted Thunder on the head(he didn't even flinch to recognize me) and turned off the light(dogs should be able to see in the dark as well as people do, so he should be able to suffice with shadows of the figures of objects to guide him.). Then I made my way to the window, stopping to look out of it before I jump, a huge bark rang through my ears. Startled I turned around to see Thunder looking at me, whimpering. "Weren't you just eating a second ago?!" I whispered, not really looking for a reply from a dog, I turned back to the window and surveyed the area around me, rechecking every single area at least three times, before I decided that the coast was clear. Rubbing Thunder on the head for a few moments(the guilt undoubtfully finding me), I placed my key into my shoe, and jumped through the window, landing on both feet with a thud, I turned back to the window, and shut it, with Thunder still whimpering behind it. I sighed, deciding that this would be the reason why I'd never buy myself a dog, I blew Thunder a kiss, not really making him feel better but it helped when covering up my guilt, and began running from the building, so that maybe he'd stop whimpering and feeling bad if he didn't see me. My eyes wide open and alert, I slowed to a jog to see exactly what was going on in the area around me. Any crime? YES, there always is. Can I detect it? Not at the moment...

Just then, I heard the cry of a baby(I think?). Stopping myself right then and there, I listened again, drawing my full attention on my sense of hearing. Faint, but definitely the cry of a baby. Trying to focus in on the sound, I began walking in the same direction I was heading, seeing if the intensity of the sound changed at all. Slowly, it began to get louder and louder. Finally, as I neared an alley, I was almost positive that it was going to be in that alley(why? I have no clue…). Poking my head around the corner, I saw nothing but the shadows of a huge alley in front of me. With a huge gulp, I made my way into the alley, the sound getting louder and louder. As I finally got to the end of it(another building blocking my way), I looked down and saw the baby, wrapped up in a blanket. I bent down, to remove the blanket from its face, and when I did, I looked at it:

The baby is fake, just a plastic baby doll wrapped up in a blanket, probably a stupid prank of some sort. Scanning my eyes down the baby, there was a sticky note on it, I squinted my eyes to see what it read: YOU'VE BEEN TRAPPED.

CHAPTER 10

The breath knocked out of me as something whacked me in the head, I fumbled to try and regain myself, another blow managed to make its way onto my face, my eyes wide as I try to get up, the taste of blood, and dirt heavy in my mouth, I flailed my arms to try and gain a hold on solid ground. I raked the ground with my hand, finally. Too late, another blow knocked me up against my head, landing me right up against a wall. Pushing my hands naturally up against the wall, I got up to try and see exactly what was going on. In front of me, stood a man. In his hand, there was a gun, and I looked down into the depths of the barrel of that very gun. My lungs screaming at me, air couldn't come soon enough as I inhaled and exhaled my breath. All I really can think about, is how I just hope it's fast and easy. In the very low light, I tried to make out who exactly my killer is going to be. He had sunglasses on, and right then and there, he smirked.

"I know you" I said, my words coming out a little more than a breath.

"Wow, aren't you smart?" he said, sarcastically. My eyes narrowed in on him, safe to say that his smirk connects him to the park, what else can I connect him to? I looked for any distinguished features that might define him as to who he is in any shape or form.

"Why don't you just shoot me already?" I said, trying to buy myself some time. There is no way that he would wear the shades without knowing that I know who he is. I just want to know now, the reason why I have been afraid for the past two weeks out of my mind. He has to be the reason.

"Because I am not the one." he said, plainly. The gun sticking straight out at me, he had to be a little more than two yards away from me, MAYBE. Excuses, excuses. He must be just a handy man of the guys, here to get me, but not kill me, he must have been ordered to do so, why, that question has to be answered sooner or later, right? I gulped, there still can't be a single person in the whole world that could stare down the barrel of a gun and not be scared out of their mind, now I am honestly beginning to miss the ruthless meat-heads that I have to fight fist-to-fist against every night, to this guy holding a gun. I want to say that I should have had a gun on me, I mean, that is the obvious smart choice to do, and I wouldn't be in this situation(he's not meant to kill me, but that doesn't me he won't shoot my foot, or something, causing excruciating pain, and probably keeping me right here), but then again, there is also the whole fact that I'd probably would have gotten in a situation like this with one of the ruthless meat-heads, only it would be MY gun that the meat-head would be holding, not his own. Trying to come up with a plan inside my head now(because trying to figure out just who he is, I come up blank), a tear rolled down my cheek as I thought of the consequences of what would happen if the plan that I create becomes an utter-failure. I felt my heart beat like a base drum in a fast-pace orchestra as I tried to come up with the best plan. I come up blank.

Biting back the thought of defeat, I said "Care to explain?", trying to see if he is gullible enough to actually tell me more information, for maybe, in some way I can get away from him and escape with the information. He shook his head slowly, obviously keen as to what I was trying to do. It was worth a try.

I looked straight into his sunglasses, practically begging him to take them off. I squinted my eyes as a couple more tears streamed out of them, I tried to un-blur my vision by doing so. As I did so, I heard the boom of a gun shot, expecting to feel unbearable pain within a second, I flashed open my eyes to see the last image of life in front of me, but was more than surprised when I heard the thud of the guy, and to see THUNDER on top of him! The skidding of the gun ran out of the corner of my eye, I bolted towards it and picked it up, the sound of growling and yelling ringing through my ears. Slowly, I made my way towards the flailing ball of fur and skin, and grabbed a hold of Thunder, pulling the growling dog off of him by his collar, I held the gun directly at the gunman. Thunder's fur was straight up and on end, anger radiating off of him like no other dog I have ever seen before, it all didn't quite make sense, but I ignored it.

"GET UP!" I yelled, making sure to stick the gun up right

towards him, in plain sight so that he would be able to see my little warning. I backed up a couple feet more, so that there was no way that he could attack me and get the gun out of my hands without fair warning of his aggressing. The figure staggered up, and even in the very low light I could see the blood oozing down from multiple cuts on his forehead. Miraculously, he still had his shades on. What were they, super-glued onto him for Pete-sake!?

"WHY are you here?!" I said, dropping my voice a good lump some so that we didn't attract any unwanted nosy people here. Thunder continued to pull on his collar as I held him there, his barking loud and vocal. He was truly infuriated. After a moment of no reply, I spat out "ANSWER ME, or you get attacked by this dog, or shot by this gun, your choice" I gestured to both of them as I said the words.

"You better hurry" was all that he said, casting a quick glance behind him, towards the streets, then back to me. A chill ran through my back.

"ANSWER ME." I said, trying to pull off a strong voice, but I am pretty sure it ended up shaky.

He just smirked again, then said "You better hurry". That was it, as I saw the flashing of lights in the distance, I realized just what he met. That son of the devil. This plan, was far too well planned out, and I don't care what someone would say, it's just plain unfair, not right at all.

Now, the gun I held in my hand began to shake, and I stuttered "Move to the wall, now". He walked casually to the wall, and almost to make a point, he waved at me. Keeping my gun pointed towards him, I began running out of the alley, and until I was able to make it out, I kept my eyes right on him. Once I was out, I sprinted with Thunder in the opposite direction that the police were coming(wiping off the finger prints from the gun and dropping the gun), drawing every last ounce of energy from every single muscle. As the lights began closing in on me, I felt the world in front of me begin spinning, it might have been from the wounds inflicted on me, or just the thought of being caught, maybe even bother, either way, I kept on bucking for it, and was more than relieved when the lights stopped getting closer, signifying to me that the car stopped and is investigating. Turning around the corner, I still kept on running, my speed slowing down by the moment as I did so, but I continued to go as fast as I could until I finally got to the place where I was keeping Thunder. I stopped, as glass crunched under my shoes, someone obviously broke in, it definitely wasn't Thunder who opened the window, and must of broke the glass in the process. I gulped as I tried to imagine who would have done something like that, definitely a robber, or maybe a druggee, either way, I am still in their debt because they are probably the reason why I am alright. But I can't leave Thunder here, not when someone broke in.

With a sigh, done with all that happened tonight, I grab on harder to Thunder's collar, and decided to walk the way home(partial was because of the fact that the wounds are still making me feel dizzy to an extent that I probably will fall if I try to pick up the pace again). There is no way that I'd be able to save someone other than myself tonight, even if I wanted to, and quite honestly, all I want to do, is go home, and go to sleep. Steadying myself with the railing, I grabbed the key out of my shoe, and opened the door, pushing Thunder in, I shut the door behind me, and locked it. My breath heavy, I let go of Thunder, and made my way to the bathroom, shutting it then turning on the light, I looked into the mirror to see what kind of damage was done this time. Small scratches were raked along my cheeks and forehead, a huge bruise on the top of my forehead underneath all of my hair that was out of my pony tail. Spitting out blood from my mouth into the sink, I realized that I must of bit my tongue during the whole thing, because it was the part of my mouth that was the most bloodied, and now that I think of it, it hurts a lot also. Rubbing my hand across my forehead, trying to wick away the sticky sweat, I managed to get a huge blood smear across my forehead. Looking at my hand, I noticed that the same spot at which I had scratches on last time, had been cut open yet again. Saving myself the time, and effort to try and clean up with the sink. I turned on the water, and got ready to take a shower. I turned off the light and opened the bathroom door and peered out to see what Thunder was doing, a light flashed off from one of the rooms telling me that I might of accidentally woke one of them up, but seeing as I told them part of what I was going to do, I didn't worry about it. I couldn't see Thunder anyway, and figuring as long as I didn't hear him, it was alright.

Going back in, I closed the door behind me and turned on the light yet again, and went to go take a shower. The warm water stung every single scratch I had on me(mostly on my head, because it wasn't much of a rough-and-tumble fight due to that lovely, sarcasm of course, gun.). As for the gaping scratch on my hand, it seared with intense pain, but of course, above all, it felt good to get all of the blood, sweat, and dirt off of me. After showering I got dressed into my pajamas and went to my bed. After a hour or so of staring up at the ceiling above me, terrified and blown out of my mind as what happened this night, I finally was able to close my eyes, and kick out most of the bad thoughts.

* * *

"ZOEY!" my eyes shot open to Summer looking straight down at me. My eyes groggy and filled with sleep I looked at the clock that read ten thirty five, work in three hours.

"WHAT?" I said, getting up, and swinging my legs over the bed, Summer backed away a foot.

"There is blood trailing from the door to the bathroom, and Thunder is here, and he made a mess of the kitchen! What on Earth happened last night?" Summer said, her eyes glancing me up and down. SHOOT. I forgot entirely about Thunder! I hope he isn't injured! Then there is the fact that I forgot to wipe away any traces of blood from the floor, probably from my hand... As I tried to figure out an excuse for what happened, Summer looked right at me, her patience must be dwindling down, she wants to know, she looks a bit worried as to what happened.

SO I figure, wing it, she is just a seven year old girl, she doesn't need every detail, right?

"Well, when Thunder and I were walking, we were attacked by someone. I think he was trying to rob me or something, luckily Thunder was there to attack him back." I said, getting off of my bed and standing up to stretch, every muscle in my body ached in protest, must have been that sprint. Never again will I push myself that much.

"Are YOU alright" Summer said, not sure if she bought it, but I guess it doesn't matter at the moment. Alright? Not necessarily the word that comes to mind when I think about the condition I am in at the moment, but yeah, I suppose I'll go with that then.

"Yeah, just stunned is all. I guess I was too tired to clearly think last night" I said, walking towards the bathroom, and as I expected there were drops of blood leading to it. I huffed in annoyance, hopefully is didn't soak into the flooring and stained it...

"She already came back and is sleeping now, I don't think she noticed" Summer said.

"Who?" I said, then I answered my own question in my head, I then added as Summer's mouth gaped open slightly "Oh yeah, Ms.Smith, my bad...", clearly I am not thinking right at the very moment either. Walking into the bathroom, I grabbed a towel and wetted it down. Crouching down on my hands and knees, I whipped away the blood from the tiles in the bathroom quite easily. Then I went onto the carpet in the hallway, after scrubbing the blood for a couple minutes, I finally got it out, then I went along the trail, scrubbing and scrubbing again, until I finally got to the hardwood flooring(type of wood is indeed a mystery), I was able to wipe it all off within a minute. Walking over to the laundry bin, I threw the towel away into there, and went back to where I left Thunder last. He made a mess on the floor, along with some old ripped up newspaper but other than that, as far as I could see, he was a good boy. The hunk of fur laid sprawled out across the kitchen floor underneath the table, I allowed him to stay asleep after what he did for me last night. I have to thank him for that. Walking over to the cupboard, I grabbed a bowl out and filled it with water from the sink, and placed it on the ground near Thunder so he could drink when he gets up.

Grabbed a garbage bag and lots of paper towels(along with some disinfectant spray of course), I cleaned up the mess Thunder made, throwing it all away, I went back to Summer. "Anything else you saw?" I asked. She looked up towards me from where she was sitting on the couch.

"Nope. That's it." she said, going back to her television, as if it was really no big deal(usual seven year old stuff of course, I can't even hope that Scott would care the same way that she did. After he sees the scratches and bruises, I am definitely going to have to take a good amount of questions.). Walking back over to the kitchen, I decided not to worry about it for now, and grabbed the chocolately cereal out(which was probably about seventy five percent gone) and poured myself a bowl. Grabbing the milk, I poured it into the bowl, grabbed a spoon and began eating. Almost on cue, I began hearing my stomach growling which seemed to remind me just how hungry I really am. So, shoveling in the last couple of scoops, I poured myself another bowl, making sure to savor it more than the last bowl, but still eating it pretty fast, above all, I felt like a huge slob once I finished but so full that I really didn't care. Putting things away, Scott came in, and stupid me, I turned around once I felt his presence shifting through the cereals, and immediately he looked up and noticed the scratches.

"What happened?" he said, as he brought the cereal that he grabbed out onto the table, his eyes dropping down to Thunder, catching a glance at him, and then back to me, well, actually back to my scratches. Worriedness definitely isn't what was on his mind when he said it, or not even suspicion, more interest than anything else(though there still might be some suspicion in there also).

"Someone attacked me when I was walking with Thunder, thankfully Thunder was there to attack him back." I said, Scott's eyes narrowed almost as if he knew that that wasn't what happened, as expected of course. "Don't believe me? Well then, honestly Scott that is your problem" I retorted back.

"Of course it is." Scott said dryly, he rolled his eyes as he went to go get milk, then he got himself a bowl and spoon, pouring the milk and cereal. I watched as he scooped a mouthful of cereal into his mouth, then he added "So, what is on your agenda for today? Can we get that video game?".

"Yes, only if you get ready now, we'll leave in fifteen minutes" I said, slightly stunned as to how he changed the subject like that. Better than more questions I suppose.

"Will do" Scott said, looking back towards me, then he added, scrolling his eyes up and down along me "You ARE going to clean up all those scratches before we go, right?".

I subconsciously moved my other hand straight towards my huge scar along my arm. Realizing what I just did, I dropped both of them and said "Of course", and left the kitchen to my room. Grabbing my day-clothes that I was going to wear today, I turned on my laptop, then headed to the bathroom. Walking in and shutting the door behind me, I changed into the clothes and grabbed the necklace that I usually wore and latched it onto my neck quickly. Then I turned to the mirror to examine the scratches, a couple of them must of bled during the night, because there were smears all over my face. Grabbing a small wash cloth from the cabinet sink, I dampened it, and then began to pat away the dried blood little by little until finally all that was left were the scratches themselves. Squeezing the water out of the cloth, I went to the laundry basket and threw it in. Then I went back to my room, and typed in the password to my laptop, grabbing the laptop from the desk, and plunking down onto my bed. Reaching over to grab my phone off the charger, and the USB port that hooks up to the computer and the cell phone, hooking them up, the computer finally flashed on all of the way. Logging on to the usual website, I went straight towards the picture, and uploaded it to my phone(took forever, but I managed to crack the code in order to do such a thing), deciding that if I am going to have to ride in a very unpleasant speeding taxi cab for minutes on end, and then stand inside a video game shop for who knows how long, then at least I could make some sort of good use out of it and examine the photo and see what I can find. Once it was complete, I unplugged it from the computer, placed the USB port back where I had it, and turned my computer off. I slipped my phone into my pocket, then walked over to the desk and placed my computer on it, making sure to plug it into the charger to juice it up a bit.

It had to have been at the very least fifteen minutes already, so, walking out of my room, I made my way towards Scott's room and knocked on the door several times before the door finally opened and Scott stood in front of me, dressed up and ready to go. Just in case though I asked "You ready?".

Scott nodded, "Yep" he said, as we walked out of the room, I turned back into my room, grabbed some money and a purse, then walked back out, taking my phone out of my pocket, and placing both the phone and money into the purse. By the time I did so, Scott was already all the way to the front door, waiting. I walked over to Summer, who was still sitting on the couch watching television.

"Mind if you watch Thunder and Tim for me while Scott and I are gone? We shouldn't be too long seeing the fact that I do have to go to work soon, and I'd probably get fired if I was late. I much rather keep my job" I laughed at the last part, making sure to persuade her the best way I could, with good humor.

"Yeah, I guess I will." she said, then she glanced over towards Scott near the front door "is Tim still asleep, cause' I don't really wanta have to entertain him or anything.". Scott nodded in reply, he then looked back towards the door like he was really anticipating going to get that game he wanted.

"Thanks, be back soon" I said, walking over to the door, Scott opened it and exited.

I was about to shut the door when I heard "WAIT!" Summer

came running towards me then stopped in front of me, Scott tapped his foot against the ground in frustration and a dwindling patience. I looked towards her with curiosity, not sure as to how I really should react to a seven year old girl running towards me screaming 'wait!' as I exit to outside. "That reminds me, where did you put Thunder's leash, I can't find it anywhere!?". I felt as if my face flushed red with embarrassment within that moment, ug, I forgot the leash! How could I be so foolish as to forget the leash from the place!? Now, how on Earth am I going to explain it? I suppose the obvious way. I took in a short breath.

"Hmmm, I don't know, forgot, sorry. I'll look for it once I have time, k?" I said, Summer laughed at how 'forgetful' I was, Scott coughed behind me, as if saying that he wanted to go. "See you later then Summer, okay? As the one in charge for the next hour or so, I expect you to be good, okay?".

Summer nodded, then I turned around and shut the door behind me, hoping for no more interruptions, Scott and I made our way to the nearest area where there'd be taxis around, in the direction of the school(MY school, not his that is). A decent distance to walk isn't too bad, especially what comes after it(the worst type of ride in history).

Scott and I didn't talk the whole way, it was complete silence between the both of us, and though it was probably my imagination, it felt sort of like Scott kept on making quick glances towards me, but not long enough for me to accuse him of looking at me in any type of moodiness. No talking, I am definitely okay with it. Being alone with my thoughts is always good, especially after what happened last night(kept both of my fists clenched just in case history repeats itself).

That guy, totally felt like he had something over me, just how he calmly said things gives me the creeps. Such a weird, twisted little demon! I hope I never see him again, I don't care if he gets away with pointing a gun right at me, and surely leading me to my death if it weren't for Thunder! I just NEVER want to see him again, not ever. As I got into the cab with Scott, I told the driver where to go, and we left. Looking down at my scratched hand to try to distract myself from the dizzy ride, I realized that there is a zero percent chance of us not meeting again, he probably knows more about me then I know about him, just like the other guy(definitely not the same one who held me to the ground and tazered me, though at the moment, they both seem to have lasting effects on me, and they both were too wimpy to come at me head on with no fancy little stupid weapon, or trap.). Now, I guess it was sort of my fault for walking into a trap in the first place, I mean, come on, now that I think about it, there were some major signs of it being a trap. Like the fact that the baby was at the end of an enclosed alley, and also the fact of how the baby's cry never really wavered throughout the whole time, it was indeed just an endless cry, but still, I hate their techniques, huge wimps indeed. The taxi driver rounded a turn, while honking the horn, shifting me across the seat slightly, and making me grip onto the seat with all the force I could, trying to steady myself, dragging out of my zoning out. Taking my phone out of my pocket, I decided maybe now was the time to drag out my secret weapon against boredom, and horrible taxi drivers. Positioning myself so that Scott wouldn't be able to see what is on the phone if he turned around towards me, I flipped open the phone, and brought up the picture.

My eyes narrowed as I tried to focus in on the picture, going from one tiny part of it, to the next. After a few minutes of looking at it and seeing no results, I decided to flip through to the small list of information I had on the case, until the taxi ride was over. I sort of memorized this portion also, so it really didn't enthrall me to be doing so. The taxi cab stopped suddenly in front of the store. Giving him the money, I walked out of the car, with Scott and we went into the store.

Following Scott idly, I flipped the phone back open, and began looking at the picture yet again. Minuscule, by minuscule, making sure that not a single piece of it was overlooked in anyway. My eyes turned towards the off sides of the picture, where it wasn't exactly focused in, where a small black thing laid. I bit my lip, trying to determine exactly what it was, not really sure what to make of it. It was most certainly not ours, that is for certain. Clicking in the zoom button on my camera, I zoomed in more, trying to make out exactly what it was. A gun? Gnawing over this for a few moments, my heart felt like it was zapped as I remember that my parents always placed their guns in a safety chest inside the house to keep them away from me(kids and guns never mix, well). That wasn't either of their guns. That gun was a Glock gun, a gun commonly used in the NYPD.

Fumbling for my phone, I went to Sam's contact and opened a new text message. "Sam, Sam, you there, SAM?!", I hit send, really wanting my answer to come up as soon as possible. After a few minutes of not another reply(and Scott still looking for the video game he wanted), I sent another one out that said "I need your help right now, please reply back as soon as possible". Within a minute, I got a reply back, "What can I do for you water-bringer? You miss me? :P", definitely

Sam. "I am serious Sam, no joke. Now tell me, do cops ever leave their stuff at the scene of a crime? Like on accident or something, without getting in trouble" I pressed send, really hoping that it was going to be a yes, and it was just some huge misperception. The sound of another reply sounded and I quickly opened the message "Ahhh, No. That would be a contaminated crime scene which would get them in huge trouble, even the newest of rookies know that. Why you ask?". My heart dropped as my worst fear finally came to surface, it was one of their fellow cops that shot them. I closed my eyes for a few seconds to soak it all in, then opening my eyes again, I honestly couldn't find the heart to reply back to Sam, so I just closed the phone and shot it back into my purse. One step closer and just as the kid said, I am beginning to regret it, but this opens up so many more things, that in the first time in a while, I TRULY believe that this case just might get solved. Holding on to my necklace, I twirled it with my fingers for a few moments.

"Okay, I am good" Scott said, standing up from where he was kneeling down and picking up a piece of paper with the video game name and number on it(at this store, to prevent stealing, they don't leave the games out on the shelves, so instead of just putting the games behind the desk, they use paper slips instead). We walked over towards the register where Scott was rang up, I handed the cashier a fifty dollar bill, then was given the change. "Thanks" Scott said, not sure whether or not he was talking to me, or if he was talking to the cashier, I didn't reply back. Walking over to the door, we exited. "Hey Zoey, I did say thanks, didn't I?" he said, snapping to get my attention.

"Ah, yes. You're welcome" I said, looking around for a taxi. The more I think about it, I think just maybe I misinterpret Scott, maybe he isn't out to get me after all. He is just a kid just like any other kid, right? I mean, he might even be able to HELP me with this case, maybe I need another set of eyes to look at it, a different angle to come from, just maybe. There was a decent crowd on the sidewalk, so I walked Scott towards the edge so that we wouldn't be trampled as people passed and we looked for a taxi. Just then, someone shoved into us, pushing Scott to the side, and grabbing the game from his hand, and ripping my necklace off of me, he ran. "HEY!" I yelled back, running as fast as I could towards the thief. People glared at me as I ran past them, making sure not to run into anyone, some even used vulgar language towards me as if I was providing them with a major inconvenience on the biggest day of their life.

But no one bothered to ask what happened, and quite frankly I didn't care, I am GOING to get him, and my necklace, there is no way that I am going to allow some jerk face to steal it from me just to make a few dollars, no way at all. That video game, I can care less about, I'll buy Scott a billion video games for all I care, but sentimental value is the true thing worth fighting for. Speeding up my pace and dodging people as I did so, I ran as fast as I could to catch up to the guy, as I began to close in on him, I heard the screeching of wheels to my side on the road. I looked over my shoulder to see a pickup truck, spinning out of control, and going right towards a cross walk, my heart dropped for what seemed to be the billionth time this week, and I stopped right in my tracks, immediately shoving aside the fact that the thief is going to make out with my necklace, and I probably never will see it again.

A small tear managed to escape my eye as I ran full-speed towards the guy on the cross walk who was completely unaware as to the danger he is in thanks to the ipod he was listening to, and the fact that he was looking straight down below him, not in front of him or anything(which really he SHOULDN'T be doing that, not the brightest guy, not to judge someone who is near death or anything) Pushing through the crowd of gasping people, and dodging a car that zoomed right past me in an effort to dodge the run-away car, I leapt with all my force towards the guy, praying that we'd clear the car in time. I heard the screeching of the car's brakes as the driver tried to stop from running into us, and then I felt the bone-cracking force as the car spun right into me, throwing both of us into the air, I landed on the ground in agonizing pain, and already by now I knew that I had to have broke the arm that I landed on.

My lungs began to hurt like a thousand elephants were stomping on them, and every time I tried to inhale, I felt like I couldn't get enough air. Blood dripped into my eyes as I looked to see if the guy who I probably just got done giving my life for is alive, my breath heavy, I strained my eyes to see, as I saw masses of blurs starting to swarm around, and the thing I was able to make out were his near-to-closing eyes, they were a hazel, but mostly green.

ABOUT THE AUTHOR

Writing is more than a fun thing to do in my spare time, writing is sort of a passion for me. I just love using my own imagination to entertain myself through out the day as a sort of escape. Interesting enough though, I never really was a huge reader much less a writer until a few years ago, in fact I hated both. I believe it was really school surprisingly enough that got me into it, being forced to read and write for various assignments over the week, every week. So, about three years ago, I slowly got into reading and writing about at the same time. Then, last summer, I decided that I wanted to write a book, because before that I was only writing poetry, and making a couple failed attempts at starting various other books, but this time it was real, thus, Bandit Flame was born. Possibly the only reason why I even thought about finishing this book was because of the loving support of my family, we are closely knit, and I practically owe all of this book to my family, thanks a lot guys!

Keep watch for the sequel to this book, Banditstorm, that is coming out in 2013!

Made in the USA
Charleston, SC
19 November 2012